THE SUMMER OF US

THE SUMMER OF US

CECILIA VINESSE

POPPY

LITTLE, BROWN AND COMPANY

New York Boston

Copyright © 2018 by Cecilia Vinesse

Cover art copyright © Lisa Kolbasa/Shutterstock.com
Cover design by Karina Granda
Cover copyright © 2018 by Hachette Book Group, Inc.
Book ornament copyright © LDDesign/Shutterstock.com

Poppy
Hachette Book Group
1290 Avenue of the Americas, New York, NY 10104
Visit us at LBYR.com

First Edition: June 2018

Poppy is an imprint of Little, Brown and Company.
The Poppy name and logo are trademarks of Hachette Book Group, Inc.

The publisher is not responsible for websites (or their content) that are not owned by the publisher.

Library of Congress Cataloging-in-Publication Data
Names: Vinesse, Cecilia, author.
Title: The summer of us / by Cecilia Vinesse.
Description: First edition. | New York ; Boston : Little, Brown and Company, 2018. | "Poppy." | Summary: Told from two viewpoints, Rae, Aubrey, Clara, Jonah, and Gabe travel through Europe by train for ten days, working through their relationships just before setting off in different directions for college.
Identifiers: LCCN 2017018095| ISBN 9780316391139 (hardcover) | ISBN 9780316391122 (ebook) | ISBN 9780316391153 (library edition ebook)
Subjects: | CYAC: Friendship—Fiction. | Dating (Social customs)—Fiction. | Railroad travel—Fiction. | Europe—Fiction.
Classification: LCC PZ7.1.V57 Sum 2018 | DDC [Fic]—dc23
LC record available at https://lccn.loc.gov/2017018095

ISBNs: 978-0-316-39113-9 (hardcover), 978-0-316-39112-2 (ebook)

Printed in the United States of America

LSC-H

10 9 8 7 6 5 4 3 2 1

For Rachel, again and always

1

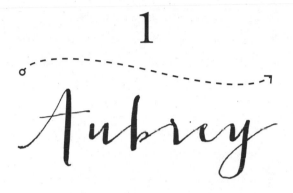

Thursday, June 30 to Friday, July 1
LONDON

When Aubrey thought about the trip, she imagined her whole life expanding.

She imagined moving beyond the walls of her tiny room in London and beyond high school and beyond everything that had seemed so important when she was a kid. She saw herself on a train, watching the world become a rush of color outside her window. Feeling like everything she'd been waiting for was about to begin.

But that didn't mean she was ready.

"Of course you are," Rae said over the phone. "You're so ready it's disturbing."

"Disturbing how?" Aubrey perched on the edge of her bed.

In one corner of the room, she saw everything she'd already packed for tomorrow: her new backpack filled with T-shirts, shorts, and SPF 50. Beside it, a stack of paperbacks from her summer reading list and a folder of all the train schedules she'd printed out over the past few weeks. In the opposite corner sat two open suitcases with a few sweaters resting inside and a different pile of books—her favorite ones, the ones she'd been carefully curating since March, the ones she would bring with her to New York.

Aubrey turned away from that corner.

"You have the organizational skills of a robot," Rae said. "You've wanted to go to Columbia since forever, and you've been planning this trip all year, and—*ow! Crap! Ow!*"

"What is it? What happened?"

"Nothing. I'm toasting marshmallows for dinner, and I burned myself."

"Rae Tara Preston. What would your mother say?"

"She's right here, and she says, 'Give me some. I'm hungry.'"

Aubrey pulled her legs onto the bed and crossed them. Down the hall, she could hear her brother, Chris, blasting *Indiana Jones and the Last Crusade* in his bedroom while her parents washed the dinner dishes in the kitchen. The kids next door must have been playing in their backyard, because squeals of laughter floated up through her open window. It all felt so normal and familiar. Aubrey swore she could close her eyes and convince herself that this was a regular summer night. That in a few weeks she would be going back to the

London American School. That all her friends would be right there with her.

"Guess what?" Rae asked, breaking the silence. "In less than twenty-four hours, we'll be in Paris!"

Aubrey sighed and lay back. "This is a good idea, right? I mean, we're not going to get axe-murdered or anything, are we?"

"Do axe murderers hang out on trains?"

"They did in that horror movie. The one Jonah and Gabe made us watch."

"Oh my God. That movie was such sexist trash."

"Fine. But what about *Strangers on a Train*? Or *Murder on the Orient Express*? More murderers, more trains."

"Aubs," Rae said, "this is supposed to be fun. We're young and we're free and we get to travel around Europe for, like, nearly two weeks. You get to make out with your boyfriend in five major European cities."

"Weird," Aubrey said. "Don't talk about me and Jonah making out in front of your mom."

"She's sketching something. She can barely even hear me. Besides, I think she knows you guys make out. She knows you're living together next year."

"We're not *living* together. Columbia and NYU aren't even in the same part of Manhattan."

"Yeah, okay, but—*Ow! These fucking marshmallows!*"

Aubrey exhaled a laugh. It was starting to get dark out, so she sat up and flicked on her bedside lamp. A pool of light illuminated her old-fashioned alarm clock and the two framed pictures beside it. One was of her and Chris at their grandparents' old house in Shelton, Connecticut. The other definitely hadn't been there earlier—her mom must have found it in the closet when she was helping Aubrey pack. It had been taken only a few weeks ago, after the last performance of the summer musical, but already that night seemed untouchable. Like something from a completely different part of Aubrey's life. Her friends were a frozen blur of messy hair and smudged stage makeup. A poster for *Singin' in the Rain* hung on the wall behind them. Clara waved a bouquet of red flowers over their heads, and Aubrey stood next to Gabe, her eyes crinkled at something he'd just said.

Instinctively, she turned off her lamp, making the image of her friends disappear. Like a curtain had fallen over them.

The room went dark, and outside the window, she could see the heavy violet of the sunset sky, bruised with clouds. She got up and peered out at the line of trees that separated her street from the ones behind it. She craned her neck, trying to see between the branches, imagining the short path that led from her house to Gabe's—past pubs and shops and bike racks, following the River Thames before finally reaching his front door.

"Aubs?" Rae asked through a mouthful of marshmallow. "You still here?"

Aubrey dropped into her desk chair. "I'm still here." She played with the keyboard on her laptop, flicking between open tabs on her browser. "Hey," she said. "Did you know that tomorrow we'll be in Paris?"

"Dude, *yes*. I am so unbelievably ready."

"Yup," Aubrey said. "Me too."

And she tried to believe it—she tried again to think of this as a beginning. As the moment her life spiraled outward into something bigger and more exciting. But now when she pictured herself on a train, all she could see was it moving quickly into the distance, everything behind her getting smaller and smaller—until it was gone.

"I made coffee," Rae's mom, Lucy, said as she opened the front door a few seconds after Aubrey had knocked.

"Thanks." Aubrey put her backpack down by the coatrack and accepted the purple ceramic mug.

"*Mom*," Rae said from the top of the stairs, her American accent contrasting sharply with Lucy's crisp British one. "We don't have time for coffee. We're going to miss our train."

"It's almost one in the afternoon," Aubrey said. "Did you just wake up?"

Rae gestured at her bed head and frog-printed pajama pants. "Your powers of deduction are outstanding." She disappeared back into her room, her dog, Iorek, trotting at her feet. Aubrey exchanged looks with Lucy, who shrugged and said, "She'll mellow out post-coffee." Rae's mom was dressed the way she always was—in an off-the-shoulder top, paint-splattered jeans, and feather earrings that made her look more like a cool older cousin than a parent. Although, to be fair, she was pretty young for an adult—Aubrey had come over for her thirty-seventh birthday party just last month.

"You should sit down." Lucy cleared a box of paint tubes from a blue velvet armchair and gestured for Aubrey to take a seat. The living room seemed even more chaotic than usual. New hiking boots and rain jackets were heaped on the floor alongside shopping bags and open shipping boxes. Aubrey had been hanging out here since she'd moved to London seven years ago, but she still couldn't get over how little the inside of the house matched the outside. Rae and her mom lived near Hyde Park in a row of terraced homes that, together, looked like an immaculate white sheet cake. The exterior of their house was all grand columns and Juliet balconies and elaborate moldings, but inside, Rae and Lucy lived among mismatched antique furniture, handmade clay sculptures, and canvases propped up against one another. Each wall was painted a different color, some of them with lines of pink hydrangeas added, others with white clouds sponged on.

"How are your parents?" Lucy asked. "They must be excited for you."

Aubrey sipped her coffee, which had way too much sugar in it. "They're—hyperventilating, I think. But okay." She didn't add that before she'd left that morning, her dad had made her recite the phone number of every American embassy in every country she was visiting.

"Don't let them worry you," Lucy said. "You'll have an amazing time. It's the perfect age for traveling around and being aimless. You don't have to make any big life decisions yet."

"Actually," Aubrey said, "I already know what I'm going to major in."

Lucy held her coffee mug over her mouth, trying to hide a smirk. *Right*, Aubrey thought. *She probably means different kinds of decisions. Bigger decisions.* Not that Aubrey could think of a bigger decision. She'd known she would major in English since she was fourteen, and she'd always hoped she would get into Columbia. After she graduated from college, she would get her master's and then her PhD. And after *that*, she would apply for jobs as either an editor or a literature professor. She had it all worked out.

"Aubrey!" Rae shouted. "I need you!"

Aubrey took her coffee and went upstairs. Rae had already changed into a pair of ripped jeans and a Sleater-Kinney T-shirt with the sleeves cut off. Her long, curly hair was twisted into a topknot now, and she was standing in the middle of her room, bed unmade and clothes strewn around her feet. "Tell me what to bring," she said.

"You're not *packed*?" Aubrey slammed the door behind her.

"No, I'm totally packed," Rae said. "This is just performance art."

Aubrey shoved the mug into Rae's hands. "Just drink this.

Your mom said it would help. And shove whatever you can into a bag. We'll sort it out in Paris."

They crouched on the floor and started cramming pajamas and cutoffs into Rae's backpack. Iorek settled his enormous form between them, thumping his fluffy white tail on the ground. Aubrey was almost glad for a few extra minutes in Rae's room. She felt like she belonged there just as much as she did in her own. She recognized each of Rae's sketches tacked to the walls and every photograph pegged to a clothesline strung across the ceiling. She knew that the beanbag chair in the corner covered a carpet burn from when Rae had attempted to flatiron her hair. And she'd been there the Boxing Day after Rae got her first camera and they'd spent hours jumping on the bed to Tegan and Sara, taking blurry photographs of each other.

"Camera!" Aubrey said suddenly. "And your sketchbook! You can't forget those."

"*Duh*," Rae said. "I packed all of that days ago."

"No clothes, no toiletries, but you remembered your camera."

"Yup." Rae stopped packing for a second and slurped the coffee. "Hey. So. You're doing better now, right?"

"Better about what?" Aubrey folded a white tank top in half.

Rae raised an eyebrow. "About college. And leaving home. All that stuff you were freaking out about last night."

"I'm fine," Aubrey said. "I had a few pre-travel jitters, that's all."

"Okay. So you're not in any way nervous about spending the next thirteen days with—"

"Gabe?" Aubrey finished for her. She stopped folding. Even saying his name made her feel dizzy, like she was standing on the edge of a precipice, gazing down. "Of course not," she said. "I can handle this. I'm an adult now."

"You're eighteen."

"Exactly! I can vote. I can drink in most European countries."

"Honestly?" Rae said. "I figured he'd be over it by now. I mean, he's a straight dude. Straight dudes can only remember things that happened five minutes ago, right?"

"They're not goldfish."

"Well, I wouldn't know. Crap! My passport! Can you grab it from my desk?"

"You were about to leave your *passport*?" Aubrey hopped up. The passport sat under a messy pile of papers, most of them from the University of Melbourne. Aubrey picked through glossy brochures and photocopied visa applications and printouts of plane reservations, the sight of it all making her feel like she was on that precipice again, reminding her that two weeks from now, right after they came home from this trip, Rae and Lucy would get on a plane and fly to Australia. Rae's school year didn't start until January, so it seemed ridiculous that she had to leave so soon, but Lucy wanted time to travel first. All last winter and spring, they'd shown Aubrey pictures of the places they were planning to go—endless golden beaches and coastal roads that seemed to fade into the sky. Soon, Rae would be there, half a world away, blending into the scenery.

And Aubrey would be somewhere else entirely.

"Dude." Rae hoisted her bag onto her back. "I think we're done."

"Definitely." Aubrey pushed aside her sticky feelings of worry and handed Rae the passport.

Rae stuffed it into her back pocket and held on to both of Aubrey's wrists. Her green eyes were bright and gleaming. "Good," she said. "Then let's get the hell out of here."

2

Rae

Friday, July 1
LONDON to PARIS

L ondon to Paris to Amsterdam. Prague to Florence to
Barcelona.

Rae knew which cities they were going to and when, but
she mentally recited them anyway as she and Aubrey rode the
tube to King's Cross station.

London to Paris to Amsterdam.

Prague to Florence to Barcelona.

She knew the exact route they were taking—a line that
carved from country to country, that bumped through cities
and skirted along bodies of water. This was the trip Aubrey
had been planning all year, the one they'd both been talking
about since *middle school*. And it was finally happening.

The tube huffed to a stop at Russell Square, letting a group of people jostle off and another jostle on. Two women wearing business suits squeezed past Rae's legs, forcing her to hug her backpack to her chest. Aubrey was looking through the map of Paris she'd downloaded onto her phone, whispering directions to herself, while Rae scrounged in her pocket for a stick of strawberry gum.

The tube started moving again. One more stop to go.

Rae wasn't nervous—not exactly, anyway. And definitely not in the same way Aubrey was. She'd gone backpacking with her mom before, and she'd always loved the whole concept of train travel.

The constant forward momentum.

The going and going and feeling like you'd never slow down.

"We made it!" Aubrey said a few minutes later. They were heading across the busy outdoor plaza that led from King's Cross to St. Pancras International, where they'd catch the Eurostar to Paris.

"We rode the tube." Rae shoved her bangs away from her eyes, making the bangles on her wrist clink together. "We do that every day."

"You're just showing off," Aubrey said, "because you're more British than the rest of us."

"Only technically," Rae countered. Because honestly, she'd never really thought of herself as British. That was her mom— Lucy had grown up in London, but Rae was born in Georgia

12

when her mom was a freshman in college. They'd stayed in the States until Rae was nine, after her grandmother died and left them an enormous house and a boatload of money.

At first, Rae had hated London. She'd missed the warmth of Georgia, and the small clapboard house she and her mom had lived in, and the weekends they'd spent driving down to the beach. Everything about England had seemed so gray to her then—the damp and the fog and the flat, metallic sky.

It seemed like the kind of place where she would never fit in, where she would feel bored and lonely forever. Until two years later, when Aubrey showed up at St. Catherine's International School. When, halfway through their first homeroom together, Rae caught her rolling her eyes at Sophie French's insistence that she was going to be cast in the next Harry Potter movie. And Rae had known it then. She'd known that this new girl was her best friend.

Now they walked into St. Pancras together, Rae breathing in the rusty city air and moving her bangs out of her face again to look up at the murky glass ceiling. The station was a cavern of clipping footsteps and humming voices. People moved through it like they were synced to its rhythm, like it was an ocean tide sweeping everyone—including Rae— along with it. She lowered her head and saw Clara leaning against a wall by the Eurostar check-in.

And that's when Rae's heart—and her lungs and probably everything else inside her—started to collapse. For a moment, the station quieted. Even the air in her chest went still.

"*Your hair!*" Aubrey said, and the station roared back to life. Someone stumbled against Rae's back, forcing her forward.

"When the hell did you do that?" Aubrey asked Clara.

"Does it suck?" Clara walked toward them, pulling her fingers through her hair, now dyed a deep cherry red. "I was thinking about it last night, and I decided I wanted something completely different for art school. But you can tell me if it sucks."

"It doesn't suck," Rae said.

"No," Aubrey said. "But it is dramatic."

"Good dramatic," Rae qualified. "Very *Run Lola Run*. It makes me want to do something radical with mine."

"No way!" Aubrey said. "You've had the same hair since middle school. You wouldn't look like Rae anymore."

Rae snorted under her breath. She didn't point out that looking the way she did *in middle school* probably wasn't a good thing.

Aubrey turned back to Clara. "Did your parents lose it?"

"The doctors were very reasonable," Clara said. "I think they both get that I'm a free woman now." She adjusted the waist of her homemade skirt patterned with a map of Europe. She was also wearing a ruffled yellow tank top and a ring on each of her fingers. Everything about her was bright and colorful. Everything about her made Rae's heart beat faster. "Anyway," Clara said, "why are we standing around? We've got a train to catch."

They shoved their backpacks through an X-ray machine,

14

and an attendant wearing a blue uniform waved them through a metal detector. Rae took her time removing her bag from the conveyor belt as she told herself over and over that everything was *fine*. After all, she and Clara were friends; they'd hung out nearly every day since freshman year.

But they'd never spent hours crammed into the same tiny train compartment, or woken up in the same hostel room every morning, or crisscrossed an entire continent side by side. This was all-new territory—this traveling through cities and whisking across borders and falling asleep against each other's shoulders. Rae had no map for it. She had no idea how to survive this trip while still keeping her biggest secret . . . a secret.

They reached the departure lounge and spotted Jonah in the far corner, waving them over. "How the hell did I beat you guys here?" he asked. "I never beat Aubrey anywhere."

"Rae made us late," Aubrey said.

"That's true," Rae said. "I did."

"You jerk." Clara dropped her bag onto the ground. "Did you seriously only save us one seat?"

"Nope." Jonah rubbed one hand over his longish, sandy hair. "I saved Aubrey one seat." He pulled her down beside him and kissed her quickly on the cheek. Clara groaned and sat on top of her bag while Rae sloughed off hers and did the same. Above them, screens lit up with new departure times and platforms. Clara was playing with the pink plastic ring on her thumb, and Rae noticed a polka-dotted Band-Aid on her index finger. "What happened to your hand?" she asked.

"This?" Clara held it up. "Sewing injury."

Rae lifted her own ink-stained finger. "I stabbed myself with a pen when I was eight. See? There's a scar and everything."

"Being an artist is so badass," Clara said, grinning. They touched their fingers together, making a jolt run all the way up Rae's arm. If this had been a normal crush, Rae would have said something flirty then. Or she would have held her hand there for an extra moment. She would have told Clara how impressed she was by her—by her talent and the incredible costumes she was always designing and the prestigious art school she was going to in LA. Rae was planning to major in art as well, but she didn't breathe it the way Clara did. She wasn't anywhere near as driven.

And she would have told Clara all of that—if she hadn't known how gushy and obvious it would sound. Because Clara wasn't a normal crush. She was one of Rae's best friends.

Rae pulled her hand back.

"So," Jonah said, "you guys haven't heard from Gabe?"

Rae and Aubrey made quick, nervous eye contact. "Nah, dude," Rae said. "We figured you'd talked to him."

"Nope." Jonah yawned. "Didn't he text you?"

He was addressing this to Aubrey, and Aubrey knew it, because Rae saw her expression freezing with alarm. Rae needed to do something—she needed to think fast. She jumped up, pointing at the screen above them. "THEY ANNOUNCED OUR PLATFORM!"

"Whoa," Jonah said. "Someone's excited."

"It's the summer before college." Rae put her hands on her hips. "If I can't be excited now, I might as well get a full-time job and a mortgage."

Aubrey shot her a relieved look as they gathered up their stuff and moved through the trundling crowd. Rae scanned the people around them, hoping to notice Gabe's dark hair or hipster concert T-shirt or the headphones he kept coiled around his neck. But all she could see was Disneyland Paris hats and bleary-eyed adults holding coffee cups and dozens and dozens of rolling suitcases. On the train, she crammed her bag onto an overhead rack and took the seat next to Aubrey. Clara was sitting in front of Jonah, but she turned around and said, "If Gabe doesn't show, I'm sitting with you."

"He'll show," Jonah said. "And no, you're not. Your elbows are pointy as fuck."

"My elbows aren't pointy." She bent her arm and stared at one. "Maybe yours are blunt. Let me see."

Aubrey played with the catch on the tray table in front of her. "What if he's not coming?" she whispered anxiously.

"Of course he is," Rae whispered back. "He wouldn't just bail on us."

A woman in a paisley summer dress walked down the aisle, her strong perfume filling Rae's nose. Rae picked at a rip in her jeans and mulled over what to say next. She could go with a traditional *maybe he got lost*. Or possibly the standard *this doesn't have anything to do with you*. But the problem was,

17

she didn't know if either of those things was true. Gabe could have chickened out. He could have decided that coming here wasn't worth the probable awkwardness.

And if he did decide that, it was definitely because of Aubrey.

Behind them, the door to their carriage breathed open.

"Holy shit, man!" Jonah stood up. "What took so long?"

Rae turned around. Gabe's bag hung from one arm, and he looked out of breath, but he also looked like him: St. Vincent T-shirt, headphones, and all. He'd gotten his hair cut recently, so it was shorter on the sides and longer on top. Rae wasn't attracted to guys, but even she could tell the haircut looked good on him. It looked like it would be nice to touch. Aubrey loosened the catch on the table again, and it bounced open in front of her. She blushed furiously, pushing it back with both hands.

"My family's still here from Madrid," Gabe was saying. "And my sister's flying back to Barcelona today, so my aunts and uncles wanted pictures. And then my *abuela* got mad because Zaida's cheeks started to hurt and she wouldn't smile anymore."

Clara absentmindedly braided a few strands of her hair together. "Is your sister going to throw us a party when we're in Barcelona?"

"No." Gabe hefted his bag onto the rack. "Why would she do that?"

"Because parties are fun?" Clara said. "Because we're high school graduates and we deserve a party?"

18

"You mean *you* deserve a party?" Jonah said.

"Shut up, Elbows."

The train exhaled and lurched forward.

Gabe took his seat and stared straight ahead, like he was doing everything in his power not to acknowledge Aubrey. And Aubrey wasn't looking at him, either—she was scratching at a freckle on her knee; she was picking at her new coat of nail polish. Rae wanted to slither out of her seat. She wanted to tell them both how blatant it was that they were ignoring each other.

Except maybe it wasn't blatant at all. Maybe it only seemed like that to Rae, because she knew what had happened three weeks ago.

The platform shifted slightly outside the window, making Clara whoop and Jonah clap his hands over his head. Rae felt a small jitter in her stomach. This was it; they were actually on their way.

"Here we go," she whispered to Aubrey, grasping her hand.

Aubrey squeezed Rae's hand back, and it reminded Rae of how they used to jump off the high dive together when they were twelve. Of how, when they hit the water, they would try to stay under and hold their breath for the same amount of time. Outside the window, the gray and brown buildings of London started disappearing behind them. Like a sped-up movie reel. Like the world on fast-forward.

3

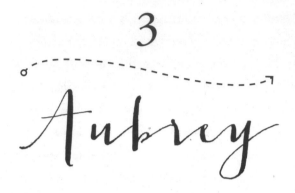

Aubrey

Friday, July 1
LONDON to PARIS

The train plunged into a tunnel, and their reflections lit up the windows around them. Aubrey's conversation with Rae had died down, so she put on her headphones and searched for the playlist Rae had made her for graduation, the one Rae had kindly called "Soundtrack to Aubrey Bryce's Sad, Forever Good-bye." Yeah. It felt oddly fitting. The fast-paced electronic sounds of Chvrches blasted into Aubrey's ears, overlapping with the steady chug of the train. The music thrummed with excitement, but also with a strain of angst. A feeling that matched the one in Aubrey's stomach. The feeling that, at any second, everything could stretch thin and snap apart.

Aubrey turned up the volume.

The train pushed toward the Chunnel, the underwater tunnel that connected England with France. The walls rattled, and Aubrey looked over at her reflection—her slicked-back ponytail and the downturn of her mouth. She saw Rae's ripped jeans and the pen she was using to drum against her knees. And she saw Gabe, too, sitting across the aisle talking to Jonah. She took in his profile: the slope of his nose and the curve of his chin, his hair falling over his forehead.

Aubrey's thoughts clouded over with guilt, but she was glad he was here. It meant the idea of being in such close quarters with her didn't make him want to run away. It meant there was hope that they could be friends again.

She closed her eyes and crossed her arms, slipping deeper into the mesh of music and train. She wondered what her sixth-grade self would have thought if she could have seen this moment. If she could have seen Aubrey at eighteen, starting to do all the things she'd promised herself she would.

Back then, she and Rae used to stay up late, watching their favorite old movies and planning the glamorous adventures they'd have as soon as they grew up. Back then, Aubrey had assumed that she and Rae would go on this trip alone. She'd had no idea that Jonah, Clara, and Gabe would be sitting with them. She hadn't even met them yet.

That had happened her freshman year, and technically, she'd met Gabe first. They'd both signed up to work backstage crew for the fall play, and by chance, they were assigned to paint the same set together—a smoggy backdrop of a city.

Aubrey remembered spending every afternoon in an empty classroom with him, applying layer after layer of gray-blue paint onto a scratchy canvas. They'd talked for hours—about where they'd grown up and how it felt to be living in England. Gabe was from Madrid, but he'd spent most of his life in Rhode Island, where his dad had taught economics at Brown. Now his family was in London so his dad could start another job at University College London.

Aubrey had been sure that her own background story (*my dad's an accountant; I'm from Connecticut*) would sound boring compared with his, but he'd seemed to like talking to her. He'd sat with her in Geometry and called her over to his table during lunch to introduce her to his other new friends—Jonah, who was an actor in the play, and Clara, who designed the costumes. When Aubrey mentioned Rae, Clara pointed out that she and Rae took Studio Art together, and everything began to fall into place. Aubrey plus Rae became Aubrey plus Rae plus Gabe plus Jonah plus Clara.

It had stayed that way ever since.

Aubrey must have fallen asleep, because when she opened her eyes again, the train had stopped. A bright bloom of yellow light poured in through the window, and people were walking up and down a platform outside.

"Check it out." Rae leaned over Aubrey, popping her strawberry gum. "It's Paris."

They headed down the platform, pigeons fluttering near the half-circle windows that ran along the station's main hall. Announcements echoed around them in haughty, musical French.

Jonah walked up beside Aubrey. "It looks like an old movie set or something," he said, sounding almost reverent.

"If Paris were a person," Aubrey said, "it would be so elegant."

"But also kind of a jackass," he said.

"Paris isn't a jackass," Aubrey gasped. "How can you say that?"

"Because," Jonah said, "it's aloof and beautiful and arrogant. Total jackass material."

Aubrey mock-scowled at him. "Fine. Then if you were a city, you would be Paris."

"And you'd be London," he said. "Hardworking. Practical. And dull."

"*What the hell?* You're so unromantic!" They walked past a baguette stand at the end of the platform and through a cloud of steam that smelled of hot coffee and warm bread.

"Anyway," Jonah said, "I wouldn't be Paris. I'd be New York."

"Because you're from there?"

"No." He waggled his eyebrows. "Because I'm sexy and dangerous."

She knocked her bag against his as they stepped onto an escalator down to the Metro.

At just after six PM, they got off at their stop and walked through sliding glass doors into a hotel lobby with black-and-white marble floors and crystal chandeliers dripping from the ceilings. Jonah whistled under his breath. This trip was expensive, and for the most part, they were doing the usual interrailing thing and staying in cheap, dingy hostels. But as a graduation present, Aubrey's parents had reserved them two nights in a hotel—in, apparently, an incredibly *fancy* hotel.

They checked in and crowded into an elevator that took them to the eighth floor. Their feet padded on lush carpet as they passed sconces glittering on the walls.

"This place is in-fucking-*sane*," Rae said. "Aubs. What were your parents thinking?"

"I feel like we shouldn't be here," Aubrey said. "Does anyone else feel like we shouldn't be here?"

"Too late." Clara grabbed the key from Aubrey's hand and unlocked their door. She ran inside, pushing back the gauzy curtains to reveal enormous windows that overlooked massive, glitzy buildings. "Everyone come look at this view!"

"And the bathroom!" Rae said. "Guys. Great news. The bathroom is the size of an apartment."

"What about food?" Jonah crossed the threshold after them. "Did they give you guys any free food?"

Aubrey was about to follow when she heard Gabe say, "Damn, Bryce. You might never get them to leave."

"Oh." Her mind went blank. "I guess they have to leave. When we check out."

There was a weird, empty silence, and Aubrey wished she could think of something else to say. Something that wasn't about hotel etiquette. Something that would keep this fledgling conversation alive. The dim hallway seemed to grow dimmer. The walls seemed to inch toward them. It all felt so stiff and formal, like they were characters in a Victorian novel. Like they'd never been close at all. Even though, of course, they had been. Only a few weeks ago, they'd been much closer than this—his hands in her hair, their lips touching.

He started to walk away.

"Doesn't this remind you of *Jane Eyre*?" she said quickly.

He turned around. "What?"

"*Jane Eyre*," she said. Rae and Clara had started playing loud music in the room, but she stepped toward him. She wasn't giving up yet. "It feels so gothic, doesn't it? Like we're all Jane Eyre, and we're going into this gigantic mansion, and we're completely unprepared for—"

"Wives in the attic?" Gabe finished for her, the corners of his mouth twitching upward.

"Right!" Hope filled Aubrey's chest. They were talking now. They were standing across from each other, and they were actually talking. "Wives in the attic. Which—doesn't make any sense. In terms of my analogy."

"They kicked me out." Jonah reappeared next to her. "They told me 'no boys allowed.'"

"Damn straight!" Clara shouted from inside. "No boys allowed!"

Jonah put his arm around Aubrey's shoulders, and Gabe's expression seemed to shut down a little. Aubrey deflated. She didn't want to make him uncomfortable, so she shifted away, glancing through the open door. Rae was pulling on a fluffy robe over her clothes, and Clara was clambering onto one of the beds. Jonah let go of Aubrey's shoulder and said, "We're going to our room. Meet up with you later?"

"Yeah. Later." She waited a beat before checking behind her again. The lights in the hallway seemed to flicker.

Gabe and Jonah were gone.

"Beyoncé sing-along!" Clara cranked up the volume on her phone.

"Oh my God!" Rae was standing inside the closet. "How is this closet the size of my house? Is it like one of those Harry Potter Quidditch tents?"

Clara jumped on the bed, belting along with the lyrics, while Aubrey put her bag on the luggage rack and unzipped it. She was thinking about how, for one moment, Gabe had acted like everything between them was normal again. Which meant he might act like that tonight. Which meant he might act like that *tomorrow*. Which hopefully meant they could undo that stupid kiss from three weeks ago—they could forget it had ever happened.

Her outfit for the evening was folded on top of everything else: a floaty skirt, a red tank top, and a pair of black sandals. She tugged her dark hair from her ponytail holder and let it fall around her shoulders.

Rae emerged from the closet, still wearing the robe and

now a pair of slippers. "This album is so freshman year. Remember when Erin Maguire sang 'Drunk in Love' in the middle of our Bio exam and didn't even realize it?"

"Was that when you had a crush on her?" Clara asked.

"What? No. I *never* had a crush on her."

Clara stopped jumping and pushed her staticky hair away from her face. "Aubrey! Verify. Did Rae have a crush on Erin Maguire or not?"

Aubrey pulled the tank top over her head, mentally riffling through her list of Rae's old crushes. "Can't remember."

"That means I didn't!" Rae climbed onto the other bed, pumping both fists in the air. "Because! Aubrey! Remembers! Everything!"

Aubrey's phone beeped, and she assumed it was her parents, asking if she'd checked into the hotel. But it was Jonah: *Aubrey Bryce, this room is NOT SMALL. also, I think I saw a bar downstairs. should we go drink in it??*

"Jonah wants to look around some more." She grabbed one of the keys. "You guys want to come?"

"Aubrey," Rae said, "you know I love you and that I would probably murder—or at the very least, *attempt* murder—for you. But there's no way in hell I'm spending alone time with you and Jonah right now."

"Ditto," Clara said. "Enjoy sucking face, though."

Aubrey flipped them off, and she could hear them cackling as she walked into the hallway, the music fading as she made her way to the elevator.

The bar, just off the lobby, was a sprawling, red-carpeted room full of couples sitting at tables decorated with votive candles. Different scenes from old black-and-white movies were projected silently onto the walls, sending shifting beams of light and shadow over everything. Aubrey chose a booth at the back and ran her hands over the plum fabric of the seat while watching Charlie Chaplin give a flower to a girl in a wide-brimmed hat. She'd never been somewhere like this on her own before, and it made her feel kind of strange—like she was a little kid playing dress-up.

Jonah slid into the booth beside her. "Are these free?" he asked, pointing to the bowl of crackers on the table.

"I would assume so," Aubrey said.

"I love this place." He popped a few crackers in his mouth. "Do you think we'll get those tiny pillow mints, too?"

Aubrey stopped watching the screen, but the images stayed behind her eyelids for a few more seconds, a hazy afterglow. Jonah had changed into the blue button-up Aubrey had bought him for Hanukkah last year, and he smelled like the bright, lemony laundry detergent she always associated with walking into his house. Even though they'd been dating since sophomore year, Aubrey sometimes found it hard to believe that he was her boyfriend. *Her serious boyfriend*, as her mom often put it. The first time he'd asked her out, she'd honestly thought it might have been a joke. When it happened, she'd been standing next to Rae, who'd had to say, *Yeah, she'll go out with you*, while Aubrey's brain tried to make sense of what was going on. She'd always liked Jonah, but she'd never considered the possibility of *like*-liking him. And it had definitely never occurred to her that he might *like*-like her. Aubrey thought of herself as the kind of girl guys flirted with so she would let them copy her homework. She wore T-shirts with nerdy literary slogans on them, and she frowned at kids who talked over the teacher during class, and she'd always enjoyed the comfort of practical shoes.

Jonah, on the other hand, was moody and artistic and seriously cute. The first time Lucy had seen a picture of him, she'd told Rae and Aubrey that he looked like Ethan Hawke in *Reality Bites*. (When they IMDb-ed it later, it turned out she was right.)

On that first date, a Saturday, a January ice storm hit. Aubrey met Jonah at the Natural History Museum, and they spent the afternoon weaving through crowds of moms and crying toddlers to gaze at bleached dinosaur skeletons and life-size whale models suspended from the ceiling. In the early evening, he walked her to the bus stop, taking her arm to guide her around icy patches on the sidewalk and waiting with her for the bus to arrive. They were still talking when its headlights flashed down the street and swept toward them. And as the bus slushed through a puddle of snow and stopped, Jonah leaned over and kissed Aubrey. His mouth was cool and wintry; the tips of his fingers touched the tips of hers.

"We should order something." Jonah crunched another

cracker, pulling Aubrey back into the moment. "How do you say *my good sir, give us the cheapest wine you've got?*"

Aubrey turned toward him. "Doesn't this make you think about New York?"

He arched an eyebrow. "Trust me. Living in New York won't be anything like this."

"Not the hotel," she said. "I meant *this*. Being by ourselves. Getting to decide what we do at any given moment— well, except for when we have to go to class."

"I'll take you to see my old apartment," he said. "My parents are renting it out now, but the doorman still remembers me. He even lets me go up to the roof sometimes."

"You have to come to the Columbia library," she said. "My mom and I went on this tour of it when we were visiting last summer. Even standing in the entrance made me feel more intelligent."

"I think I've been there. But when you come downtown, we can go to all the weird little theaters they have there. We'll see a new show every week."

"And we'll go to the Statue of Liberty. And get a couple of those Statue of Liberty hats."

"Aubrey. No."

"Okay. But we can *at least* get matching 'I Heart NY' ponchos, right?"

His eyes crinkled at the corners, and he took her hand under the table. "No tourist garbage," he said.

"But I'm a tourist!"

"No, you're not. You're going to live there for the next four years."

"Maybe even longer than that," she said and instantly felt shy about it. They'd never talked about it explicitly, but it did make sense that they'd stay in New York after they graduated. Jonah was studying drama at NYU, so it seemed logical that he'd go on auditions in the city. And Aubrey could apply to do her English lit master's at Columbia—she'd already researched how to get into the program.

Just like that, it glowed to life in her mind, this future they would have together: Aubrey taking the subway from Columbia to NYU to see him in the evenings; the two of them walking across the Brooklyn Bridge on chilly autumn nights and going out for soup dumplings in Chinatown; Aubrey having a key to Jonah's dorm.

Jonah's phone buzzed on the table, and Leah's name popped up, the screen turning bright and garish. Jonah let go of Aubrey's hand to check the message, and Aubrey felt the little bubble she'd created around them burst.

"She's asking what kind of drinks she should buy," Jonah said. "For when we're at her place Monday night."

"Cool!" Aubrey tried to sound enthusiastic as she poked a few crackers around the bowl. Leah was Jonah's friend from the London American School, but she'd graduated a year earlier, and now she was at NYU, doing the exact same drama program Jonah was going to start. Aubrey didn't exactly *dislike* Leah, but she did resent the fact that when Leah was around, the focus of everything seemed to shift to her. And, *of course*, Leah was interning at a theater in Amsterdam that summer, which meant they would have to see her in a few days. Which was annoying.

Jonah was still texting, the black-and-white images from the silent movie gliding over him, forming triangles of light against his skin. Aubrey wished she could reach over and pull him back to her. She wished they could go back to talking about New York—the New York that belonged to the two of them, the New York where they were the only people who existed. She blurted out, "You can't be New York."

"Huh?" He looked up from his phone.

"The conversation we were having earlier," she said. She could feel her face getting flushed. "About which city we would be. You can't be New York, because it puts us on uneven footing when we move there, and that isn't fair."

"Okay." Jonah looked baffled, but he reached over to touch her cheek. "So we're both New York." Aubrey felt the bubble growing around them again, blocking out Leah and the rest of the world. The images from the movie grazed Jonah's lips; they got caught in his eyelashes. And Aubrey tipped her head toward his. She let her eyes drift shut.

4

Friday, July 1
PARIS

"This," Clara said, "is *exactly* how I imagined tonight would be."

Rae walked between Clara and Gabe down a wide Parisian avenue. Clara was wearing a short silver dress she'd sewn herself with a vintage black fascinator clipped into her hair. The warm night crackled with energy. Clara was so close to her it made Rae feel feverish. She tried to distract herself by snapping pictures of all the things they passed: yellow lights in windows, opulent buildings, cafés with bright-red awnings. Everything vivid and dramatic. Everything like a living work of art.

Rae jogged a few steps in front of them and held up her camera. "Look over here!"

Clara stuck out her tongue as Gabe mussed up her hair, making her screech and duck just as Rae snapped the picture. The two of them a whir of motion against the elegant city.

"Nice," Rae said.

"Very funny." Clara patted down her hair while Gabe stuck his hands into his pockets and whistled.

Since they'd stopped, Aubrey and Jonah had gotten even farther ahead, walking with their arms around each other's waists.

"Typical," Clara said, gesturing at their friends. "Abandoning us already."

"Probably because we're so immature." Gabe skipped ahead and kicked a stone down the sidewalk. If Rae hadn't known about what had happened between him and Aubrey, she might have thought he was being his normal jokey self. But she could hear an edge of hurt in his voice. She contemplated taking a picture of him. Something artsy and in profile.

A boy hiding his thoughts.

A boy pretending nothing has changed.

Humidity from the day lingered in the night air. She noticed couples smoking cigarettes on their apartment balconies, a girl fastening her helmet before climbing onto her motorbike, and groups clinking wineglasses together at café tables.

Clara linked one arm with Rae and the other with Gabe. "If either of you had a girlfriend right now, you'd ignore everyone else, too, and only pay attention to her."

"Doubt it," Rae said. *I would*, she thought, *if you were my girlfriend.*

"I don't need an excuse," Gabe said. "I could ignore you right now."

Clara sighed and shoved his arm. Gabe and Clara were constantly teasing each other, but Rae knew there was nothing more to it. Clara had told her a dozen times that she thought of Gabe and Jonah more like brothers. In fact, she'd never dated *any* of the guys who went to their school. She said LAS boys were full of drama. But she had hooked up with a couple of guys from different London schools, and she'd even had a long-distance boyfriend in California for a few months during freshman year.

Rae reminded herself of all that. It made her wish—for the hundredth, maybe thousandth time—that if she had to fall for a friend, it hadn't been one who seemed one hundred percent straight.

"Well, I think they're lucky," Clara said. The curve of her elbow tightened around Rae's. "Going to college must be a lot less terrifying if you go with someone you love."

"Sure," Gabe said. "But technically they're not going together. They're going to different schools that happen to be in the same city."

"Ha," Rae snorted. "You sound just like Aubrey."

"Really?" Gabe asked.

"Yeah." Rae flicked her camera off and then on again. She probably shouldn't have said that. It was probably a major

Best Friend Violation to talk about Aubrey with Gabe. She was about to change the subject when she realized that they had almost caught up with Aubrey and Jonah, who were waiting for them outside a restaurant on the street corner.

"Ladies and gentlemen," Aubrey announced when they stopped in front of her, "welcome to your first official night of freedom."

A waiter led them to an outdoor table covered by a white tablecloth with leather-bound menus at every place setting. In the center, a candle sat inside a globe, its flame muted by frosted glass. The waiter pulled out their chairs for them, which made Rae feel super awkward. She half slid, half tripped into hers. "Thanks—*garçon*," she said. Gabe smirked at her, and she kicked him under the table.

"Okay." Aubrey unfolded her napkin. "I know this place *seems* expensive."

"That's because it is." Jonah gawked at his open menu.

"But we don't have to worry," Aubrey said. "Rae and I looked up this place weeks ago. We already figured out what we should do."

"Yes!" Rae said. "I totally remember that!"

Gabe folded his hands on the table. "Do you now?" he asked. She kicked him again.

"We can order one bottle of wine," Aubrey said, "and a main course each, but we'll choose from the ones that are less than twenty euros. That way, we'll have enough left to share a couple of desserts." She took out her phone to show them the budget she'd drawn up.

"Great plan." Clara flipped her curtain of dyed-red hair over her shoulder and waved down the waiter. The silver on her dress shimmered like water, and Rae felt helpless. And seriously ridiculous, like there were actual hearts in her eyes or something. Like she might as well get a T-shirt printed with *Ask me about my soul-absorbing crush on Clara!*

The waiter came back, and Clara said something to him in rapid, convincing French.

Rae picked up her fork and banged it against the side of her water glass. She tried to ignore how perfect Clara looked this evening—the way her hair had turned an even deeper shade of red, how the candle illuminated a small half-moon scar at the corner of her eyebrow. "All right," she said. "This is our first night, so I think we should set down a few ground rules. I'll start. Rule number one: No one currently seated at this table is allowed to discuss theater or musicals of any kind. This definitely includes *Singin' in the Rain*."

"That show only ended three weeks ago," Jonah said. "I'd say it's ripe with conversational possibility."

"If we're making a list," Gabe chimed in, "let's add *what are you majoring in?* I could use a break from that question."

"You still haven't picked one?" Clara asked.

Gabe leaned back, tipping his chair onto its two back legs. "My mom's gunning for political science, so I'll probably just go for that. Make her happy."

"You should make yourself happy," Clara said.

"Hey." He pointed at her. "This is on the list. No more talking about majors. Anyway, maybe I won't major in anything. Maybe I'll skip Reed altogether and become a roadie. Follow some band around the country."

"Cool!" Rae said. "Can I join you?"

"You two are going to give me a heart attack," Aubrey mumbled at her menu.

"Okay, okay," Jonah said. "We'll talk about something else. Gabe, I'm kicking your ass at *Battlefield* the second we get back."

"No!" Rae said. "No battlefields, no assassins, no street fighters. Those are going on the list."

Gabe snorted. "Who still plays *Street Fighter*?"

"I'm serious," Rae said. "We're taking a vote. Everyone who agrees to follow the rules say *aye*."

"Aye!" Rae, Clara, and Aubrey said at the same time.

Rae banged her water glass again. "Sorry, gentlemen. The ayes have it."

The waiter appeared again, this time carrying a bucket of ice and a bottle that looked suspiciously like champagne. Aubrey sat up straight. "How much is that?" she asked.

Clara ignored her, but there was a spark in her eyes as she

directed the waiter to set a flute in front of each of them. A moped droned down the street, and bubbles rose through the liquid in Rae's glass. Clara held her own glass in the air, and for the briefest second, her eyes met Rae's. "What should we toast to?" she asked.

"I don't know." Rae shrugged. "Graduation? Or our futures? Or some other bullshit like that?"

Clara turned to Aubrey. "Or I was thinking... to Aubrey's budget."

Gabe choked on his water.

Jonah laughed. "Oh yeah, I'll definitely drink to that."

They held their glasses high and concentrated their stares on Aubrey, who groaned and shut her menu. "You guys are the fucking worst," she said. But she threw her shoulders back and cleared her throat before saying, in the loudest voice she possibly could, "*TO AUBREY'S BUDGET!*"

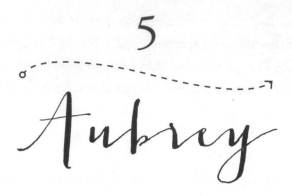

5

Aubrey

Friday, July 1
PARIS

The champagne was, in fact, expensive.

But also, it made walking easy.

Walking was so easy!

Aubrey felt like she was practically flying. It helped that Jonah was there, his arm wrapped firmly around her. They were in the middle of the place de la Concorde, brightly lit fountains on either side of them, and cars and motorcycles nudging their way around even this late at night.

"I love Paris!" Aubrey exclaimed.

Jonah smirked. "You love everything right now."

"That isn't true. But I'll tell you what I do love: I love

tonight, and I love how *shiny* everything is, and"—she felt a swell of emotion—"I love you."

She tripped a little, and he caught her, his expression warm. "Love you, too, Aubs. Even if you won't remember any of this."

"Hurry up!" Clara shouted in front of them. "Or we're leaving you behind!"

"Come on." Jonah dragged her forward. The plaza led to a long, wide avenue with two rows of leafy trees running along either side of it.

"This is the Champs-Élysées," Aubrey explained. "I recognize it because it's on the Internet. Also, because it's *super* famous."

"Uh-huh," Jonah said.

"Everything's on the Internet!" Aubrey slowed down a little. "It's like I've been here before, but I actually haven't." Although, she had to admit, Paris seemed so much bigger than she thought a city could be. Bigger than London, even bigger than New York. Of course, she knew that wasn't *technically* true. She'd been on Wikipedia before; she knew Paris was actually kind of small. But it *felt* true. Being here made her feel so close to the image she'd always had of her life after high school. It was glamorous and romantic and brimming with unknown possibilities. Aubrey could feel how important this night was. She could feel how it really was a beginning.

Rae shouted behind her. "Clara says stop staring at shit! She wants to go somewhere."

Their friends sped up, so Aubrey and Jonah went faster, too, the colors of the city bleeding past them. They were on the part of the Champs-Élysées that ran parallel with two tidy, green parks, and then they were on the part crowded with flagship department stores and tiered restaurants. The sidewalk was just as jammed with activity as the road, but Aubrey wasn't overwhelmed. Jonah was holding her hand. She could see Rae's topknot and the sparkle of Clara's dress.

They raced all the way up the long boulevard, skittering to a stop at the roundabout that marked the very end of it. In the center of it all—larger than everything else around—was the Arc de Triomphe, an enormous stone arch that burned with light against the dark. Traffic spun and spun around it. The city felt as wide open as the sky.

Clara propped her elbow on Gabe's shoulder. "Amazing, right?" she said. "I thought we should see it up close."

Rae cut her and Gabe a quick glance. "Sure," she said. "It's rad."

Aubrey was watching them, too. Clara wore heels, and, for the first time ever, Aubrey noticed that she was almost the same height as Gabe. She noticed how glamorous they looked together. And how Gabe didn't try to move away from her.

He was staring across the road, the hair above his ears sweaty from running. "I bet you can see everything from up there," he said.

"Gabe!" Clara said. "You are totally, one hundred percent

right!" She crouched down to adjust the backs of her heels and then quickly stood back up. Before Aubrey could put together what was going on, Clara took Gabe's arm and pulled him through a brief lull in traffic, heading straight toward the Arc. Car horns shrieked and angry voices shouted through windows.

"Damn," Jonah said. "How does she do that without dying?"

"Don't you think they look great together?" Aubrey blurted.

"Who?" Rae asked, looking warily at the constant stream of cars.

"Clara..." Aubrey paused. "And Gabe. Wouldn't they make the most perfect couple?"

Rae's head snapped away from the road, and her mouth fell open in shock—Aubrey wasn't sure why. Maybe Rae was worried that she was about to say something stupid about Gabe in front of Jonah. But that wasn't going to happen. Aubrey had finally seen a way for everything to work out—maybe Gabe and Clara liked each other; maybe, if they became a couple, any weirdness left over from her kiss with Gabe would disappear.

"Seriously?" Jonah asked. "What makes you say that?"

"They just—fit together," Aubrey said. "And they're both *tall*. Have you ever noticed that they're the two tallest people in our group?"

"And you and I are the shortest," Rae said. "But I am so not marrying you."

Jonah watched them as they stood in the space around the Arc. Clara's hair was blowing in her face, and Gabe grinned at something she'd said. The circle of cars was a tornado around them. It seemed like they were right in the middle of the entire city. "I hate to break it to you," Jonah said, "but I know for a fact that Gabe doesn't feel that way about her."

"How could you know that?" Aubrey said. "Have you ever *asked* him?"

"Uh," he said. "No?"

"Guys!" Rae said. "Eyes on the road! Let's go, go, go!"

They shot across the cobblestones, hot car exhaust blasting against Aubrey's legs. When they reached the other side, she felt a little wobbly from adrenaline. She fell forward into Clara. "Hey, drunky," Clara teased.

"I'm not drunk." Aubrey fixed the sides of her skirt. "I had just as much champagne as everyone else."

"I know," Clara said. "But you're, like, a notorious lightweight."

"Holy shit!" Jonah scraped both hands through his hair, and he and Rae gaped back in the direction they'd come from. Aubrey turned as well, and her breath stopped. Because even though they weren't on the top of the Arc de Triomphe, and even though she was still seeing everything at eye level, it seemed as if all of Paris was staring back at her. There was the long, vibrant stretch of the Champs-Élysées and, to the right, the distant, gleaming Eiffel Tower.

Aubrey could have stayed there for hours, basking in the enormity of it along with everyone else, but she needed to do something first. She worked up her nerve and tapped Gabe on the shoulder. "Could I talk to you for a minute?"

He pulled his eyes from the view, but his expression didn't change. It was the same neutral look he'd worn around her since that night after the musical—the same one he'd worn at graduation two weeks ago and at the party at Jonah's house afterward and every time he'd seen her since. "Go ahead," he said.

She swallowed the lump in her throat. "Actually, could I talk to you for a minute—alone?"

She waited for him to ignore her or to say no or to talk to Clara instead. But he didn't. "Over there?" he said, walking off to the side. Relief washed through her as she followed him. The Arc had low stone ledges built into its sides, and Gabe perched on one. Aubrey did the same, although she was careful to leave lots of space between them.

"This is seriously incredible." Gabe's focus was fixed in front of him again. Aubrey watched, too—it felt like all the streets were rotating. Like the world had become a carousel.

"It's really pretty," she said, placing both hands on the ledge. She wondered if she had it all wrong—maybe the city wasn't spinning at all; maybe she was.

"Do you remember when we had to dissect that fetal pig in Bio?" she asked. "And how looking at all the tiny knives made me nauseated?"

45

Gabe knitted his eyebrows together. "Yeah," he said. "Of course."

"I feel that way now." She gripped the ledge tighter. "Can you get motion sickness when you're not the one moving?"

"Sounds like you need a distraction," he said. "Like that day in Bio. Remember I convinced you to skip class?"

"We didn't *skip class*," she said. "You took me to the nurse's office, and we watched *Marcel the Shell* on repeat for forty-five minutes."

"Bryce," he said. "That's skipping class."

"Well, yeah," she said. "But it sounds better when I rationalize it."

He scratched the back of his neck and smiled down at his feet. The night seemed to open up even more. Aubrey felt a tiny bit steadier. "And you made me watch all those old music videos, too," she went on, "of that singer from the eighties you had a crush on."

He shrugged one shoulder. "What can I say? I was going through a Blondie phase."

"Right!" Aubrey let go of the ledge. "And I told you she kind of looked like Clara."

Gabe's face flickered with confusion. "You did?"

"Actually, that's what I wanted to talk to you about." This was going to work out—Aubrey could feel it; she just knew it. "I was wondering if, maybe, you have a thing for Clara? Because the two of you get along so well, and you've been friends for years, and you're both—cute. You'd be really, *really* cute together."

Gabe's smile faded. The movement on the road created a breeze that sent goose bumps up Aubrey's arms. Only a few feet away, Clara and Jonah were laughing while Rae took pictures of everything. But their voices were lost to the wind. They seemed so far away.

And Aubrey hated this—she hated the weight that hung over her and Gabe now, the way their easy relationship had changed practically overnight. She hated that one dumb, meaningless kiss could ruin so much so quickly.

"Okay." Gabe stood up. "Was that it?"

"No." Aubrey stood up, too, desperate. "Wait. *No.* I was just thinking, you'll be in Oregon next year, and Clara will be in LA, and that's not exactly opposite sides of the universe. And the summer's not even over yet. There's still time for something to happen."

Silence stretched between them, vast and terrifying. Making Aubrey feel like there was nothing to grab onto. Making her feel like she was about to be pulled into a whirlwind of night and noise and tangled city streets.

"I think," Gabe said finally, "we should get back over there."

"Why?"

"Because you're clearly drunk."

Aubrey took a sharp breath. "Like I told Clara. I didn't drink any more than everyone else."

47

"Yeah, I heard what you told Clara. I was standing right there."

"I didn't mean to piss you off," she said, but there was annoyance in her voice. "It was just an idea."

"A pretty fucking weird idea."

"*Why?* Because Clara's not good enough for you?"

"Because it isn't any of your business who I do or do not date," he snapped.

Aubrey's face crumpled. She turned her head away so he couldn't see.

"Shit," he said softly. "Bryce. I'm sorry. That came out all wrong."

She crossed her arms. "Don't worry about it."

"I was just thrown by what you said." He rubbed his hair where it had been clipped short. "Jesus. This really isn't easy."

"But it could be, couldn't it?" She took a small step toward him, still determined to say this. "I keep thinking about everything we've done together. All those *Evil Dead* marathons we used to have on Halloween. All the times you called me at midnight when you got bored with your homework. That doesn't just disappear, does it? It doesn't have to change."

"We're going to college," he said blandly. "Everything has to change."

"But we can still keep in touch." Aubrey's heart slammed against her rib cage. "And we can still be friends. Can't we?"

Gabe tugged at the collar of his shirt. Aubrey's hands

felt cold. But she had to believe it would be okay. She had to believe that he would say yes. "I'm sorry, Aubrey," he said. "But I really don't think so."

"What's *up*, you two?" Jonah rushed over. "And what the hell are you doing all the way over here? Aubs, are you sick? You don't need to puke or anything, do you?"

"Everything's fine." Gabe headed toward Clara and Rae, leaving Aubrey and Jonah behind. Aubrey stood still, trying to understand what had just happened. Trying to feel it.

"Oookay," Jonah said. "You sure you're all right?"

Aubrey's eyes were hot, so she blinked up at the Arc. She could see the smooth curve beneath it. And she could imagine standing on top of it, Paris a blanket at her feet.

"Aubs?" Jonah touched her arm this time. And since she didn't know how she could answer him, she kissed him instead. His mouth relaxed against hers, and his hands reached for the hem of her shirt. Her eyes were closed, but Aubrey didn't feel like she was on solid ground anymore. She could almost see the millions of dizzying, twinkling lights beneath her. *It doesn't matter if Gabe hates me*, she said to herself. *It doesn't matter, it doesn't matter, it doesn't matter.*

Jonah pulled back, his expression hazy. "What was that about?" he asked.

"Can we stay here?" She held on to him as if he were the only thing keeping her in place. The only thing that could stop her from falling. "I want to stay here a little bit longer."

6

Friday, July 1
PARIS

Rae, Clara, and Gabe stood across the river from Notre Dame. Jonah and Aubrey had stayed back at the Arc de Triomphe, where, Rae assumed, they were still making out. She leaned over the wall in front of her and looked at the Seine below, at its dark, glassy water. They'd been walking for over an hour, and her feet *killed*.

"My feet *kill*." Clara slumped beside her. "How far did we walk?"

"It's almost midnight," Gabe said, "so—pretty far? I guess?"

"Pretty far," Clara whimpered. She pressed her weight into Rae's side, her skin warm and her hair draping over Rae's arm. It felt stiff and waxy from the recent hair dye. It reminded Rae of the way her own hair used to feel after a day at the beach in Georgia. Or maybe she was only thinking about that because the air around them smelled damp, the same way it used to when Lucy would drive them to the beach, all the windows of their old car rolled down. Rae's limbs grew sleepy and comfortable.

"Rose and I came to Paris a few summers ago," Clara said, staring up at the massive stone cathedral. "Right before she went to college. My parents let us come by ourselves, and we spent the whole time pretending we lived here."

"In an old cathedral?" Rae asked.

"In *Paris*," Clara said. "Wouldn't you love to live in Paris?"

"I don't know." Rae considered it. "Maybe? I want to live as many places as I possibly can. What about you, Gabe?"

"Not sure," Gabe said, but Rae didn't think he was really listening. His eyes were fixed beyond Notre Dame, and he seemed distracted.

Rae wondered if he was thinking about Aubrey. She wondered if Aubrey had tried to set him up with Clara and if he'd totally freaked out. She wondered if maybe she should have done something to stop her. Maybe she should call Aubrey right now to find out what had happened. But—selfishly—she didn't want anything about this moment to change.

"Where should we drink these?" Gabe held up the bag of beers they'd bought at an all-night grocery store.

"Down there." Clara gestured at a staircase built into the side of the bridge. They walked to the riverbank, and Rae saw the tops of parasols, a few tall palm trees, and a line of flapping, blue flags come into view.

"What the hell is all this?" Rae asked.

"I guess we're about to find out." Clara adjusted her fascinator.

They hopped down the final step and landed next to—a beach. But not a real one. It was a raised wooden platform drenched in sand and dotted with lounge chairs and umbrellas in the same dark violet color as the deepening sky. Even at midnight, couples and tourists ambled down the pathway by the river.

"They put up actual palm trees," Gabe said. "Talk about committing to a theme."

Clara kicked off her heels, climbed onto the platform, and lay down in the middle of a circle of chairs. "If Aubrey were here, she'd be *so* pissed at me right now."

"She would tell you going barefoot is a tetanus risk." Rae settled on a chair, taking off her camera bag and placing it beside her.

Gabe sat between them and checked over his shoulder to make sure there were no guards around before passing out the beers. A boat drifted past, its deck dripping with twinkling lights, and water splashing in its wake. Rae reached over to dig her fingers into the sand. Tetanus be damned.

"All right." Gabe lifted his beer. "Here's to the first hangover I don't have to hide from my parents."

"Cheers to that." Clara clinked her can with his, and they

opened theirs together, slurping the foam away before it could spill onto their hands.

Rae held on to hers but didn't open it yet. The air dipped and bobbed around her like water. She tucked a loose curl behind her ear and took it all in: the ornate carvings on the side of Notre Dame, the glittering colors reflecting on the bridge.

"You know what we should do," Clara said. "We should make a pact. We should promise each other that a year from now we'll come here again and sit on this exact beach at midnight."

Gabe raised an eyebrow. "What if we all hate each other by then?"

"We won't *hate each other*," Clara said. "Why would you say that?"

"No, he's right," Rae said. "Lots of people end up hating their high school friends. It's a statistical likelihood."

Clara kicked sand in her direction. "You're both so morbid."

Their conversation drifted to a pause, and Rae heard water lapping against the concrete barriers. Gabe's phone rang, and he shimmied it out of his pocket. "Zaida," he said to them. "My parents probably asked her to check up on me." He stood, brushing sand from the back of his jeans.

"Tell her to throw us a party!" Clara called after him.

He shook his head as he answered in Spanish, walking away down the beach. Clara and Rae watched until his silhouette disappeared past the palm trees, and then Clara turned back to Rae. "Okay," she said. "You have to tell me. What was Aubrey talking to him about back there? And why did they both look so miserable?"

"Oh." Rae's gaze fell to the sand. Clara's eyes were so bright and earnest that Rae didn't think she could lie to her. "I'm not exactly sure. But I think it had something to do with—you, actually."

"Me?"

"Yeah. Aubrey might have asked whether you and Gabe liked each other. Or something."

"She *did*? Where the hell did that come from?"

"I believe from her good friend Too Much Champagne."

Clara laughed, and Rae slid from her chair to the ground beside her.

"But I don't see Gabe that way." Clara wrapped her arms around her legs and rested her chin on her knees. "I can't even imagine kissing him. It would be so creepy."

"I know," Rae said. "Remember when Aubs and Jonah got together? You said you'd never date someone from our friend group. You called it a 'recipe for awkwardness.'"

"Oh yeah." Clara turned to face the water, and the light from the bridge illuminated her profile.

Rae hadn't fallen for Clara because she was beautiful, but once she had fallen for her, the beautiful thing had become impossible to ignore. Even now, Rae couldn't help noticing the sweep of her eyelashes, the dip of her collarbone. Another boat passed by them, its light reflected on the water's surface.

"What about you?" Clara asked, watching it pass.

"Do I have a crush on Gabe?"

"No." Clara looked back at her. "Do you like anyone? Or did you? Before we left school?"

Rae rolled her warm can of beer on the ground. "Not really."

"Typical Rae. So many girls, so little time."

"That is *not* typical me."

Clara smiled. "It really is. You fall hard for someone, but then the relationship lasts approximately ten seconds. You've clearly forgotten all about Emily St. James."

"What about her?"

"You *kissed* her at prom."

"Yeah, but she kissed me first. What was I supposed to do? Pretend I didn't notice?"

"Because that doesn't prove my point at all," Clara said flatly.

"Well, you kissed your prom date, didn't you?"

"Jack?" Clara stretched her legs across the sand. "I did. But he was pretty boring."

"So boring you dated him for a month?"

"He was a cute college guy. I was *infatuated* with him. But then I realized he wasn't deep or poetic—he was just dull."

Rae traced a few lines in the sand. "I think you made the

right call. You don't want to move to LA with a boyfriend. You want to be free to meet lots of hot art-school guys."

"I guess," Clara said.

The blue flags snapped in a gust of wind. Rae kept rolling her beer can. She felt a dull ache at the base of her ribs, the same one she got every time she thought about Clara leaving. Or meeting some stupid perfect guy. But she had to remind herself that this feeling was good. This was the feeling of moving on.

She and Clara had been friends since their first semester at LAS, but Rae's feelings for her hadn't changed until the summer after junior year. Their friends were off traveling with their families, but Clara had stayed in London to do a fashion internship at the Victoria and Albert Museum while Rae worked part-time at her mom's antique store. They began spending all their free time together—floating between each other's houses and staying up till three AM to watch old movies like *Moulin Rouge!* in Clara's room.

Her room was crowded with a sewing table, dress mannequins draped in patterned fabrics, and inspiration photographs pinned to a bulletin board above her desk. Being there made Rae feel like the world was made of such vivid colors. Like everything was a little more intense, a little more concentrated there, in that tiny space with Clara's purple-painted walls and the high window above her bed. It was the first time since meeting Aubrey that Rae felt another person slip so easily into her life.

Except being with Clara was nothing like being with Aubrey.

It was like being with a girl Rae wanted to kiss. Because Clara had been right earlier—Rae did harbor intense, all-consuming crushes. And those crushes usually became intense, all-consuming relationships. And those relationships always ended. But since she and Clara had no hope of dating, Rae was stuck here, in the pining stage, waiting for the day her feelings would finally burn out. "We should do your pact," she blurted.

Clearly, that day was not today.

Clara dusted sand from her knees. "Really? You want to meet again in Paris?"

"Sure. How do we make it official? Do we sign it in blood or something?"

Clara scooted across the sand. "Or we could drink to it."

"Better idea." Rae opened her beer, and instantly, warm, foamy liquid sprayed everywhere.

Clara covered her mouth with her hands. "Oh no!"

"Shit!" Rae held the can away from her, beer sputtering onto her arms and legs.

"Quick! Take this." Clara grabbed a towel someone had left on one of the loungers, but already the beer was soaking into Rae's clothes. She wiped some off her lap. "Great," she said. "I'm going to smell so wasted."

"I guess that's what happens when you roll a beer around for ten minutes," Clara said. "But it's okay. We can share." She started to hand over her drink but paused for a second, her arm suspended between them. "But only if you really mean it," she said. "Only if you want to come back here sometime. Even if it's only the two of us."

Another boat appeared from under the bridge, stirring the night breeze—a breeze that touched Rae's cheek, that moved through Clara's hair. It rippled the river beside them, the water as dark as a pool of black ink.

Rae took the drink from Clara. "Yeah," she said. "Even if it's only the two of us."

7

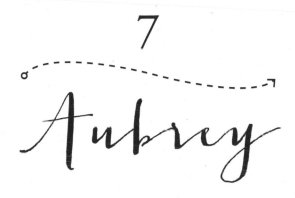

Aubrey

Saturday, July 2
PARIS

"Come on, Aubrey! Keep up!"

Clara stood as she pedaled, her bright-red ponytail snapping against her back. Jonah was right behind her, and Gabe and Rae were behind him, cycling next to each other. Gabe said something and she laughed, wobbling on her bike. Aubrey squinted and bent her elbows, begging her legs to work harder. Her head throbbed as sunlight reflected off the passing cars. She swore that the smell of champagne was everywhere.

"How are you doing back there?" Rae called.

"How are you not hungover?" Aubrey called back.

"I can't hear you." Rae dropped back to wait for her. "Jesus. Are you dead?"

"Getting there," Aubrey muttered.

Rae, of course, looked great. She was wearing cute cut-off overalls, and her long curls had been wrangled into two braids. Early that morning, Clara had woken them all up so they could get coffee and bike to the Centre Pompidou. Aubrey had been shocked that Clara hadn't seemed even remotely queasy. And that neither Clara nor Rae looked tired.

Aubrey glanced up at the nearest street sign. They were on the rue de Rivoli, moving away from the Centre Pompidou and getting closer to their next stop: the Louvre. Construction cranes loomed in the sky, and the lunch rush-hour traffic clogged up the road. Aubrey winced as cars swerved around them; she hated that the bikes they'd rented hadn't come with helmets.

"So," Rae said, "tell me about last night."

Aubrey squeezed her handlebars. "You were with me last night."

"Not for all of it. What happened when we left?" Rae's words were muffled by roaring jackhammers, which gave Aubrey a moment to think. She wanted to tell Rae what Gabe had said, but she couldn't face it yet. The embarrassment felt too fresh. "Is it TMI if I tell you I puked in a Starbucks bathroom?" she asked.

"Ew," Rae said. "Yes."

"Well"—Aubrey felt her sunglasses slip down her nose—"that's what happened."

Afterward, Jonah had taken them on the Metro back to

the hotel, where they'd hung out in Aubrey's room and he'd found an old French movie on TV. Aubrey had fallen asleep to the muted, underwater sound that black-and-white movies always seemed to have and whispered conversations in a language she couldn't understand.

"Sounds romantic," Rae said.

"Watch it, or I'll push you off your bike."

"You can't even let go of the handlebars!" Rae lifted her own hands and briefly held them overhead. A railing separated this part of the bike path from the rest of the street, but Rae still looked brave. Young and wild and unafraid of anything. She moved her fingers like she was trying to catch the air.

"Please stop," Aubrey said. "I can think of a thousand ways this could end horribly."

Rae stopped and grinned with all her teeth.

"Turn left!" Clara called from up ahead. They went through a long, cool archway that led to the place du Carrousel. Aubrey saw everything all at once: the long line of tour buses, the shining glass pyramid, and the Louvre itself, zigzagging around the plaza's perimeters.

Aubrey's bike hobbled to a stop.

"Damn," Jonah said to her. "You don't look so good."

"She's totally great," Rae said. "I hear near-death experiences make you stronger."

"Bad news," Gabe said, holding up his phone. His eyes skimmed straight over Aubrey, and her embarrassment felt new and raw all over again. She picked at her handlebar with her thumbnail. "We can't park our bikes here," he said. "We have to go somewhere else and come back."

"Oh God." Aubrey collapsed against Jonah. "Why isn't today over yet?"

Clara shaded her eyes; an image of the pyramid was reflected in her sunglasses. "Aubrey. It hasn't even begun."

But, somehow, it did end.

Hours and hours went by, hours they filled wandering the unending corridors of the Louvre and sitting on the Right Bank eating falafel. As soon as the sun set, they returned their bikes and traipsed back to their hotel to change for the night.

Now it was after eleven PM, and the nightclub they were in was crowded. People filled the dance floor—girls wearing skintight jeans and strappy tank tops, guys with their hair gelled up straight. Music played over the speakers, but Aubrey couldn't tell if the lyrics were in English or French.

She was standing against the back wall, holding a soda, while Rae, Clara, and Gabe danced with everyone else. Jonah had gone outside to answer his phone—probably to reassure his mom that they were all safe and currently sober.

Aubrey sipped her watery soda. She saw Gabe grab Rae's hands and spin her in a circle. It was strange, because Rae and

Gabe had never really hung out without Aubrey before. She'd always considered herself the thing that linked them together, that made them friends in the first place. But maybe that was selfish. Clearly, they got along just fine without her.

"Taking a dance break?" Jonah dodged around two girls bobbing their heads to the electric beat and took his place beside her.

"I got soda." Aubrey held up her glass. "Was that your mom?"

"Leah."

"Oh."

Jonah was wrapped up in the music and everything going on around them, so Aubrey let herself roll her eyes. Of course it was Leah. Getting in the way even when she wasn't here. Making everything about *her*.

"She wanted to talk about the apartment," Jonah said. It was so loud he had to speak next to her ear.

"The apartment?" Aubrey shouted.

"You know. The three-bedroom place her friend rents in Alphabet City? Leah's moving in next year, and she said she'd put in a good word for us."

"A good word about what?"

"About us moving in with them."

For a moment, Aubrey was grateful for the noise. It gave her time to gather her thoughts. For her mind to tick through a series of memories—of the spring when she got accepted to Columbia; of their whole senior year, when she and Jonah would talk about New York. It ticked back to junior year, when she and Jonah would hang out at play rehearsals and Leah would drag him away to tell him some gossipy, pointless secret. He always glowed when Leah paid attention to him. And sometimes, it made Aubrey wonder if he secretly liked Leah more. Which was ridiculous—after all, *she* was Jonah's girlfriend—but still. Leah could make her feel so small.

"Let's get out there." Jonah laced his fingers with hers. "Or we'll miss everything."

A rap song was playing now, one that Rae and Gabe knew all the lyrics to. They blasted through each line while Clara cheered them on. Bodies slammed against Aubrey's back. She thought about what she would be doing if she were home instead—probably reading a book in bed, or maybe watching *The Temple of Doom* with Chris, arguing with him over whether or not it was the worst Indiana Jones movie (she was a firm yes; he was a firm *Kingdom of the Crystal Skull*). She knew she should dance, too, but she didn't exactly feel like it, so she just nodded her head a lot.

The song ended, and Gabe held up his hand for Rae to high-five.

"Why are you so tall?" she asked, jumping up to meet him.

"Don't know, Preston," he said. "Why are you so short?"

Preston, Aubrey thought. Usually he only called *her* by her last name.

"Does anyone want water?" Clara fanned her face with

both hands. That afternoon, after the museum, she'd painted each nail white with a neon-green line down the middle. She turned toward the bar and stopped cold. "Oh my God." She tugged on the bottom of Rae's shirt. "That girl is totally checking you out."

Everyone stared in the direction Clara was looking. "Smooth, guys," Rae said. "Very subtle."

"What's with the haircut, though?" Jonah asked.

"I kind of like it," Gabe said. "Very young Carrie Brownstein."

Rae buried her face in her hands. "Jesus Christ, you're all exactly like my mother."

Another song started, but none of them were dancing; they were a beat of stillness in a sea of motion. Gabe and Jonah talked over Aubrey's head. She looked down and saw the pink laces on Gabe's shoes and the stripes on Jonah's old sneakers. Their voices collided above her. It was almost like she wasn't even there.

"I need some air," she said.

Instantly Rae said, "I'll come with you."

And Aubrey felt absurdly relieved. Outside, the night was lukewarm, and she slumped against the beige wall beside the club's entrance as tiny cars and scooters zipped down the street. The sky was smoggy and dense with clouds.

"That place is so tacky." Rae dug around in her pocket for a stick of strawberry gum.

Aubrey still had her drink, which she placed on the

sidewalk. "Jonah wants to move in with Leah next year," she said.

Rae stopped digging. "No effing way."

"Yeah," Aubrey said. "Or I should say, he wants *us* to move in with her. They were on the phone tonight, planning it all out."

"What a control freak!"

"Leah? Or Jonah?"

"Definitely Leah. No offense, but Jonah's too hapless for that."

"That's not offensive." Aubrey held out her hand, and Rae gave her a stick of gum. They both stood there for a minute, just chewing, waiting for the sugary taste to fade. Aubrey couldn't imagine going back inside that nightclub. "Gabe doesn't want to be my friend anymore," she said.

"What?" Rae asked. "When did that happen?"

"It happened last night. At the Arc de Triomphe. I wanted to tell you about it this morning, but I could barely even think about it. Plus, I was super hungover."

"So, hold on. Are you upset about Jonah? Or about Gabe?"

"Maybe both."

"Or maybe you're just upset because everything's so different now."

Aubrey watched someone across the street flick a cigarette butt to the ground. Rae was definitely right—everything was different.

It had been for three weeks. It had been since the last

night of the musical, when, in a darkened backstage room, Aubrey and Gabe had kissed. When, just like that, the space between them had evaporated to nothing. His mouth on hers. Her mouth on his. It had lasted only a few seconds, but that didn't matter. It was still a kiss.

A kiss that Aubrey had spent every day of the past three weeks trying to figure out. She'd sprawled out on the grass in her backyard, going over and over that moment. Like there was some secret meaning to it. Like, if she could just find that meaning, the kiss would suddenly make sense, and she could forget all about it.

She thought over the silly crush she'd had on Gabe freshman year. She remembered the afternoons they'd spent painting sets together and the weekend mornings she'd biked over to his house so they could spend all day sitting on his living room floor, listening to the old, folksy records his dad collected.

But then, during their sophomore year, Gabe stopped inviting her over so much. He'd get this distant look in his eyes and make up excuses whenever she asked if he was free. Eventually, she realized: He must have figured out that she liked him. He must have been trying to tell her he only thought of her as a friend. And by the time Jonah asked her out a few months later, Aubrey only thought of him as one, too.

Or, at least, she thought she did. So why had she kissed him? How had she let all of this happen?

"Okay." Rae blew a curl out of her eye. "You want me to tell you something you don't want to hear?"

"No," Aubrey said. "Of course I don't."

"Well. Tough love, baby." Rae stood in front of her and snapped her gum. Her cheeks were still bright red from dancing. "Maybe this whole thing with Gabe isn't about him despising you. Maybe it's—the opposite."

"The opposite *how*?" Aubrey asked.

"Aubs, have you ever considered the possibility that Gabe likes you? You know, as more than a friend?"

A motorbike stopped in the street, its engine popping. Frenzied energy built up in Aubrey's chest. "There's no way," she said. "He wouldn't be treating me like this if he did."

"Maybe he would. Maybe he didn't expect to kiss you that night. It's probably a lot for him to deal with."

"I know he didn't expect to kiss me." Aubrey shook her head. "Because it was a mistake."

"Look, I know this seriously sucks, but"—Rae blew another bubble—"maybe what you need to do is give him space. Let him work this shit out by himself. If he still doesn't want to be your friend, forget him."

Aubrey pressed her hands to the wall—she was surprised by how cool it was. "I can't forget him," she said shakily. "I can't forget any of you."

Rae didn't speak for a moment, her expression full of sympathy. "Dude. I never said anything about forgetting me."

That made Aubrey laugh, and the panic inside her loosened a little. She looked out at the busy bars and clubs of Paris, and it occurred to her that maybe Rae was right—maybe she was trying too hard to make things how she wanted them to be. Maybe she needed to leave Gabe alone.

Give him space.

The door to the club burst open, and a group of people emerged. Behind them was Clara, her face falling when she saw Aubrey. "What happened?" she asked. "You look so bummed out."

"I'm fine." Aubrey pushed herself off the wall and smiled. Because, for that moment at least, it felt true.

8

Sunday, July 3
PARIS to AMSTERDAM

The train from Paris to Amsterdam left late at night, so it was completely dark out as they made their way between countries. Rae sat by herself, a sketchbook open in her lap, tapping her pen against the page. Gabe and Clara were across the aisle from her, and Aubrey and Jonah were in the row in front, all of them asleep.

Rae kept tapping her pen. And she kept thinking about yesterday. She thought about how she'd told Aubrey to leave Gabe alone, and she thought about how unbelievably stupid that was. Of *course* Aubrey shouldn't leave Gabe alone! Rae should have told her to kick his ass for saying he didn't want to be friends anymore.

No. Actually, Rae should be the one kicking his ass. She was Aubrey's best friend—that kind of stuff was her job.

Clara slid into the free seat beside her, kicking off her flip-flops and pulling up her legs. "What are you working on?" she asked.

Rae looked over in shock. "Nothing," she said. "Well, nothing serious." Which was true—so far, it was only a few rough palm trees and the skeleton of a boat floating on a river.

"No, it's perfect." Clara leaned over the paper to get a better look. Her hair was pulled into a side braid with a few strands that must have fallen loose while she slept. Rae could smell the orange and raspberry perfume Clara always wore. That morning, she'd put some on standing in front of the hotel mirror, and it had lingered in the room until they had to leave.

"What about you?" Rae cleared her throat. "What have you been doing?"

"Sleeping. But I should be sketching like you. I have this idea for a series of mermaid-themed dresses—real mermaid dresses, with glittery tails and seashells sewn into them and everything. But I don't know. I think maybe it's a little over the top."

"That's still cool," Rae said.

Clara sighed. "I keep imagining myself walking in on the first day of school and just . . . not knowing what to do. Not even knowing how to use a pen or a pair of scissors."

"Never gonna happen." Rae shifted so her back was against the window. The train hummed against her skin.

"Maybe I'll have to transfer," Clara said. "My parents would love that. Where do you think I should go? Somewhere else in California, right?"

Rae tossed the cap of her pen at her. "Stop being so negative. You're not going to transfer. I won't allow it."

"What are you two talking about?" Aubrey sat up in front of them.

"Oh my God," Rae said. "Wasn't everyone asleep, like, two seconds ago?"

"I was." Aubrey yawned. "But your mom keeps texting me. She told me to tell you to turn on your phone."

"My phone *is* turned on. It's also on silent."

"So tell her yourself."

Rae took out her phone and saw a series of photographs that Lucy had been sending her, all of them of an apartment decorated with sea-green furniture and vases of white flowers. The text read: *Melbourne apartment. Could rent for all of December. What do you think???*

Rae typed back, *yeah, mom, looks cool.*

Her mom's response: *NOT ENTHUSIASTIC ENOUGH!*

YEAH, MOM! LOOKS COOL! Rae tossed the phone back in her bag.

"I still can't believe it," Clara said. "In less than two weeks, you'll be in Australia. You're going to have the coolest life."

"I'm spending the next six months with my mom," Rae said. "How is that the coolest life?"

"Lucy's cool," Aubrey said. "She's definitely cooler than

my parents." There was a whooshing sound as someone opened the door connecting their carriage to the next. It closed, and the train went quiet again.

"And mine," Clara said. "The most fun pre-college activity we have planned is making Rose come from Stanford so we can all go shopping at Bed Bath & Beyond."

"Sure," Rae said. "But that's because your parents are reasonable adults."

Aubrey reached over to prod Rae's shoulder. "Lucy's an adult."

"She was *nineteen* when I was born."

"So?" Aubrey poked her again. "She raised you by herself. She moved you back to London, and now she's moving you to Australia. You can't diss that."

"Yeah, yeah," Rae said, pretending to be exasperated. But honestly, she knew Aubrey was right. Her parents had dated for a while when they were both students at the University of Georgia, but they were never serious, and her dad was firmly out of the picture long before Rae was born. And here was the truth: Rae was fine with that. She liked the weird life she had with her mom—their house full of junk, and Lucy's tiny antique store, and the small studio space in their guesthouse where Rae would sit with Iorek and do homework while her mom painted.

"Anyway." Clara's eyes went mischievous. "Rae just wants her mom out of the picture so she can find an Australian girl to fall in *loooove* with."

"Well," Aubrey said, "that's definitely true."

"*Ugh.*" Rae slid down against the window. "Why does everyone really enjoy making fun of me?"

"We're not making fun of you," Clara said. "We're talking about how much crush potential is in your very near future."

"Remember the California art-school guys?" Rae said. "Can't we talk about them?"

Clara waved one hand to the side. "But I want to talk about Melbourne girls. Hot, artsy Melbourne girls with cute accents and tattoos."

"Not my type," Rae said dismissively. But the thing was, she had wondered about this before: What would happen if she met someone in Australia? Before Clara, she actually used to like having crushes. She liked the butterflies-in-her-stomach feeling whenever she ran into one of them; she liked the rush she felt every time they had a conversation or not-so-accidentally touched. And she liked obsessing over those crushes with her friends—texting Aubrey the second she saw Jane Carpenter at an art supply store in Covent Garden, or running up to Clara's locker sophomore year when she'd just had a five-minute conversation with the pretty senior girl in her ceramics class. This was another reason Australia was a good thing. Distance would help her get over Clara, and then she could finally be open with her friends again.

The train started to slow down.

"You'll see," Clara said. "You're going to meet so many cool girls. Way cooler than the entire population of LAS *combined.*"

"Oh yeah. I can already see it," Rae deadpanned. "Get in line, ladies."

Clara tipped her head to the side as a few people in surrounding seats began to get up and stretch. She seemed to be contemplating something. "Rae," she said, "you do realize you're kind of a babe, right?"

Rae's pulse raced. Out of the corner of her eye, she saw a question form on Aubrey's face. And seriously, she had no idea what to make of any of this. Was Clara flirting with her? Had Aubrey noticed? Rae knew how to handle flirting, but she had no clue how to handle flirting *with Clara*.

In front of Aubrey.

She racked her brain, trying to come up with something to say, but luckily, she didn't have to.

The train let out one final breath before clunking to a stop.

They'd arrived in Amsterdam.

9

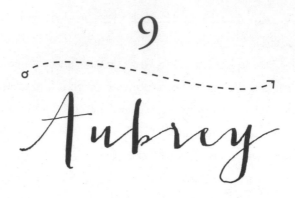

Aubrey

Monday, July 4
AMSTERDAM

Aubrey woke up at seven AM, worrying about Rae.
 She turned over in her bunk and let her eyes adjust to the hostel room around her—the triangle of light filtering between the curtains, the banged-up set of dresser drawers, the bunk bed where Clara and Rae were curled up under polka-dotted sheets. They hadn't arrived until after midnight, so Aubrey knew she should still be tired, but she wasn't. She'd slept fitfully, obsessing over how weird and distant Rae had acted when they'd brought up Australia on the train.

She couldn't shake the feeling that maybe Rae was keeping something from her. Something about Australia? Something about leaving? Aubrey tossed and turned. Rae was so evasive when it came to college. The first time she'd told Aubrey she was considering Melbourne, she'd sounded uninterested in the whole idea. Like it was no big deal to her. Like she would be living in a separate state rather than a separate hemisphere.

Aubrey pushed back her covers and climbed down the ladder of her bunk, bare feet padding along the cold linoleum floor as she went to sit on Rae's bed. "Wake up," she said. "We're in Amsterdam."

Rae smashed her face into her pillow. "I don't believe you."

"Don't you want coffee?" Aubrey asked. "Or waffles? I bet they have waffles in Amsterdam."

"Why are you awake right now? It's evil and it's wrong."

Aubrey's eyes fell to a spot on the wooden bedpost where someone had scratched two sets of initials inside a heart. She traced her thumb over the indents, feeling a little let down that Rae didn't want to hang out with her. Feeling a little like it was a sign that Rae was already pulling away, growing distant.

"Fine," Aubrey said. "I'm going to take a shower." She grabbed her toiletry bag and some clothes and slipped into the hallway. The bathroom was quiet this early in the morning, and she watched as steam clouded up the light fixtures above her. She let herself think about how much she was going to miss Rae. Soon, she wouldn't automatically know everything that was going on in her best friend's life. She wouldn't be a fixed part of her world anymore. It was like they were both speeding toward a dead end. Like the ground was slipping out from under their feet.

She banged her elbow on the shower's narrow walls, then stared at the dingy tile and considered how germ-ridden it must be. This was nothing like the spacious shower in the hotel in Paris—it was probably more like the one she would have to deal with in her dorm in New York.

When the water ran cold, Aubrey turned it off and changed into the T-shirt and shorts she'd hung on the back of the stall door. Her dark hair dripped as she combed it out and then put on sunscreen. When she left the bathroom, she instantly walked into Gabe. He stumbled backward, and so did she, toiletries spilling out of her bag.

She ducked down to pick them up. "I'm so sorry," she said.

"Not your fault." Gabe leaned over to help, their heads bending toward each other. "So"—she neatly arranged all her tiny bottles of shampoo and soap—"what are you doing here?"

"Showering," he said. "Or I was about to. In—um—the bathroom."

They stood again, Gabe holding her conditioner now, and Aubrey clutching her toothbrush to her chest. He was wearing only boxer shorts and a T-shirt, so she concentrated on the wall beside her, which had a flyer on it advertising an outdoor music festival.

"Gabe?" she said.

"Yeah?" He shifted from foot to foot, obviously uncomfortable.

"Um, you still have my conditioner—"

On the floor above them, a door banged open. In the

nearest room, Aubrey could hear someone strumming an acoustic guitar. But her thoughts were louder than anything else: *Leave him alone. Give him space.* "Anyway"—she grabbed the conditioner from him—"thank you." And then she ran all the way back to her room.

Aubrey yanked back the curtains and shoved open the window to let in the morning noise.

Clara whimpered and pulled the covers over her head, but Rae barely moved. Neither of them got up.

This was starting to piss Aubrey off. They only had one full day in Amsterdam, and they needed to make the most of it. Her phone buzzed and she lunged for it, desperate for someone to talk to. It was a text from Jonah. He was downstairs and wanted to know if she was awake yet. She grabbed her key and left the room before she'd even replied.

Their hostel sat on the edge of the Vondelpark, and Aubrey opened the front door to see tall, skinny trees and scrubby purple wildflowers, with a rush of bikes clipping past it all.

Jonah was sitting on the front steps, playing with his phone. His hair was pushed back from his forehead, and he was wearing a forest-green shirt—a really cute one that matched the color of his eyes. He stood up when he saw her and handed over a small paper cup. "Good morning," he said. "They had free coffee in the lobby."

Aubrey sipped it and coughed.

"Sorry," he said. "I should have warned you: It's pretty gross."

"Yeah." She tried to swallow the burnt taste in her mouth. "You definitely should have."

"So, guess what?" He bounced up and down on his heels. "I've been looking stuff up, and I've come up with a whole plan for today. And I know exactly where we should go first."

"*You* came up with a plan?"

"Yeah, you're not the only one here who can make plans."

She felt her mood lift. "Clearly."

They threw their cups in the trash and made their way through the park. Past lush green lawns and small lakes and dainty, idyllic gazebos. It all looked like something from a tourist brochure. Aubrey could picture herself doing this kind of thing soon in New York—probably in Central Park. She and Jonah would crunch over autumn leaves or go ice-skating before winter break or bring a picnic in the spring and do their homework in the sunshine.

They'd been walking for about twenty minutes when they reached a clearing taken over by a group of treehouses, all of them balanced on stilts with rope bridges and ladders hanging from their sides. It was the first part of the park they'd been to that was completely empty.

"What do you think?" Jonah said. "It's rad, right?"

"Is it a playground?" Aubrey asked.

"A *treehouse* playground. Don't you wish you'd had a place like this when you were a kid?"

Aubrey eyed one of the rope ladders. "I was actually pretty afraid of heights."

"Somehow, I'm unsurprised by that." Jonah nudged her shoulder. "Okay. Follow me."

The ladder creaked and shuddered under his weight while Aubrey stood at the bottom, hands braced on the rung in front of her. Of all the things that might happen to her before college, *death by horrible treehouse accident* wasn't her favorite option. The ladder slackened when Jonah reached the top. "You have to come up," he called down to her.

"This seems unsafe," she called back, gripping the rope as she climbed. "Maybe we're not supposed to be here."

"We're *definitely* not supposed to be here. We're not child-size anymore." He scooted out of her way so she could crawl inside. The walls of the small room were made of slats of wood that let in long stripes of light, and the sanded floor was covered in a layer of sawdust. Even on her hands and knees, Aubrey had to duck so her head wouldn't hit the low ceiling.

"See?" Jonah sat back. "Told you I'm full of plans."

Aubrey tipped her head to watch a burst of sun appear between two slats. Silhouettes of leaves shivered against one another. "I can't believe everyone is missing this," she said.

"I don't think we'd all fit."

"No, I know. It's just—I thought we'd all go out together this morning. See the sights. Isn't that what we're supposed to be doing?"

Jonah shrugged. "I guess they're still tired."

"I guess." Aubrey sat beside him. She wanted to tell him about the feeling she'd woken up with—the feeling that Rae was keeping something from her. The feeling that, when Rae left, Aubrey might begin to lose her best friend. But she couldn't get into all that with Jonah. The nuances of girl friendships tended to confuse him.

"Aubs." Jonah leaned over to tug on a strand of her hair. "Don't worry so much."

"I'm not worrying."

He tugged her hair again. "You're always worrying."

She smiled and rolled her eyes.

"Anyway," he said, "maybe we don't want anyone else here."

Aubrey looked over at his teasing eyes, at the small, adorable lines that appeared by the sides of his mouth whenever he smiled. She realized that, for the first time in a while, they were alone. Not the way they'd been that first night in Paris. Not *vomiting* and alone. But *alone* alone. The treehouse was dark and cool, and Jonah was brushing his fingers through the ends of her hair.

"I've never seen you like this before," he said.

"In a treehouse?"

"No." His voice went low; he seemed to get shy. "By ourselves. First thing in the morning."

She moved toward him; their mouths touched. And in that single breath, all of Aubrey's anxiety faded away. The tiny room was crowded with the two of them, so she moved one leg over his lap, and he pulled her closer. The bottom of her T-shirt slid against the bottom of his. Her hands traveled into his hair. . . .

And then his phone vibrated between them, making Aubrey jump, her head smacking the ceiling. *"Ow."* She reached back to rub her head. "Jesus."

She had to move out of his way so he could shimmy his phone from his pocket. "It's probably just Leah," he explained.

"Leah?"

"Yeah, I told her to text when she was at the hostel. But I figured she'd be a while."

Aubrey stopped rubbing her head. "So, Leah's at the hostel? Right now?"

"I think so. She's got the whole day off, so I said she should come over here. Show us around."

"I thought *you* came up with a plan for today."

"Exactly. That is the plan."

A bird fluttered over the treehouse, its shadow moving across the floor. Everything went quiet as Jonah's thumbs flew over the screen of his phone.

"Actually," Aubrey said, "I had a few places I really wanted to see."

"Uh-huh," he said. "But Leah will know all the non-touristy ones. She does live here."

"She interns here," Aubrey said, and she could hear the bitterness in her voice. Not that Jonah was listening anymore.

She adjusted her shorts and crawled off his lap. The silence in the treehouse felt overwhelming now. And Aubrey couldn't seem to shove aside her most anxious thoughts about Leah. Thoughts that Leah would take up all of Jonah's time and attention. Thoughts that Aubrey would be the one left behind.

Instead, she tried to imagine what this place would be like in a few hours—kids crawling all over it, disappearing in and out of the trees. A day from now, Aubrey wouldn't even be in Amsterdam anymore. She would be catching another train, racing off to Prague. A few weeks after that, she and her parents would be at Heathrow, boarding the plane that would bring her to New York. But now Aubrey couldn't shake the thought that maybe *this* was what her life in New York would be—not the one she'd daydreamed about on their first night in Paris, but one that kept getting interrupted with texts. One that was all about NYU and Alphabet City apartments and Jonah-and-Leah.

Jonah-and-Leah going to hipster bars and concerts downtown. Jonah-and-Leah hanging out while Aubrey studied in the library and stressed out and ate dinner by herself in the school cafeteria. Maybe next year, Jonah would move into that apartment without her.

Maybe he and Leah would grow closer and closer. While he and Aubrey grew further and further apart.

10

Monday, July 4
AMSTERDAM

When Rae finally woke up, Aubrey was gone and Clara was still burrowed under her blankets. The window was open, a breeze skittering over Rae's top sheet. She got out of bed and grabbed her clothes to take to the bathroom—no way in hell was she getting changed in here. What if Clara woke up?

Way too awkward. So not worth the humiliation.

She brushed her teeth and stared at herself in the mirror over the sink. It was humid, which made her hair even curlier than usual. Rae thought she looked young. Or like a creepy horror-movie doll. She held her hair behind her neck and spat into the sink.

After she got dressed, she headed down the creaky stairs into the lobby. Gabe was sitting on a threadbare couch wearing headphones and reading a creased paperback he must have picked up from a pile by the window. She considered slipping past him—after all, he wasn't exactly her favorite person right now—but there was something undeniably sad about the fact that he was sitting by himself. His shirt was rumpled, and the skin around his eyes looked dark, like he hadn't slept much.

Rae walked over and sat down, kicking her feet onto the coffee table. "Happy Fourth of July," she said.

He pushed off his headphones. "Are you even allowed to celebrate that? Because you're, like, British."

"Come on. I'm American, too," she said. "But honestly, I celebrate nothing until the matriarchy takes over."

"Sounds about right."

"So," she said. "Where is everybody?"

"Out," he said. "Leah came to the hostel, and Jonah and Aubrey went somewhere with her."

"Why didn't you go, too?"

He shut the book and leaned back in his chair. "Would you voluntarily spend an entire day in a foreign city with Leah?"

"Fair point." Rae reached over to snag his book and skimmed the back cover—it was a true-crime story from the 1980s. "Is this what you've decided to do for a living?"

"Become a serial killer? Nah. Too messy."

"Um, *no*. I meant, like, read books. Or, you know, *study* books. Whatever it is people do."

"Reading books," he said. "I don't think they offer that exact major at Reed. But who knows? The world is our oyster, right?"

"That's what they keep telling me." Rae flipped through the onionskin pages, swishing them against her fingers. She wasn't sure what to say to him now. He'd hurt Aubrey, which meant she was supposed to hate him. But he also seemed so pathetic. She couldn't help feeling a little sorry for the guy.

She kicked the underside of his foot. "Okay. Let's go out."

"I don't know," he said. "I was getting pretty into that book."

"Oh please. You can read all the time in college. But we're only in Amsterdam until tomorrow. There has to be a better place to hang out than this hostel."

The skepticism vanished from his face. "Fine." He hopped out of his chair. "You win."

"I'll text Clara to let her know we're heading out." Rae got up, too. "That way she won't think we got serial-killed."

The morning was gorgeous. Rae put on her sunglasses and took in all the adorable brick houses lining the sidewalk, their windows and doors trimmed in white. It was cuter than Paris and quainter than London, but it still felt like a city. Sunlight bloomed over everything.

"I can't handle how precious this is," she said. "It's like the whole place is made of gingerbread."

"Except less edible," Gabe quipped, dodging a cyclist who'd momentarily ridden onto the sidewalk.

They picked up breakfast at a coffee shop with beech-wood walls and then followed the map on Gabe's phone toward a ring of nearby canals. Light sparkled in the water, and trees on the banks shook out their airy, green branches.

Gabe stopped at a railing, and since Rae had left her camera at the hostel, she tried to remember a few details she could draw later: potted plants on the decks of houseboats, red doors on brown and gray buildings, grass growing through the cement by the canal's edges.

"Uh-oh," Gabe said. "Someone's got Drawing Face."

Rae slushed her straw around her iced coffee. "What the hell is that?"

"It's when you're thinking about something you want to sketch." Gabe let his mouth soften and brow furrow and squinted around them, like he was trying to memorize what he saw. "See? Drawing Face."

"I am *not* that obvious." Rae propped her elbows on the railing. Gabe was wearing neon-framed sunglasses and a Nirvana T-shirt, which made him look extra hipster—even more so than usual. Rae could already picture him in Portland, riding bikes or hanging out with Fred and Carrie on the set of *Portlandia*.

"You know what I'm going to love about Melbourne?" she asked. "How little people will know about me. I'll be a complete mystery."

"Me too," he said. "Such a mystery even I don't know what classes I'm taking."

"I'm not talking about school." Rae watched a couple of bikes whip over the bridge. "I'm talking about important stuff. Meeting new people. Figuring out a city I've never lived in. You must want all of that, right? I mean, why else would you pick Oregon when you don't know anyone else there?"

"*You're* the one going to Australia."

"Yeah, but now we're talking about you." Across the canal, Rae spotted a cute girl walking out of a hair salon, wearing low-slung jeans and a tank top, her hair dyed bright pink.

"Fine," Gabe said. "I picked Reed because it's part of a city but there's still wilderness around."

"You like wilderness?"

"I like the *concept* of wilderness. But I've never lived in it." He paused. "Your turn. Why Australia?"

Rae sipped the last of her coffee and shook the ice in her plastic cup. "Why did we stop? We should be walking."

They headed down the red-brick sidewalk. White and blue flowers hung in planters attached to the bridges. A group of kids their age sat at an outdoor café, smoking cigarettes and eating pastries.

Rae felt a little bad for avoiding Gabe's question when he'd answered hers. She decided to throw him a bone. "I want to be somewhere new," she said. "That way, I get to be completely different, too."

"Different how?"

"In—lots of ways." The number one way being that she could actually move on from Clara. But she wasn't about to bring that up. Suddenly, she remembered the girl from the hair salon. "Like, I really want to cut my hair short, but my mom would probably think I'd betrayed her or something."

"Betrayed her? That sounds pretty extreme."

"Trust me, she'd hate it. The Rae you see now is the one I've been my whole life."

Gabe stretched his arms over his head, which reminded Rae of exactly how tall he was compared with her—her head barely reached his upper arm. "You could totally pull off short hair," he said. "Why don't you just do it?"

"I will. Someday. But I've already mentioned it to Aubrey a few times, and all she says is, *You wouldn't be Rae anymore.*"

"Huh," he said.

She could hear him retreating from their conversation. It had happened the second she mentioned Aubrey.

God, he was confusing. She still couldn't tell if he wanted nothing to do with Aubrey or if it was the exact opposite. Honestly, that would explain why he'd told Aubrey he didn't want to be friends anymore. Not because he didn't like her, but because he liked her *too much*. Because the idea of staying just friends was painful to consider.

Rae could definitely relate—which was maybe why she decided she had to snap him out of it.

"Okay, fine," she said. "I'll do it. I'll go full *Roman Holiday.*"

"What? *Right now?*"

"Yup. Before I change my mind." She stomped off in the direction of the salon, dumping her empty coffee cup in a trash can along the way. A few seconds later, he raced to catch up with her. The bell above the door rang as they entered a room decorated with retro pink wallpaper and chairs upholstered in green vinyl. A girl with a half-shaved head sat behind a desk at the front. Immediately, Rae's palms began to sweat. This was so stupid. She didn't want to cut her hair. Not on a whim. And definitely not to make Gabe *feel better* about Aubrey. That made no sense!

But here they were. The girl at the desk spoke perfect English and told them that, yes, she could fit Rae in now. She stood to get a black gown and Velcroed it around Rae's neck before leading her to one of the chairs.

"I'll be right back," she said, turning to answer the ringing phone. Rae focused on a comb in a jar of water in front of her. She squeezed the squeaky vinyl armrests.

Gabe took the chair next to hers. "You look nervous," he said. "I thought you wanted to do this?"

"Of course I do," she said. "It's going to be great. Chin-length. With a shaved patch right at the back. It's going to be rad and radical and super queer."

"You sound like you're trying to convince yourself." Gabe shoved his sunglasses onto his head. "You can always back out. I won't judge you."

"Seriously, bro. Stop talking." Rae scowled at her reflection— at her small, slightly upturned nose (*her aristocratic nose*, Lucy

91

called it) and her pale freckles. She pulled her hair out of its topknot, and it fell past her shoulders, all horizontal and fluffy, like Hermione's in the first *Harry Potter* movie. "I've always had long hair. Always. What if I hate it?"

He snapped his fingers. "You should try to distract yourself. Quick. Talk about something else—the first thing that comes to mind."

"Good idea." She took a deep breath and said the one thing that had been bugging her all morning: "So, are you going to stop ignoring Aubrey or what?"

In the mirror, Gabe's eyes widened. He seemed embarrassed, which made Rae feel kind of bad. But whatever. She couldn't stop now. And besides, he needed to hear this—if it didn't come from Aubrey's best friend, who would it come from? "Remember graduation?" she said.

"You mean that big important ceremony we had?" He sounded wry. "I have a vague recollection of it, yeah."

"You barely spoke to her. Couldn't you tell how heartbroken she was?"

Gabe sighed and looked down at his hands. "She really hates me, doesn't she?"

Rae swiveled her chair to face him. "I know for a fact that she doesn't. She misses you. She wants to talk to you again. Do you even know how jealous I got when you started hanging out with her freshman year? I thought you were going to replace me. You were Best Friend 2.0. A taller, more masculine version. But then I realized she just had a big, stupid crush on you and..."

Rae choked on her words. Gabe's eyebrows shot up.

Holy. Shit.

Holy shit!

What the hell had she just said? She'd been so determined to protect her friend that *she'd blabbed one of her biggest secrets*?!

The stylist walked back from the phone. "Let's get your hair washed," she said.

Rae stood and opened her mouth, but her mind went blank. And Gabe wasn't paying attention to her anyway. He was sitting forward, staring at the mirror like he was trying to look through it. Like he was watching something Rae couldn't see.

11

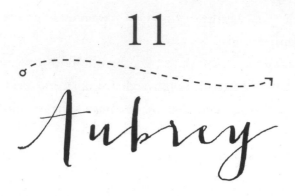

Monday, July 4
AMSTERDAM

Aubrey stood on the top deck of the houseboat and peered over to the deck below. A string of red, white, and blue paper lanterns was wrapped around the boat's guardrail, and the water glowed amber in the early evening light. She spotted a few different groups of college kids: boys taking selfies with a blocky Polaroid camera, tattooed girls waving tiny American flags and dancing barefoot. Leah was renting the houseboat with a group of NYU students interning in Holland for the summer, and when she'd met them, Aubrey had instantly felt like she was five years old. She'd wished she'd worn something cooler than a striped A-line sundress and cardigan.

"Shut *up*." Leah shoved Jonah's shoulder. "I can't believe you remember that!"

Jonah huffed out a laugh. "It's hard to forget the day you called our drama teacher a 'thwarted misogynistic manbaby.'"

"Jesus," Leah said. "You were a freshman then. I should have covered your ears."

"I was a sophomore."

"You were a *baby*." Her hand rested lazily on his shoulder. His eyes didn't move from her face.

Aubrey took a long drink of lukewarm beer.

It had only been a year since she'd last seen Leah, but she looked different now. Rows of silver hoops glinted in each of her ears, and a patch was shaved into the back of her long hair. It reminded Aubrey of Rae's new hair—except Rae's was a lot shorter. When Aubrey had first seen it, she'd stood there for a moment, dumbfounded. She couldn't believe Rae would just *cut* it like that. Without even asking for her opinion first.

"So, Aubrey," Leah said. Her voice sounded lower now and a little raspy. "Are you ready for Columbia?"

"I picked all my classes," Aubrey said. "Bought a warm coat."

Leah turned her head to the side and blew out a cloud of cigarette smoke. "You'll be amazed by how far Columbia feels from NYU. It's like this whole other universe."

"I bet." Aubrey glimpsed over the railing again. Rae was down there somewhere, probably charming hordes of college girls with her funky hair and her flirty *I'm-not-trying-to-impress-you-but-I-totally-am* attitude. Clara sat cross-legged on the deck, doing Jell-O shots with a guy in a flannel shirt with the sleeves cut off. And a few feet away from her stood Gabe. Looking up at Aubrey.

She wrenched her head away, blinking into the sunset to get her bearings. After a moment, she glanced back down, expecting him to be gone—but he wasn't. He jerked his head to the side, indicating the party around him, and rolled his eyes. Aubrey bit her lip. She nodded in agreement.

"Right, Aubs?"

"What?" She turned around, startled.

Jonah and Leah were staring at her.

"Fake IDs," Jonah said. "Leah knows someone who can set us up."

"Of course," Aubrey said. "Breaking the law. That sounds excellent. I just—I'll be right back." She slipped through the sliding glass door before Jonah had a chance to react, shutting it tightly behind her. Inside, the air felt close, and it was clear no one had bothered to clean up for the party—cereal bowls and balled-up hoodies covered every surface, and there were dust bunnies languishing in the corners. *Maybe this is okay*, Aubrey thought. *Maybe this is what college living is supposed to be like.* But God. It really was disgusting.

She left her beer beside a pile of dishes and walked down the narrow staircase. At the bottom, she met Rae and Gabe.

"There you are." Rae punched her shoulder. "We were on our way to rescue you."

"You were?" Aubrey rubbed her arm.

"Yeah." Rae tipped her head toward Gabe, making her new chin-length curls bounce. "Gabe told me we should."

"Thanks." Aubrey directed this at Gabe without actually making eye contact.

"You're welcome." He did exactly the same.

They were standing in the miniature living room, which smelled like incense and alcohol. The coffee table had been pushed out of the way to make room for a dance floor. The three of them stood awkwardly to the side while someone cranked up Arcade Fire on an iPad linked to speakers and people shimmied against one another in this half-joking, half-serious way. Rae drank from a plastic cup.

"What is that?" Aubrey asked her.

"Cranberry juice," she said over the music.

"With vodka," Gabe added.

"You never drink vodka," Aubrey said.

Rae shrugged. "Just trying something new."

"I can see that." Aubrey eyed her hair. Across the room, a girl in a straw hat and pinstripe pants kept glancing in their direction, checking out either Rae or Gabe.

"Look," Aubrey said. "Is it okay if we go somewhere else?"

"Like, now?" Rae asked.

"Yes, please," Gabe said loudly.

Rae looked at the girl in the pinstripe pants, who'd taken off her hat and was placing it on a boy wearing aviator sunglasses. She took another slurp of her drink and fixed her camera bag on her shoulder. "Yeah, fine. Anywhere's got to be better than this heteronormative wonderland."

They stepped off the houseboat and onto a gravel road, leaving behind the thrumming beat of Arcade Fire and watching the area turn quiet and residential. A little girl and her mom walked their dog, and a man haphazardly balanced an armful of groceries as he unlocked the door to his apartment building.

"This is the way back to the bus stop," Aubrey explained.

"You want to catch a bus?" Rae asked.

"I was with Leah all day, and I didn't get to go anywhere I'd planned. So, yes. I want to catch a bus."

Rae scrubbed at her hair. "You're in charge, I guess."

Gabe shoved his hands into his pockets. "Okay, Tour Guide. What's on your list?"

"A lot of museums. But they're probably closed by now. I guess we could walk around the city center. See what's open."

They arrived at the bus stop just as one was pulling in. Rae headed straight to the last row and flopped down, resting her legs over the two seats beside her.

"You're one classy lady." Gabe pushed her feet off so he could sit down.

"And you're a bastard," Rae said, but she made room for him.

Aubrey sat with them but turned toward the window. He and Rae were already wrapped up in a debate about the best albums of an all-girl punk band they both liked, and Aubrey didn't want to interrupt. She watched their bus crawl over a bridge. From here, it looked like there was nothing but water beneath them, stretching toward the horizon, trying to cover the whole city.

It made her feel like she was floating.

They arrived at Centraal Station in the heart of town. As soon as they got off the bus, Aubrey checked her phone, but Jonah hadn't texted. Which meant he wasn't pissed at her for leaving. Or that he hadn't noticed. Or that he was getting spectacularly wasted. (Or probably all three.)

"Guys," Rae said. "Look at this. Drunk British people as far as the eye can see."

"I think some of them are American," Gabe said.

"My two countries are truly representing themselves." Rae held up her camera, catching different scenes. A woman with dyed-blond hair sung in a slurring voice while her friends carried her down the street; a group of guys stumbled from a bar, toasting each other with the pint glasses they must have stolen. Last night, Aubrey hadn't really been able to look around the station since she'd gotten straight on a bus that took her to the hostel. But now she was looking, and honestly? The city center wasn't exactly what she'd imagined.

"I assumed it would be cuter," she said.

Rae patted her on the back. "Now you know what happens when the museums close."

"Oh!" Aubrey veered toward a green-painted entrance. "A coffee shop. Let's stop in there for a minute, figure out where to go next." She opened the door of a dimly lit café and stepped into a cloud of overly sweet air and soft electronic music. The tables were all taken up by people having mumbled conversations. Before Aubrey could head to the counter, Rae put a hand on her elbow.

"Wait," Rae said. "I don't think this is a coffee shop. I think this is a *coffee shop.*"

"What do you mean?" Aubrey asked.

Rae mimed smoking a joint, even though Aubrey knew she never had. Or, at least, she was pretty sure she hadn't. She'd also been pretty sure Rae wouldn't chop off all her hair at a moment's notice.

Gabe made a coughing noise under his breath. "I think people are staring at us."

It was true. A group of twentysomethings was definitely giving them stink-eye, and Aubrey realized they were still holding the door open.

"This might be a good time for a hasty exit," Rae said, taking Aubrey's arm and sprinting outside. Gabe called out an apology as he left, too. They kept running, passing neon-lit bars on one side and a canal on the other. A few clearly intoxicated people cheered and clapped for them, and Aubrey waved back for no other reason than it seemed polite. She looked up at the signs on buildings, at a red-and-blue one with a woman's figure in silhouette. All of a sudden, it clicked—she knew *exactly* where they were.

She stopped dead in the street and doubled over with laughter.

Gabe and Rae stopped, too, and Rae took a second to adjust the straps of her tank top. "Should we have looked at a map or something?" she asked. "Because I think maybe we're in the—"

"Red Light District!" Aubrey collapsed against the brick wall beside her, laughing so hard her stomach cramped.

"What gave it away?" Gabe asked. "Was it the incredibly explicit window displays in all of the sex shops?"

"I can't." Aubrey hiccuped. "I just...I can't."

"You're both such prudes," Rae said.

Aubrey scoffed. "Says the girl who made us run out of a *coffee shop*."

"I was protecting your delicate sensibilities." Rae climbed the stoop of a building and took a picture of the street. Aubrey smoothed back the flyaways from her face. The area was still raucous, but she didn't find it intimidating anymore. She felt as if she were at a party—the kind of party where she didn't have to try to fit in. Where she could just stand and observe and feel like she belonged anyway.

She took the step below Rae's. "I can't get over your hair!" she said. "I thought you liked it long. It was your thing."

"Not anymore." Rae looked down and took a picture of her.

"What do you think Lucy will say?"

"She'll tell me I don't look like her daughter anymore. Or maybe that I look like my own evil doppelgänger."

"I mean, that's the obvious reaction," Gabe said, stepping up to join Aubrey.

"Well, I hope she's not too mad," Rae said. "Or she might refuse to come with me when I get my tattoo."

"Hold on," Gabe said. "You were losing your shit over a haircut, but you're getting a *tattoo*?"

This time, Rae took a picture of him. "Needles don't scare me."

"But scissors in your hair?" Gabe said. "That was terrifying?"

"Maybe you were nervous because it was a metaphor," Aubrey said. "It represented the transformation from childhood to adulthood."

"Exactly!" Rae said. "Thank you."

Gabe shook his head at Aubrey. "You're such an English-lit major."

She smiled out at the canal, watching it slide peacefully down the center of the wild street. If someone had asked her right then, she would have said this moment was perfect: She was out with two of her closest friends, talking and joking around, exactly the way they used to. Standing in a city that—for the moment, anyway—felt like it was theirs.

"So, Preston," Gabe said. "How did you convince your mom to let you get a tattoo?"

"Are you kidding?" Aubrey said. "Her mom *designed* it."

"Okay." Gabe laughed. "That's pretty badass. What are you getting? Where?"

Rae stretched out her left wrist. "It's going to be these two shadows standing together. Mom drew it from one of her favorite movies, *The Big Sleep*. She named me after Raymond Chandler, because he wrote stories for all these old film noirs she's obsessed with. She thinks the cinematography in those movies is, like, the best thing ever."

Gabe examined Rae's wrist, as if the tattoo were already there. "What about you?" he said to Aubrey. "What's yours going to be?"

Nothing about him seemed hesitant. He wasn't talking to her because he thought he should. He was talking to her because he wanted to.

"Probably a skull," she said. "You know, a big one."

"Yeah?" he said.

"And you should get something outdoorsy. Or Oregon-themed. A lumberjack?"

"How about a flannel pattern?"

"On both your arms!"

"With buttons down my burly chest."

Aubrey cracked up. She felt her whole body lighten. And even though she didn't know exactly what had changed, she knew he wasn't the Gabe he'd been in Paris. He was the one he used to be. The one who would ride his bike along the Thames with her to pass the time after school; the one who would sit at her kitchen table showing her Wikipedia pages of national parks in Oregon; the one who made her listen to P. J. Harvey on his family's record player, both of them sitting on his living room floor, eyes closed, talking about her scratchy voice and her guitar that grumbled like an engine.

On a balcony above, someone played a loud punk song. Gabe cupped his hands around his mouth and shouted along with it. Rae held her camera above her head, taking a picture of the street, the night, everything. And Aubrey caught herself wishing that the party at Leah's would carry on and on. She wished that they could stay out here for hours, waiting for the sun to rise, waiting for the glimmering canal to turn pink, red, yellow.

And then her phone chirped, shocking her back to reality. She saw Jonah's name pop up on her screen along with a message she didn't expect: *this is leah. jonah and clara are fucking trashed. take them home NOW.*

12

Monday, July 4
AMSTERDAM

Rae hated to admit it, but Leah was right. Jonah and Clara were shit-faced.

The sun had set completely by the time she, Aubrey, and Gabe got back to the party. Leah was standing outside the houseboat, smoking. Clara spun to the music still coming from inside while Jonah tried to climb onto someone's bike.

"Jesus," Aubrey said under her breath.

"How much did they have to drink?" Gabe asked.

"Too much," Leah said, taking a long drag of her cigarette.

"Yeah, but they never drink *this* much," Aubrey said.

Rae smirked. "Oh, come on, Aubs. Have you forgotten the graduation party already?"

Aubrey shot her a *not-helping* look. Clara spun over and into Rae. They both lost their balance, and Rae's camera bumped against her hip as she held on to Clara's arms to keep her steady.

"You're here!" Clara said. And in that single moment, Rae let herself imagine what it would be like to slide her hands around Clara's back, to feel Clara lean into her grip.

"Yeah." Rae dropped her hands, hooking her thumbs through her belt loops. "I am."

There was a crashing sound as Jonah tipped the bike over. Leah, Aubrey, and Gabe rushed over to help him, all of them yelling over one another.

"I keep not recognizing you," Clara said. "Your hair—it's so different."

"That's what I was going for," Rae said. "Full-on disguise mode." She didn't want to think too much about how close they were standing, so she scanned the row of houseboats instead, counted each of their lit-up windows. The water was much glossier and blacker than it had been a few hours ago.

"Forget the fucking bike, Jonah!" Leah was saying.

"Don't snap at him!" Aubrey said. "He wouldn't even be drunk if he hadn't come here."

"Sure, Aubrey. He'd probably be home *right now* knitting a sweater."

Clara leaned forward, her breath in Rae's ear. "Don't tell," she whispered, "but everyone here is an asshole."

Jonah talked loudly the whole bus ride back to the hostel,

leaning heavily against Aubrey. She and Gabe led him back to his room while Rae took Clara to theirs. They'd only been there one night, but already, dirty clothes and pajamas were lying across the floor; pots of glittery makeup and bags of trail mix cluttered the windowsill. Rae closed the door behind her, and Clara skipped over the mess, collapsing onto Rae's bunk. "Where were you guys?" she asked, splaying her arms out. "You missed the whole party. You didn't even dance."

Rae put her camera down and took off her sandals. "I don't dance where people can see me."

"But you danced in Paris. And at the Sleater-Kinney concert!" Clara cried. "You can't fool me, Rae Preston. I have seen your moves."

Rae rolled her eyes. But she remembered the concert, too. Aubrey and Clara had schemed with Lucy to buy tickets for Rae's sixteenth birthday, and they'd all danced so hard, every muscle in Rae's body had throbbed for days. "That was different," she said. "Sleater-Kinney is a badass feminist band. This was just some college kids swaying on a boat."

Clara sat up, hair messy and cheeks flushed. Her lips were stained blue from so many Jell-O shots. "Do you ever think we should have applied to college together? All five of us?"

"I don't know." Rae was surprised. "Applied where?"

"It doesn't matter. As long we were all in the same place. As long we could live in the same dorm and eat breakfast every morning and go to all the same parties. It would be just like high school."

"Oh goody," Rae said.

Clara chucked a pillow at her. "You're such a bitch."

"That's an antifeminist term!" Rae tossed the pillow back, and Clara moved over so Rae could sit on the bed, too. "The thing is," Rae said, "I don't think college is supposed to work that way. It's supposed to be a fresh start."

"Is that why you cut your hair?" Clara reached over to touch one of Rae's curls.

"Something like that." Rae's words sounded fuzzy in her ears. She could feel her heart rate increase.

"Well, whatever," Clara said. "Everything's perfect right now, and that's all that matters. In fact, you know what? We should take a selfie. I need to be in one of your Amsterdam pictures so you remember I was here." She gingerly picked up Rae's camera. "How do you work this thing again?"

"I'll do it," Rae said, laughing. It was hard to take a selfie with her heavy camera. She had to hold it with both hands and guess at the right angle.

Clara placed her arm around Rae's waist, pulling them together. "Smile!" she said, reaching over Rae's hand to press the button. A flash popped in their eyes. Rae turned into Clara's shoulder.

"Christ!" Rae said. "That was awful!"

"No, it was great," Clara said. "It's my new favorite picture ever." Their arms were still around each other, their faces inches apart. Rae saw Clara's blue lips and soft eyes, the strands of hair that fell next to her mouth. It would have been so easy for Rae to fall into that, to let herself believe that they were this close and touching because it meant something to both of them.

But that wasn't the truth. And Rae couldn't pretend it was—she couldn't torture herself like that. She moved away, pretending to examine the sets of initials etched into the bedpost. She wondered why they'd been carved there in the first place—what had happened to make someone feel the need to sit here and scratch and scratch until the letters became permanent.

"Rae?" Clara asked.

"Yup?"

"Do you think Leah's a bitch?"

Rae bit the inside of her cheek and wished she didn't feel so disappointed at the change in subject. "I think you know her better than I do. So I shouldn't comment."

"Okay. But she ignored me all tonight."

"In that case, yeah. She's a bitch."

"Antifeminist," Clara teased. Then she lay back on the bed again. "Honestly, I'm not surprised. It's always been obvious that she likes Jonah more than she likes me."

"Why does everyone care so much what Leah thinks of them?" Rae asked. "She smokes, like, a thousand cigarettes a day. She makes annoying references to books that might not even be real. All in all, I'd say she's pretty terrible."

"I know." Clara sighed at the underside of the bunk above her. "But why does she act like she never even kissed me?"

The room lurched and started spinning. Rae dug her fingers into the mattress, trying to hold herself still. "Leah *kissed* you?"

"Last year." Clara yawned. "A few months before her graduation. It was fun, but now she seems determined to pretend it never happened." She sat up again and scooted down the bed until there was only a sliver of polka-dotted sheets between them. "Who was the first girl you ever kissed?"

Rae blinked hard. "Dana Silverstein. Eighth grade. But you knew that."

"Yeah, I did." Clara's knee was almost touching Rae's thigh. Her blue lips were slightly parted. "But you were sure then? You were definitely sure you wanted to kiss girls?"

The room kept moving. All Rae could think to say was "Yes."

Clara pressed her palm against the bed and leaned in. And this time, Rae didn't think she was making it up. Because she'd been in positions like this before. Because girls had looked at her in *exactly* this way before. Clara's voice lowered to a whisper. "If you could kiss anyone right now, who would it be?"

The door opened, and Aubrey walked in.

Rae jumped off the bed. "Aubrey! You scared us."

"Oh. Sorry." Aubrey took off her shoes, placing them neatly by the door. She went to the sink and pulled her contact case out of her toiletry bag.

Rae's skin was still tingling from what had just happened.

She could still feel the warmth of Clara leaning toward her and the certainty that they were about to kiss. But that was impossible. Because—Clara was straight!

Or was Rae the one being heteronormative now?

Because Clara had kissed Leah, so how straight could she be?

"Why is this place already such a mess?" Aubrey asked.

"It's a mystery for the ages." Rae tried to sound upbeat. "Scientists will study this room for years to come."

Clara yawned again and dropped back onto the pillow. "Too tired for talking. Night night."

Since Rae had nowhere else to go, she climbed to the top bunk. She didn't want to focus too much on how these bunched-up sheets were the same ones Clara had slept in the night before. Or on how Clara was currently sleeping in *Rae's* sheets. *Or* on how Clara had potentially, maybe, almost kissed her.

Seriously, though, Rae thought. *How straight could she be?!*

"Is everything okay?" Aubrey asked.

Rae slid off her armful of bracelets and tucked them next to the wall. "Why? Does everything seem not okay?"

"I don't know," Aubrey said. "You just look—awake."

If any other girl had almost kissed her, Rae would have told Aubrey all about it—she would have sat up through the night with her, drinking coffee in the hostel lobby and obsessing over every detail. But Rae couldn't talk about Clara like that. Not with Aubrey, not with anyone.

"It's the vodka I drank," she said. "Maybe it had Red Bull in it? I should probably sleep it off."

Aubrey opened her contact case. "Is it okay if I leave the light on for a minute?"

"Yeah, go for it." Rae plumped up the pillow and kicked the covers farther down the bed. She closed her eyes, but her mind refused to go still. She heard Aubrey turning on the sink. She heard cars speeding down the road and trees rustling. Her thoughts bloomed with full-color images—canals and houseboats and bridges over jet-black water. But mostly they bloomed with Clara—Clara's hand on the polka-dotted sheets; her hair brushing the crook of Rae's elbow; her voice asking—again and again—who she would kiss if she could kiss anyone.

The light clicked off, but Rae couldn't sleep. She climbed down the ladder as quietly as she could and padded across the room to get her sketchbook and a pen. When she got back to bed, she tilted the sketchbook toward the window so it would catch a thin stream of moonlight, and she drew until the sun began to saturate the room. Until, eventually, she fell asleep, her bed filled with dreams made of ink.

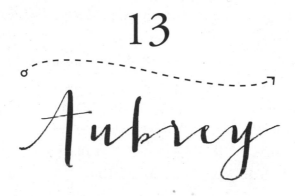

13

Aubrey

Tuesday, July 5
AMSTERDAM to PRAGUE via BERLIN

That night, Aubrey's dreams were made of something soft and drowsy. A stage lit with shimmering lights. A set made to look like a city with every detail exact: rain gutters on the buildings, scuff marks on the sidewalks. Everything in blues and grays. Aubrey wasn't an artist, but somehow, she knew she'd designed it all. She'd filled the canals with water; she'd hung the stars from the rafters and whispered voices into the cardboard buildings. This was her city, she thought. It would be here even when she left it behind.

She woke up, but the dream lingered around her. It distracted her as she packed up her stuff and took the bus to the station with her friends. It followed her when they boarded the train, and she sent her mom a text to let her know they'd made it okay.

Their compartment was small, with two rows of three seats facing one another. Jonah and Clara sprawled out and crashed before they'd even left the station. Rae stayed awake for a little bit longer, but she seemed exhausted, too. Her eyes kept closing, her head dipping toward the window. Aubrey couldn't sleep. Maybe because traveling always made her extra panicky. She had this feeling that she'd forgotten to do something important, that something wasn't quite right.

She checked over the train schedule on her phone to make sure their layover time still looked okay—they would arrive in Berlin early that afternoon and then they would have nearly an hour before their connection to Prague.

Was that what was bugging her? That they could some-how miss their train? Or was this really just about last night?

About how, when she and Gabe had helped Jonah to his room after the party, he had only talked about one thing: Leah. Her amazing internship, what classes she'd taken last year, what shows she wanted to see with him in New York. He stirred in his sleep now, and Aubrey touched the tips of his hair, which looked golden in the early-morning sun. The fabric of his favorite navy-blue hoodie was soft and faded in patches. It smelled like his cologne and like his room in London. It made Aubrey remember borrowing it from him in cold movie theaters and the times she'd worn it to walk home in the rain, the hood pulled tightly around her ears. These were the things she was worried about forgetting— these small, familiar pieces of her old life. These fragments of moments she would never get back again.

"Hey," a voice whispered.

Aubrey looked over Jonah's head at Gabe. "Hey," she whispered back.

"Everyone's asleep," he said. "Should we, like, draw on their faces?"

"Do you have a Sharpie?" Aubrey asked.

"No. But do you have nail polish? We could use that."

"Hmmm. The fumes might give us away."

Gabe rested his long legs across the aisle. He wasn't hungover, but he looked a little crumpled, like he'd probably rolled out of bed only a few minutes before leaving the hostel that morning. "How's it going, Bryce?" he asked. "You seem worried."

"I'm not really." She glanced down at her lap, some of her hair falling out of her ponytail and in her face. "I was just thinking—we don't have *that* much time left together, and everyone keeps sleeping through it. Doesn't that seem like a waste to you?"

"I don't know. People do need sleep. And this is only the train part."

"But the train part is half the point," Aubrey insisted. "I mean, that's why people go interrailing in the first place, isn't it? So they can look outside at everything they might never have seen otherwise. And have all these extra hours to talk to each other. That's the romance of trains. That's the whole reason we're here." She felt silly for getting so swept away—these were her sixth-grade fantasies of what this trip would be like. She'd never talked about those with anyone except Rae. And even then, it was when they were twelve years old, watching movies like *North by Northwest* and planning for their grand, mysterious futures.

Gabe looked at her intently. "Okay." He reached over Jonah's sleeping body. "Let's do this."

"Do what?"

He wiggled his fingers. "Isn't it obvious?"

"Are you trying to high-five me?"

"Bryce! Yes! It's guaranteed to wake everyone up. That way, we can talk and bond and look at the country and whatever else you said we should do. Awesome idea, yeah?" His eyes pleaded.

Aubrey twisted her lips to the side. It was kind of a stupid idea, actually. But it made her think of last night, of the tenuous connection they'd somehow managed to form again. She raised her hand and clapped it with his, the sound reverberating through the compartment.

Clara groaned. "What *the hell* was that?"

"Nothing," Aubrey said.

"Maybe birds?" Gabe said.

"Right!" Aubrey choked down a laugh. "Birds."

"The infamous clapping birds of Europe," Gabe said.

Clara pouted and slumped lower in her seat. "Are you two drunk?"

"Hate to remind you," Aubrey said, "but I think you drank enough for all of us last night."

"I can't take your jokes right now." Clara pushed her cat-eye pink sunglasses from her forehead down to her nose. The train bumped along, and Aubrey and Gabe exchanged quick, amused looks. Outside the window, a small cluster of houses appeared by the tracks and then disappeared into a blur of trees. Aubrey felt guilty for thinking it, but she wished Clara hadn't woken up. It was easier to talk to Gabe when it was only the two of them, easier to feel like their friendship made sense again.

"*Shit.*" Clara jumped up and ran out of the compartment. The door slammed shut behind her, bouncing in its frame.

"S'okay." Rae groggily stood up. "Everything's okay. I'll go check on her."

Jonah woke up, too. "I thought I was home," he mumbled. "I thought I was home, and I was eating one of those fucking awesome grilled cheese sandwiches my mom makes. You know the ones I mean?"

"Four different types of cheese and a bag of Doritos." Gabe nodded solemnly. "I'm well-acquainted with the Jonah Hangover Special."

"That you are," Jonah said. He and Gabe fist-bumped.

Aubrey felt herself bristle a little. Maybe she'd been right before. Maybe her mood did have something to do with

Jonah—with the fact that he'd been so drunk last night, or that he'd spent almost an entire day and evening ignoring her. And worst of all, he didn't even seem sorry about it.

Gabe stood and stretched. "I'm going to the dining car. You guys want anything?"

"Soda," Jonah said. "Lots of soda. And Doritos if they have them. Thanks, man."

Gabe looked at Aubrey before he left, but she just gave him a small smile and shook her head.

"This feeling is . . . not great," Jonah said.

"Yeah," Aubrey said. "That's what drinking most of the tequila in Holland will do to you."

Jonah pulled the cuffs of his sweatshirt over his palms. "Where did you guys end up last night?"

"Nowhere."

"Well, you clearly ended up *somewhere*. You were gone for hours."

She shrugged. "We went for a walk."

"*Okay*. But just so you know, you did kind of hurt Leah's feelings."

Aubrey glared out the window, her jaw clenching. "Somehow, I think she'll survive."

"What's that supposed to mean?" Jonah asked.

"Nothing. Forget it." The countryside was speeding by so fast, too fast for her to catch on to. She didn't want to pick a fight with Jonah—but also, she couldn't pretend everything was okay.

"Did Leah do something to piss you off?" he asked.

"Not exactly," she said. "But it's not like she was so desperate to spend time with me or anything."

Jonah frowned. "She spent all day with you."

"She spent all day with *you*. I was—extra baggage."

He sat forward. "You didn't say any of this yesterday."

"How could I? You were both so absorbed in each other I could barely get a word in edgewise. You didn't even listen when I told you which museums I wanted to see."

"Those museums were expensive and overrated," he said. "Leah explained that. Besides, there are tons of museums in New York."

"But we weren't in New York," she said. "We were in Amsterdam for *one day*. I might never get another chance to see the Rijksmuseum."

"Come on, Aubs. We didn't go on this trip to have an educational experience. We're here to find out what the world is like when we're on our own. Not just do all the bullshit things our parents tell us we should."

Aubrey felt stubborn. "Well. I wanted to see museums."

Jonah grunted. "I don't get where all of this is coming from. I mean, you've always been sort of weird around Leah, but I figured you'd be over it by now. I figured you'd be more grown up."

"*Grown up?*" she snapped. "And by *grown up*, do you mean I wouldn't notice the way you worship at her feet? Or the way you hang on every word she says?"

"No," he snapped back. "It means you'd be able to include yourself in our conversation. You'd be able to say something when she talks to you."

"I'm sorry. So I'm only *grown up* if I can sit in a dingy bar, drink cheap wine, and have super-obnoxious conversations about Anton Chekhov? Is that right?"

"That isn't what we're like."

"It's *exactly* what you're like. Whenever you're around *her*."

"Yeah, well! She's my friend!"

Aubrey stood now, her breathing rapid, her legs wobbly as the train took a turn. "I know that, Jonah! But I wish it didn't feel like she's the person you imagine being with when you imagine living in New York. I wish you didn't expect me to just fit into the life you're planning to have with *her*."

Jonah pressed his fingertips to his forehead. The train sounded like a storm beneath them. And he seemed so exhausted, so hungover, so weighed down by everything she was saying. But Aubrey had to tell him this. She had to let him know what she was terrified of before she gave up her whole world and everything that felt like it belonged to her.

"Whenever we talk about next year," she said, "we talk about you. We talk about NYU and theater and what you want your life to be like, and that's great. But I'm going to Columbia. I want to study. I want to work hard and spend hours in the library and take really difficult classes that will change my life."

"So do that." He refused to look up. "I'm not stopping you."

"But you won't be with me. You won't come uptown to hang out with me after class. You won't spend a weekend getting to know the friends I make there. Will you?"

"I have no clue how you want me to respond to that," he said.

She wanted him to say *Of course I will.* She wanted him to say *It would never be like that, because I care about you. Because I think about what you want just as much as I think about what I want.*

But he didn't say any of those things.

And all of a sudden, Aubrey knew what had been bothering her all morning. What she hadn't been able to put her finger on: Jonah didn't picture their lives together the way she did—he never would.

"Jonah." She sat down across from him and took a long breath, then let it out slowly. "I think we should break up."

His head snapped up. *"What?"*

"We should break up," she said again. "If college is going to be anything like yesterday, I'm going to hate it. And if I hate it, you'll hate me, so why don't we save ourselves the trouble and get it over with now?" Her chest was compressing; she couldn't get enough air. Even though she was saying all this, she didn't actually want to break up with Jonah. She didn't want to lose him. But also, she didn't have a choice. If she stayed with him, she'd feel the way she had at that houseboat party for the next four years. She'd never think of herself as anything except small and unimportant.

"Are you really breaking up with me?" he asked. "Is that really what's happening?"

"*No,*" she said. "I mean, I don't know. Just—tell me that all the things I'm worried about aren't real. Tell me that you'll come to Columbia. That you'll be a part of my life there, too."

"Aubs." His expression went heavy. "I want to be there for you, but I can't just run uptown all the time. NYU's a really big deal for me. I need to concentrate on that."

Everything inside of her began to unsnap. "Okay," she said. "So. That's it. We're done."

He got up. "I need to walk. I need to get the fuck out of here right now." He left Aubrey alone, in a compartment where all her friends should have been, too.

She inhaled. She exhaled. She tried to remind herself that she wasn't actually alone. But that wasn't true.

She was.

14

Tuesday, July 5
AMSTERDAM to PRAGUE via BERLIN

Rae sat across from the bathroom door, waiting for Clara. She'd knocked a few times, but Clara kept insisting she was fine. Even though she clearly wasn't.

Rae folded her legs on the gray-striped carpet and leaned back against the wall, the train grumbling in her ears. In the almost silence, the only thing she could think about was last night—about sitting in the hostel room with Clara, about the cool sheets beneath them, and Clara shifting toward her. But this time Aubrey didn't walk in on them. This time Clara's knee brushed Rae's thigh; her breath was warm on Rae's mouth.

A guy knocked on the bathroom door, snapping Rae out of it. "Hey," she snarled. "Can't you see it's occupied?"

He frowned at her before walking away. And as he did, Rae told herself a different story: Last night Clara had been *drunk*. The truth was, she might not even remember what had happened.

Rae scratched at the shaved patch in the back of her hair. She tried to focus on Australia—on limestone cliffs and blue stretches of ocean and Melbourne alleyways brimming with thrift stores. *Come on, Rae,* she thought. *Focus on the future.*

"Rae," Clara's voice whispered from the other side of the door.

"Yeah?" Rae moved forward.

"Is Aubrey there with you?"

Clara's voice was almost too quiet for Rae to hear. "No," she said. "It's just me."

"Is she not there because she's mad at me?"

"Why would Aubrey be mad at you?"

"Because I'm hungover," Clara said. "Because I'm totally ruining her perfect trip."

"It's not *her* trip. And you're not ruining anything. Jonah's hungover, too."

"But you're not," Clara said miserably. "You never are."

"Dude, I definitely am," Rae said. "And remember Aubrey's eighteenth birthday? When that gallery owner gave my mom those free bottles of wine and we snuck some into my room?"

"Oh yeah," Clara said.

"And remember the next day? When Aubrey's parents

took us on the Harry Potter studio tour, and they thought I had the flu. They even tried to call a doctor."

Clara giggled a little. "I can't believe they didn't figure it out."

"They rarely do." Rae picked at a thread in the carpet. "Having Aubrey for a daughter makes them think all teenagers are responsible."

Clara didn't respond for a moment, and Rae worried she'd said the wrong thing.

"No one thinks that about me," Clara said eventually. "Everyone knows I'm the dumb, ditzy party girl with a super-weird wardrobe."

"Clara," Rae said. "That's not true."

"Of course it is. If I were sick on a Harry Potter tour, no one would assume I had the flu."

Rae touched her fingers to the grainy plastic door. "For what it's worth, I promise I will always assume the flu."

Jonah came out of the nearest train carriage, startling Rae away from the door. His neck and cheeks were flushed, and he seemed disoriented. Rae waited for him to stop and talk to her, but he didn't. He stormed into the next carriage over.

What the hell was that? she thought, staring after him.

Just then, the latch clicked on the bathroom door, which slid open. Rae turned and saw Clara sitting on the floor, her skin washed out from crying, the backs of her hands smeared with makeup.

"Jesus." Rae squeezed inside, locking the door behind her. "Why are you crying?"

Clara rubbed her face into the collar of her shirt. "I k-keep trying to stop, but I can't."

Rae kneeled down across from her. There wasn't much room, so her head was lodged directly beneath the sink. "Is this about the Harry Potter thing?"

Clara shook her head.

"Or about ruining the trip?" Rae asked. "Because, I swear, you didn't. This isn't even embarrassing! Junior year I made out with Alicia Green at that party before winter break. Now *that* was embarrassing."

Clara's face clouded over. "Why do you always have to remind me of how many girls you've hooked up with?"

Rae felt her mouth open in shock.

"Oh my God." Clara's gaze dropped down. "What's wrong with me? I didn't mean that. I'm saying stupid things, and I'm crying in a bathroom. And I haven't even washed my face today!"

"It's okay," Rae said, but she was still confused. Since when did Clara get upset over who Rae had kissed?

"It's not okay." Clara sniffled. "I'm such a mess right now. I'm disgusting."

"You're still Clara," Rae said. "You're—the opposite of disgusting."

Clara glanced up.

The train hitched, and Rae knocked her head on the bottom of the sink, her top teeth cutting into her lower lip.

"Rae!" Clara leaned forward. "Are you all right?"

"Totally fine." Rae wiped her hand across her mouth to make sure it wasn't bleeding. "Anyway, forget about me. What's making you cry?"

"Well," Clara said, "today. For starters."

Rae looked around them. "I'll admit sitting on a bathroom floor isn't exactly a high point."

The hint of a smile flashed across Clara's face. "Everything is just going by so fast," she said. "We're already leaving Amsterdam, which means I'm one step closer to California. Which means I have to start school soon. I've wanted to design costumes since I was ten years old, but what if I can't keep up with my classes? What if I'm not as good as I always hoped?"

"But you are. You don't have to stress about that."

Clara played with a sequin on her purple ballet flat. "It's different for you. You're so fearless."

Rae looked up at the small window beside them—at a single, shifting rectangle of blue sky, at the tops of trees that were laid against it. "Clara," she said. "I'm scared, too."

"But you can't wait to go to Australia. You looked at a map, and you found the farthest place you could possibly go, and now you're going there. That's so brave."

"It wasn't like that," Rae said. "It was more like—I saw this version of myself who would go to Melbourne, and she was the version I wanted to be. She was confident and smart and she was—kind of like my mom, actually. You know, Lucy moved to the States when she was eighteen, even though her family didn't want her to. I figured if I could convince myself to be like that, maybe leaving wouldn't suck so much."

Clara pushed her feet across the floor so the tips of her flats almost touched the tips of Rae's flip-flops. It reminded Rae of last night—and it made her wonder if maybe Clara did remember what she'd said when they'd sat on that bunk together. And if she did remember, maybe she didn't regret it. Rae slid her feet forward, too.

"It's really weird that we're sitting here, isn't it?" Clara said.

"Yeah." Rae laughed. "It really is."

"I don't want to go back yet, though."

"Me neither." Rae looked down at their legs, at the shadows of passing trees that rushed over them. It was hard to believe that outside, the world was moving as fast as it could. Because in here—for now, at least—they were holding still.

15

Aubrey

Tuesday, July 5

AMSTERDAM to PRAGUE via BERLIN

No one had come back to their compartment yet.

It was just Aubrey.

Aubrey and the numb, gaping hole in the center of her chest.

Aubrey stuck on a train, speeding toward a place she didn't know. She'd always wanted to go to Prague—in seventh grade, she'd even written a paper on it, complete with a poster board covered in pictures she'd found online. She could list every landmark she wanted to visit. She could close her eyes and see the way they all connected, everything neatly arranged the way it would be on a map.

But that wasn't the same thing as knowing it.

She put in her earbuds and lay down across the empty seats, watching power lines twist and loop above her, like figure-skater tracks drawn in ice. She listened to a girl with a sweet, high voice sing about saying good-bye to someone she loved. And she thought about what would happen if Jonah came back to talk to her—if he sat down and told her he was sorry. If he told her that everything would be okay.

The door to the compartment opened, and she turned her music down. But it wasn't Jonah who walked in. Aubrey could hear Rae and Clara talking to each other, and, a few minutes after that, Gabe's low voice joining in. Aubrey squeezed her eyes shut and thumbed the volume back up until her friends were drowned out completely. She pretended to be asleep.

An hour later, the train began to slow into the Berlin station. As it ground to a stop, Aubrey sat up and pulled out her earbuds.

"Jonah isn't here," Clara said instantly.

"We've been trying to call him," Gabe explained, "and I walked around a couple of times, but I couldn't find him."

"He's not hurt," Rae said. "There would have been an announcement if someone was hurt, right?"

"Exactly!" Clara said. "They would have asked if there was a doctor on board."

"I thought that only happened on planes?" Rae said.

"Bryce?" Gabe said. "Did he tell you where he went?"

They were all staring at Aubrey, waiting for her to say what had happened. Maybe waiting for her to panic. But she couldn't do either of those things. She knew he was avoiding her, and she wondered how long he could keep that up. Maybe until they went home. Or maybe he was staying away now so she would have to tell their friends that they'd broken up. Get it over with for him.

"Let's take his bag," she said. "I bet he went ahead to the next train."

They walked to another level of the station, Aubrey's gaze roaming the walls of glass panels, listening to the German voices around her.

Gabe and Rae found their platform and their seats, and they all piled their stuff onto a luggage rack. The rest of the carriage was still empty.

"Maybe we should look around," Gabe said. "Jonah could be sitting somewhere else, I guess."

"Great idea." Clara smiled encouragingly at Aubrey. "He's probably trying to find us right now."

"Okay," Aubrey said, but her voice sounded flat.

Rae's forehead scrunched up. She probably wanted to ask Aubrey what was really going on, but Aubrey hoped she didn't. She couldn't lie to Rae, but she also couldn't stand the idea of saying any of this out loud.

"We can go in opposite directions," Gabe said. "Cover the whole train."

"I'll go with you." Aubrey turned from Rae, following him into the next carriage and touching the top of every seat they passed. The deserted train made her think of these photographs Rae had shown her once of abandoned amusement parks. Wooden roller coasters with grass growing over them. Swan boats stuck in murky water. Places that should have been full of life left still and silent instead.

"It's like *Snowpiercer*," Gabe said.

"What?" Aubrey asked.

Gabe glanced over his shoulder. "This French comic my dad gave me when I was in middle school. It's about a train that keeps circling the earth after it's all frozen over. I think they made it into a movie."

Aubrey touched another seat. "How is this anything like that?"

"I don't know. I guess because the characters can't ever leave the train. That's almost what this feels like, isn't it? Like we're just going from train to train. Like we live here now."

"Maybe." Aubrey looked toward the window.

"Bryce." Gabe stopped walking. "What's going on? Do you know why Jonah disappeared?"

Aubrey gripped a seat. The lights above them were off, making everything look too dark. Too dark for the middle of the day. Too dark for the middle of a bustling station. "You want to know what the worst part is?" she asked.

He cocked his head. "About Jonah leaving?"

"The worst part," Aubrey said, ignoring his question, "is that all morning, I was so worried we wouldn't make this train. But look at us. Look how early we are. I waste so much energy panicking about things that don't actually happen. And the things that do happen never even occur to me."

"Sorry," Gabe said, "explain that again?"

Aubrey blinked down at the scuffed carpet. "JonahandI-brokeup," she said, like it was all one word. Like she was trying to get it out as quickly as possible.

"Christ." Gabe pushed his hair away from his forehead. "Are you sure?"

Aubrey raised an eyebrow. "I was there, Gabe."

"But how? When did this even happen?"

"A few hours ago." Aubrey sat down in the closest seat.

"Wait, wait, wait." Gabe sat across the aisle from her. "You mean when I left to get a soda? You just—broke up?"

Aubrey nodded. "We had this big dumb fight about Leah."

"Why? What happened with Leah?"

"Nothing." Aubrey turned, her knees jutting into the aisle. "That's the whole point. I spent an entire day with Jonah and Leah, but they barely even noticed I was there. And when I brought it up with Jonah today, he made it pretty clear that's who he wants to be now. The person he is when he's with Leah."

Gabe played with the armrest, pushing it up and then back down. "That just sounds like a fight. Jonah doesn't really want to break up with you."

"It doesn't matter," Aubrey said, "because I want to break up with him." As soon as she said it, she knew it was true. She didn't want to be with Jonah anymore. She knew—she'd known for a while now—that something wasn't right. That all her daydreams about what next year would be like could never be real. That things could never have gone the way she'd always planned.

Gabe's knees faced hers now. "You seem eerily calm about all this. The last time I broke up with someone, Jonah took me out and we drank five pints of Guinness each. And, Bryce, I do not recommend that at all. But are you sure you don't need anything?"

"I'm sure," Aubrey said. And then she burst into tears. She doubled over, catching her face with both hands.

Gabe jumped out of his seat. "Damn. I didn't mean to do that."

"You didn't," Aubrey said through her fingers. "This isn't because of you."

And it wasn't. It was because it felt real now. She and Jonah were *done*. She was moving to New York all by herself. And she didn't want that—she'd *never* wanted that. She'd never wanted her future to feel this blank. She'd never wanted to face it alone.

Gabe knelt in the aisle beside her. "Text him," he said. "Text him and tell him this whole thing was a big fuckup. Tell him he was dumb about Leah and hungover as hell. Just talk to him."

"*I did.*" Aubrey wiped her eyes with her arm. "I—I asked him if he wanted to be part of my life next year. But, Gabe—he didn't. He couldn't even pretend."

Gabe touched her elbow, and just like that, her mind went quiet. And in that quiet, a memory rushed in.

Just over three weeks ago—on a Friday in June, on a night when everything was different—she'd been standing backstage after the closing show of the musical. She'd been crying then, too, holding a bouquet of orange flowers a few underclassmen had given her. She kept trying to brush off the heavy sadness she felt, but she couldn't. She could only think about how this was the last time she would ever turn off the stage lights, or check to make sure all the props were put away, or even stand backstage. Theater wasn't her life's passion or anything, but this was a place where she'd felt like she belonged. And now it was gone for good.

When Gabe had walked past her, he'd rolled his eyes and gone in to hug her. Instead, they'd kissed, Aubrey's flowers pressed between them. Everything dim as they held themselves together, kissing like it was the only kiss either of them would ever have. Eventually, they broke apart, breathless and confused.

"Aubrey?" Gabe said now, drawing Aubrey out of her memory. He looked at where his fingers still rested on her elbow. "Should we try calling Jo—"

She kissed him. She kissed him, and immediately he kissed her back. Her worries about Jonah sank away. She felt Gabe's hands move to her sides, and her arms wrap around his neck, tugging his lips closer to hers. And for those few seconds, these were the only things that mattered: his mouth, his skin, his warmth. She disappeared inside of them; she let them swallow her whole.

Until she opened her eyes.

Until she saw Jonah standing in the door of the train, gripping his bag with both hands.

"Jonah," she said, and her mouth went cold. The rest of her body followed, all of her skin turning to ice.

Jonah shook his head. "I'm going," he said. "I have to go back."

"No." Gabe stepped forward. "*Fuck.* Please just—wait a second."

But when Jonah's eyes met Aubrey's, she knew it was too late. She watched him jump back onto the platform. She watched him fade into the crowd as the train began to fill with people. They hadn't left yet, but it didn't matter. Jonah was already gone—he was a thousand miles away.

16

Tuesday, July 5
PRAGUE

At the beginning of June, on the night that Aubrey kissed Gabe, Rae could tell something was wrong.

She hadn't known what exactly—Aubrey hadn't told her yet—but she could still *tell*. She was practically psychic when it came to Aubrey.

They'd gone to a cast party at a pub, and after that, Aubrey and Clara had come over to stay at Rae's house. Clara fell asleep on the couch, watching Lucy's DVDs of *Twin Peaks*, but Aubrey and Rae were wide-awake. *What's wrong?* Rae mouthed. Aubrey scratched Iorek behind the ears and nodded toward the back door.

It was raining, so they put on coats and Wellies before

heading across the lawn toward the tiny guesthouse, where Rae's mom had her art studio. Rae turned on the Edison bulbs that hung from the ceiling and the lamp on her mom's drafting table. Aubrey just stood there, water from her coat and boots dripping onto the floor. After the room had been lit up, section by section, Aubrey said, "I kissed Gabe."

"*What?*" Rae nearly fell over. "Wait, dude, *what*? Are you being serious?"

"When am I ever not serious?"

"Okay, okay. I officially need more information. You have to tell me everything."

Aubrey sat on the ground. "It was right after the play. He kissed me—or maybe I kissed him. I think we both went for it at the same time."

"Holy fuck!"

"Exactly." Aubrey looked so depressed. Outside, rain drummed against the windows. The room was filled with art books and pots of brushes and sketches tacked to the walls. Some of them were of Aubrey and Rae when they were kids, sharing ice-cream bars and sleeping on the couch with Iorek. Rae's favorite was of the two of them dressed as Sherlock and Watson on Halloween five years ago.

"I have to tell Jonah," Aubrey said.

"Aubrey," Rae said, "not to be dramatic or anything, but why the hell would you do that?"

"Because I have to. I cheated on him. I cheated on my boyfriend—I can't lie about that."

"It's only lying if you say *good news, Jonah, I never kissed Gabe.* What I'm suggesting is you avoid the topic altogether."

Aubrey pulled the hood of her raincoat over her head and crossed her arms. It was officially summer break, and the days were starting to get warm, but the rain had cooled down the air again. "I can't believe I'm such a skank," she said.

"Don't say that," Rae said. "I hate that word."

"What else do you call someone who cheats on their boyfriend?"

"I call them a person. A person who got carried away, because graduation is coming up and Gabe is one of your best friends and the two of you have this whole weird history together."

Aubrey's eyes filled with alarm. "But I shouldn't have weird history with my boyfriend's best friend."

"Of course you should! Women can have weird history with whoever they want."

Aubrey shrank further into her coat. "You're only being nice about this because you care about me. And because you've kissed so many people."

Rae scoffed. "Guys can kiss as many people as they want. Why can't we? Anyway, kissing is just—faces smashing against each other. It's the same thing you do with an ice-cream cone. One kiss means nothing, Aubs. Unless... I mean, unless you *want* it to mean something?"

"No." Aubrey frowned at the carpeted floor, at the dark spots of water that kept falling from her clothes. "I really don't."

Rae didn't say anything else, although she wanted to; she could tell that Aubrey needed a while to think.

The rain grew louder, and Rae got up to dig through her mom's stuff, looking for the bags of candy Lucy kept hidden there. They spread their raincoats out like picnic blankets and lay down on them, eating mini Mars bars and listening to the gusts of wind that creaked in the studio walls. Toward morning, the storm finally began to clear. And Aubrey and Rae went back inside, where Clara was still sleeping and Lucy had made them breakfast.

Just like that night in June, Rae could tell something was wrong.

But this time, Aubrey wouldn't talk to her about it.

The whole train ride from Berlin to Prague, she just curled up by the window next to Rae, not saying a word, looking like she was about to start crying. Gabe wasn't saying anything, either. He disappeared into his headphones, eyes blank as he stared at the back of the seat in front of him. Rae was floored. *Why on earth had Jonah left?* And what was Aubrey hiding from her?

The only conclusion that made any sense at all was that Aubrey and Jonah had broken up.

And that maybe Gabe had something to do with it?

"Broken up?" Clara asked when they were finally in Prague.

She and Rae sat on the front steps of their hostel, sharing a bottle of soda they'd bought at the station. It was evening, and the sky above the buildings was stained lavender and red. Broken bottles and cigarette butts littered the cobblestone ground, and across the street, Rae could see a few cheap souvenir shops, the space between them tagged with graffiti. But when she tilted her head back, all of that went away. The world transformed into buildings painted pistachio green and rose pink. It became clock faces set in gold, and pigeons landing on elaborate, curling cornices. The city was so ornate and old-fashioned, it reminded Rae of a music box.

"I guess so," she said, still staring at the buildings. "Why else would Jonah run away like that?"

"But they're *Jonah and Aubrey*," Clara said. "They never even fight."

"It's the summer before college. Tons of people break up now."

"But where did he even go?" Clara asked.

"No clue." Rae looked down, rubbing the bottle of soda between her hands. "He could be anywhere, I guess?" But she had to admit, it was weird. She'd never imagined Jonah and Aubrey breaking up like *this*—dramatically, in the middle of a foreign country. As a couple, they'd always been pretty low-key, so how could they just end everything? Had Jonah found out Aubrey had kissed Gabe after the musical? And if so, why wouldn't Aubrey just tell her about it?

The door to the hostel opened, and a group of college-age

kids tromped down the steps to the sidewalk. Some of them were already drinking cans of beer, and they were all arguing about what bar they should go to. Clara stood up, and Rae's heart sank. Obviously, Clara wanted to talk to them. Maybe she wanted to tag along to the bar, which sucked, because Rae had liked hanging out alone. Clara dusted off the back of her dress and slung her vintage purse over her shoulder. "Let's do something," she said.

"Like what?" Rae asked.

"I don't know." Clara threw up her hands. "Let's get food. Or see Prague. I can't sit around like this anymore. It's making me antsy."

Rae played with the cap of the soda bottle. "What if Aubrey tries to find us? What if she wants to tell us what happened?"

"No problem. We'll go for a quick walk and we'll come right back. Besides, when will you get another first night in Prague?"

Rae looked back at the blue-painted door of the hostel. But she knew Clara was right—they wouldn't be gone for long. She got up, and the two of them wound through a maze of narrow cobblestone streets. The buildings they passed were lit up like parts of a theater set: gold letters stenciled onto their façades, carved angels perched on their window ledges. None of it seemed real. It was an image taken straight from a fairy tale.

Clara tugged at one of her long, silvery leaf-shaped earrings. "If Aubrey and Jonah are really broken up, do you think we'll have to choose sides?"

"It's not really a choice, is it?" Rae said. "We'd obviously take Aubrey's."

"But we don't even know what happened."

"They broke up. What else is there to know?"

Clara chewed her lip. They walked under a streetlamp, which cast a spotlight over both of them. "But it's complicated," Clara said. "I mean, Jonah's our friend, too. And I've known him since middle school. He was so small and cute then. He used to embarrass himself in PE all the time."

"Aubrey embarrasses herself in PE, too," Rae said. "You can't make this decision based on athletic ability."

Clara tugged at her earring again. "But if you automatically take Aubrey's side, and Gabe automatically takes Jonah's, my vote is extra important. It tips the scales."

Rae had never thought of their friendship dynamics as particularly complicated before, but maybe they were. "It probably doesn't matter," she said. "We're all leaving soon anyway. Technically, everyone is breaking up with everyone, right?"

Clara's face fell.

Rae cringed. "Sorry. I didn't mean to make it sound so depressing."

"No, no," Clara said. "It's fine."

But clearly it wasn't. "I think I'm just hungry," Rae said. "Should we get food?"

They walked into a square where all the stores were closed except for a small donut stand in the center. "See!" Rae said. "It's a sign."

"A sign of what?" Clara asked.

"A sign of donuts! A sign of sugar! The greatest signs of all time, if you ask me."

Rae ordered two donuts, which came wrapped in thick, greasy paper and warmed their fingers. They made the summer air smell like cinnamon. *"Amazing,"* Clara said, her voice muffled by a bite.

"It's like funnel cake," Rae said, "but with jam. Don't you think everything is better with jam?"

Clara laughed through a mouthful of dough, putting Rae at ease. They were standing on the edge of the quiet square now. "Is it just me," Rae said, "or does this place feel kind of fake to you?"

"Fake?" Clara swallowed.

"Not in a bad way. It's like a set. Actually, it made me remember something: When my mom and I moved to London, one of the first things she did was take me to a ballet. And obviously, I thought it was terrible—so unbelievably boring—but I did like the sets. They were—otherworldly. They felt like this."

Clara smiled softly. "And you pretend you're not a theater nerd."

"Yeah, well. It's my deepest, darkest secret." They'd both finished eating, but they were still standing there, still watching each other. Rae thought back to this morning on the train and last night in the hostel. She felt like something was changing. She cleared her throat. "I guess we should head back now?"

But as she stepped away, Clara blurted, "Let's not?"

Rae stopped, giving her a curious look, and Clara fixed her hair around her ears. "I mean, we've barely seen anything yet. We should keep walking. Just for a few more minutes."

"Sure," Rae said. "A few more minutes sounds good."

The streetlights burned orange against the stone; they brought out its texture as Rae and Clara approached an archway leading into another square. They stepped through, and Rae's breath caught.

The cobblestones stretched to the corners of her vision, silhouettes of churches and bell towers cresting the square's edges. In the center, a band played—a boy hunched over a keyboard and a girl in a long, drapey dress played the violin, occasionally stopping to sing into a microphone.

Rae and Clara stepped closer.

"I love the way her dress moves," Clara said, her voice a whisper.

Rae had forgotten her camera, but she didn't need it. When she drew this later, she knew she would remember every detail: the heavy lines of the churches; the fluid lines of the singer and her dress; the small crowd huddled by the band; and the kids that broke off, chasing pigeons through pools of golden light.

And she would remember Clara: her bright-pink lipstick and her dress printed with bluebirds; the way her hair was pulled back by that single bobby pin; the way her lips were parted in awe.

Maybe this was why Prague felt like make-believe to Rae. So impossible and unreal. Because she was alone with Clara. Because this whole city could have been set up for them, each place waiting for them to find it.

"Come on." Clara nodded toward an alleyway between two buildings. "That church looks pretty. We can probably still hear the music, too." They walked until they couldn't see the square anymore, but Clara was right: They could still hear the music. Rae perched on a stone shelf that jutted from the side of the church, and Clara stood in front of her, twisting a strand of hair around her index finger.

"This is better, isn't it?" she said. "Less crowded?"

"Way less crowded," Rae agreed. She kicked her feet against the stone while Clara kept twisting her hair and looking up at the church that Rae was leaning against. Rae wanted to say something—something funny and charming, something that would calm the nervous fluttering in her stomach. The music echoed off the walls as if it were playing just for them.

Clara let go of her hair. "Could I ask you something?"

"Go for it." Rae tried to sound light, like she hadn't

noticed how private this place was. Like that didn't matter to her at all.

"You never really explained this, but—why Australia? I mean, I know you wanted to go somewhere different. But of all the places in the world, why there?"

"I told you," Rae said. "It's just where I imagined myself."

Clara ran her hands down the front of her dress. "But you didn't tell me *why* you imagined yourself there. And you also said you were scared to go."

Rae frowned. The music had stopped for a moment, and the instruments were tuning. "I wanted a blank slate. And anyway, isn't that the whole point of graduating and leaving home? Isn't this when we're supposed to do things that are different and scary?"

"I guess," Clara said, "but you don't have to go to Australia for that. There are a thousand good schools in a thousand places you've never lived. And you're really talented, Rae. You could have gone anywhere you wanted."

Rae crossed her arms. Why was Clara lecturing her on making good life choices? "Maybe," she said, "but you're talented, too, Clara. Why did you only apply to schools in California? What about ones in England? Or *New York*?"

"All my aunts and uncles live on the West Coast. And my sister goes to Stanford. I know I joke about having an overprotective family, but I still want to be close to them."

"Yeah," Rae said bitterly, "but if you went to New York, you could be close to Leah."

Clara's expression was stunned. "Why would I want that?"

"Maybe you don't remember"—Rae hopped down from the stone—"but you told me that you and Leah were, like, an item or whatever."

"Rae. Leah and I were *never* an item."

Rae shoved her hands in her pockets. "Look. We don't have to get into it. And if you're worried I'm going to tell everyone that you're queer, you don't have to be. I wouldn't do that."

"I'm not worried." Clara looked so upset that it made Rae feel nauseous. But she couldn't take this anymore. She couldn't take the constant push and pull, the constant hope of thinking that maybe Clara liked her, the constant disappointment of realizing, yet again, that she didn't. Rae just wanted to go back to the hostel—to focus on Aubrey's issues instead.

She started to leave, but Clara reached for her arm. "You never answered my question last night," she said.

Rae was thrown. "What question?"

Clara flushed. The music started again and cascaded down the walls. "You know which question. I asked you, who would you kiss if you could kiss anyone?"

The humidity in the air was suddenly unbearable—Rae's skin had turned hot, her breathing constricted. "Okay," she said. "I think maybe you're trying to make me feel better. But you don't have to do that. In case you haven't noticed, I'm being pretty surly right now."

"No," Clara said. "I'm not trying to do that."

And then she kissed Rae.

Rae froze in place.

The music rushed into her ears, and, slowly, her lips began to soften. Her hands touched Clara's arms, and Clara's touched hers. But Rae's mind was still racing—it was reminding her of all the girls she'd kissed before. Girls at school dances and in front of tube stations and in the quiet art room after school. It brought up a memory of the first girl she'd ever kissed. Dana Silverstein had invited her over for a *Grey's Anatomy* marathon when—halfway through the second episode, while some doctor was yelling at some other doctor—they'd leaned together, their lips meeting for a few brief seconds. Ever since then, Rae had kissed girls and they'd kissed her, and it had always been fun and sweet and perfectly right.

But not as right as this.

Not as right as Clara's lips tasting like cinnamon sugar, or her hands fluttering to Rae's waist, or the way her hair moved across Rae's shoulders.

They backed against the stone, the building keeping Rae steady as she fell deeper into this—into this dark corner, this night, this kiss. The fabric of Clara's dress pressed up against her bare legs; her hand now rested against the side of Clara's neck. The night felt heavy, like it was draped over them, protecting them. And the world was spinning so fast, it was shaking beneath their feet.

"Rae," Clara murmured against her mouth. "I think that's your phone. Your phone is vibrating."

Rae blinked drowsily. "My phone?"

It had to be her mom. Oh God, Rae was going to be *so mad* if it was her mom. Clara stepped back a little, but her hand lingered on Rae's hip. She was still right there, lipstick smudged, eyes shining. Rae yanked the phone out of her pocket, and Aubrey's name jumped out at her. She fumbled to answer it.

"Aubs?" she said. "What's going on? Are you okay?"

"Rae?" Aubrey asked, but there was too much background noise. Her voice was garbled with sobs, and Rae could barely make out what she was saying. "I—I'm at this—this bar. I don't know where it is. Please. Wherever you are, please come find me."

17

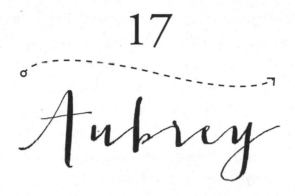

Aubrey

Tuesday, July 5
PRAGUE

It was past sunset when Aubrey got up. Despite the open window and the fan in the corner, the air felt humid. Claustrophobic. She looked outside at the shapes of opulent rooftops and down to the street, where a group of people stood drinking and talking.

Rae and Clara had been gone for a while, and Aubrey didn't want to be here when they got back. She needed to get out—out of this hostel and out of this room, where every cinder-block wall had been painted in layers of thick blue paint. It made her feel like she was having a fever dream.

She went to the mirror and looked at her wrinkled clothes and blotchy red cheeks. She wiped away the mascara printed under her eyes and tugged out the tangles in her hair. For once, she didn't care about combing it or parting it in the exact right place. She didn't care that she was alone or that Jonah was probably halfway back to—wherever by now. He'd only said that he was going, not where he was going to. And every time she tried to picture him in any particular place, she couldn't. She imagined him hopping from train to train instead, losing himself in city after city.

But Aubrey couldn't obsess over that. She needed to think about tonight. She needed to learn how to be by herself.

How to be a grown-up.

She grabbed her room key and opened the door—right onto Gabe.

His hand was raised like he was about to knock, but he dropped it by his side instead. "Hi," he said.

"Hi." Aubrey's breath felt trapped inside her rib cage.

Gabe scratched the side of his head. On his wrists, he wore a few old festival bracelets, and he'd changed into this old Brown University T-shirt he used to wear a lot after he'd first moved from Rhode Island. The pale blue material was almost threadbare at the collar, and for a few light-headed seconds, Aubrey imagined what it would feel like against her skin. But she shook the thought away.

"So," he said. "Should we talk? Because I want to tell you how sorry—"

She held up her hand to stop him. "Don't. I *really* can't talk about this right now."

"Okay." He paused. "Are you going out?"

She stepped into the hallway and pulled the door shut behind her. It locked automatically. "I think so."

"You think so? You mean you're still deciding?"

"No. I've decided. But—I don't know where." They walked into the stairwell, a light jittering to life above them. They'd been in Prague for a few hours, and Aubrey wondered what Gabe had been doing all this time—sitting alone in his hostel room, maybe. Unpacking his stuff, checking his phone, and feeling complete disbelief that his best friend wasn't there with him.

"What you're telling me," Gabe said, as they went down a flight of concrete steps, "is that you don't have a *plan*?"

"It's Prague. I'll figure something out."

"Yeah, but, Bryce. You *always* have a plan."

"I do not. At least not anymore."

Aubrey maneuvered around a girl carrying a basket of clean laundry and skipped out the front door. The same group of people she'd seen from her window was still there, having a loud conversation in English. Aubrey stepped over an old soda bottle someone had left on the stoop and walked up to a guy with his hair in a ponytail. Her resolve wavered, but she refused to let anxiety win. She tapped him on the shoulder.

"Hey?" There was a question in his voice, like he was trying to figure out if he knew her.

"Are all of you staying here?" she asked, pointing back at the hostel.

"Yeah," the guy said. "You?"

Aubrey nodded.

A girl with a nose hoop turned around, too. "We're going to a bar," she said. "You two should totally come with!"

"Us *two*?" Aubrey checked over her shoulder and saw Gabe, hands casually slung in the pockets of his jeans. "*You're* coming as well?"

He shrugged. "I don't have anywhere else to be."

Aubrey bit down on her tongue. On the one hand, this was something she'd wanted to do alone. She'd wanted to be bold, to play the part of the girl she would have to become as soon as she got to New York. And also—he was Gabe! A few hours ago, they'd kissed. A few hours ago, Jonah had left because of that kiss.

But on the other hand—*he was Gabe*. Gabe, who'd spent long afternoons reading on the sofa in her living room. Gabe, who made her feel comfortable. Who made her feel safe.

Maybe it was better having him with her.

The streets of Prague were a maze, and Aubrey was too on edge to keep track of any of them. She and Gabe followed the rest of the group to a bar sandwiched between a currency exchange and a store with a display of marionettes in the window. Their strings glinted like spiderwebs, and their painted eyes stared blankly outside.

"Creepy," Gabe said to Aubrey.

"No kidding," Aubrey said. "It's like they know all my secrets."

"Aubrey," he said in a creaky voice. *"Aubrey, I know about that bio test you never studied for."*

She elbowed him in the stomach.

Inside, the bar was warm and rustic, with farmhouse tables, wagon wheels suspended from the ceiling, and vintage advertisements hanging on the walls. Their group gathered in the center, but Aubrey headed straight for the bar, where a bartender with a shaved head stood cleaning pint glasses. Aubrey asked him for a beer, clutching her passport to her chest, expecting him to check her ID.

But he didn't. He filled a heavy tankard and handed it over.

"That was fast," Gabe said, walking up next to her.

Aubrey lifted her drink. "Cheers."

"Hold that thought. I need one, too." He ordered a beer as well, then folded his arms on the counter. She thought, *I really like his hair that way, all long and messy on top.* And she liked his Brown T-shirt, because it was nerdy and it reminded her of when they'd first started hanging out. And she liked that if she'd asked him right then, he probably could have told her the name of the song playing over the bar's speakers.

"I'm really glad you came along," she said, tightly gripping her cold glass.

A spark of hope flashed in his eyes. "You are?"

"Sorry," a guy from the hostel group said, squeezing through the crowd to reach the bar. He had spiky dark hair and sounded American, but he ordered his drink in Czech.

"I'm Henry, by the way," he said, turning to Gabe and Aubrey after he'd paid. "So you guys go to Brown?"

Gabe glanced down at his shirt. "No," he said at the same time that Aubrey said, "Yes."

Henry glanced between them. "You do or you don't?"

"We do." Aubrey tapped her foot against Gabe's. She wanted him to understand—tonight, she wasn't High School Aubrey. She wasn't the bored, childish girl she'd been at the Amsterdam party.

"Yeah," Gabe said. "We're—uh—we're going to be sophomores."

Henry's brow pinched. "But you said you didn't go there?"

"What can I tell you?" Gabe shot Aubrey a look. "I'm full of contradictions."

Henry nodded wisely. "That only gets more true, man. I just finished my junior year at Northwestern."

"That's such a great school," Aubrey said.

"It's all right," he said. "But I'm not sure I'll go back. I'm actually taking a little time off."

"And that's allowed?" Gabe asked.

"Sure. College is a lot of pressure. Sometimes you have to step back, examine things from a new angle. I'm traveling this summer, and then I'm going to WWOOF in Italy."

"Woof?" Aubrey asked.

"Yup. You live on a farm for a while, volunteer there. A buddy of mine did it a couple semesters ago—picked crops, baked his own bread, shit like that. Said it made him realize there was more to life than just studying crap." Henry pointed at them. "Don't forget that."

Gabe smirked. "You should definitely talk to my parents."

"And mine," Aubrey chimed in. Henry was saying something else, but she stopped listening for a moment. She was thinking over what Lucy had said the day they'd left London—that it was good for her to take this time, that she needed to travel and be aimless before making the decisions that would define the rest of her life. But Aubrey had assumed she didn't need that kind of time. She'd assumed she'd made those decisions already.

More people congregated around the bar. Aubrey couldn't hear the music as well, but she could feel it—persistent, sad, weary. It was a strange contrast to the buzz she felt at her future opening up, at seeing all these new possibilities she'd never even known about.

And the most exciting part was, tonight held those possibilities, too.

Aubrey put her empty glass down on a paper coaster. She was two beers in and sitting with Gabe at a table now, with Henry across from them talking to the girl with the nose hoop. He and Nose Hoop Girl seemed to be hitting it off, actually. Aubrey wondered if they would kiss.

"Okay." Gabe showed her the mouthful of amber liquid at the bottom of his own glass. "Your turn."

They'd been playing a game to pass the time: Whoever finished their drink first had to make a prediction about the other's future—and that person had to accept it. No questions asked.

"Easy," Aubrey said. "Next year, when it's cold and raining in Oregon, and you've had enough of hipsters and trees, you're going to look up pictures of all these other places in the world and realize that Portland is exactly the right one for you. And you'll be so happy, because in your whole life, you won't have one single regret. That is the truth. The end. Good night."

"Or maybe," he said, "I'll be full of regrets. Maybe I'll book a flight to Italy."

"To go BARKING?" she asked.

"You mean *WWOOFing*?" He laughed.

"Uh-huh." She bit back a smile. "That's what I said."

He turned his coaster on its side and rolled it across the table. "Seriously, though, I wish I knew what I'd end up doing."

"That's easy. You'll do something you're good at."

"And what, exactly, do you think I'm good at?"

Her eyes went straight to his lips, which made her cheeks flame. She looked pointedly at a vintage advertisement hanging on the wall—at its depiction of green hills and daisies. "How about painting sets?" she asked.

"Preferably of cities," he said. "And preferably only when it's *really obvious* where I should paint."

"Or political science? Or art history?"

"Interesting, I guess?"

"Okay. Hold on." She closed her eyes and massaged her forehead. "Here's my real prediction: In your freshman year, it'll become clear that studying literature is perfect for you. Because you love to analyze and pick things apart and figure out what you like about them, and that's basically what the entire major is. And the thing is, you already do that with music, but you can do it with books, too. It's like music but minus the instruments." She opened her eyes. "That's what you told me a couple of months ago, right? That if you could do something that was like music but without having to play an instrument, you totally would."

The bar was packed with people—holding full glasses over their heads, singing along with the music, talking over menus—but Gabe wasn't looking at any of them. Only at her. He brought his mouth to her ear; his voice traveled down her neck. "Do you want to go outside?"

She pushed open the door of the bar and stepped into the cool and the quiet. The street was empty. All the streetlamps looked lonely. Aubrey stuck out her arms and spun in a circle the way she'd seen Clara do the night before.

"Having a good time?" Gabe called after her.

"The best," she said, still spinning.

She stopped, but the world kept going—it was lights bleeding together; it was bright, intangible ropes twisting around her. "Dizzy." She touched the top of her head. "Why would Clara do that?"

"Let's sit down." He led her to the wall by the bar's door, and they slid to the ground, which was probably dirty, but Aubrey didn't care.

"Remember our friends?" She gestured at the marionettes across the street.

"How could I forget?" Gabe lifted a hand. "How's it going, guys? Still being disturbing as fuck, I see."

Aubrey laughed.

"Okay. Come on," he said. "It's my turn."

"For what?"

He bumped her shoulder with his. "I get to make a prediction about you."

"Nope! You have to finish a drink first. I'll go get us some." She started to stand, but he touched the back of her wrist. "My prediction," he said, "is that you are going to fit perfectly in New York."

"Ha."

"No, I mean it. I can see you walking down Broadway. Or going to the farmers' market to buy apples—people in New York are big on apples; just ask my sister about that. And you can go to as many museums and concerts as you want, and afterward you'll ride a bus home in the dark, still thinking about everything you've seen. You'll probably miss your stop, but you won't mind. I think you'll like that feeling, actually. The letting-go feeling."

Aubrey looked at the shape of his hands, which were now resting on his knees. She took one, sliding her fingers between his. He swallowed, his Adam's apple bobbing up and down. Memories of the rest of the day taunted Aubrey from the corners of her thoughts. They begged for her attention. But she didn't want to give in to them. She wanted this night exactly as it was—so hot and thick she felt like she could swim in it.

Gabe let go of her hand. "Maybe we shouldn't."

"You're right," she said.

But she kissed him anyway, and he kissed her back—frenetically and passionately, his hands trailing up the back of her neck. She climbed into his lap, and the air felt even warmer, so much warmer than it had a few seconds ago.

The door to the bar opened, and Aubrey jumped up, tugging the hem of her shirt back into place, getting ready to explain herself. But the people who'd left the bar had no idea who she was. They were already walking away, footsteps snapping as they turned a corner.

"Oh no, no, no." Everything she'd been feeling—the elation, the hope, all of it—was gone. The only thing she was left with was the memory of that afternoon.

Of Jonah.

Gabe stood, too. "Everything's fine. You'll stay over there, and I'll stay here, and we're both fine."

"*No, no, NO.*" Aubrey paced the cobblestones. In the darkened window across the street, the marionettes gawked at her. "I can't do this. I can't be here."

"No problem," Gabe said. "We'll go back to the hostel."

She stopped pacing. "We can't go back there together!

What if Clara and Rae see us? What if they figure it out?" She stopped pacing. Her thoughts roared. Why had she just kissed him?

Why had she kissed him *twice*? *In one day!*

"We can't go separately," Gabe said. "It's dangerous, Bryce."

"I can't do this. I need to think." She walked to where the street narrowed into an archway and stood beneath it. Everything was changing so quickly. This day was going by so much faster than she knew how to deal with.

Gabe came to stand across from her. "We can go back now. I promise I won't even talk to you. And Clara and Rae might not even be there yet."

"Why did you kiss me?" she demanded.

His face blanched. "You mean tonight?"

"I mean tonight. And this afternoon. And at the beginning of the summer. Why did you kiss me when I was dating Jonah?"

"Aubrey," he said, "I don't know."

"How can you not know?"

He fussed with his bracelets. "I just—don't. It happened, but I didn't want it to."

"So you're saying you didn't want to kiss me?"

He let out a frustrated breath. "You're not making this easy."

"You ignored me," she said, leaning all her weight against the archway. "For weeks you ignored me, and then yesterday you start talking to me again. You start pretending like everything is fine."

"I wasn't pretending. I thought we could go back to the way things were."

"Well, clearly"—she gestured between them—"we can't!"

Gabe kicked a stone down the street. "Look," he said, "I ignored you because I thought you wanted some distance. I thought I was making things simple for you."

"By treating me like crap?"

"By making it clear I wasn't interested in you."

It was a blow to Aubrey's stomach.

She couldn't even look at him.

She went back inside the bar, swerving through the crush of people, the heat of their bodies, the too-bright lights that beat down above her. She waited until she reached the bathroom to let herself sob, ducking down beneath the hand dryer, pushing both hands against her mouth. Even here, she could hear the music playing.

This wasn't supposed to happen. She wasn't supposed to cry over Gabe. She was supposed to cry over Jonah.

A girl came out of one of the stalls and gave Aubrey a weird look before washing her hands. The girl left, and Aubrey tried to pull herself together. She needed to do something; she needed to at least get back to the hostel. With shaking hands, she took out her phone. "Rae?" she said the second her best friend answered. "I—I'm at this—this bar. I don't know where it is. Please. Wherever you are, please come find me."

18

Wednesday, July 6
PRAGUE

T a-da!" Clara raised her arms with a flourish.

Rae examined the map on her phone. "And what exactly are we looking at?"

"The Astronomical Clock!" Clara paused. "This is the Astronomical Clock, right?"

She was asking Aubrey, but Aubrey didn't hear—she was watching tour groups walk across the square. It was the same square Rae and Clara had stood in the night before, but it looked different now. Brighter. Filled with vendors hawking sun hats and people filming videos with their cell phones. A break-dance troupe performed where, last night, the band had played. Rae tried to clear it all away, to let memories of the evening before flood back in—darkness and light, music and silence. She tried to feel like it was all here again.

"Rae?" Clara said. "Does that look like the right clock to you?"

"Yeah, I think so." Rae's arm was right beside Clara's—the backs of their hands brushing together. The daylight and the crowds seemed to evaporate completely as Rae remembered Clara's hands moving lightly to her sides, the press of her bright-pink lips.

"We should get closer," Aubrey said suddenly. "It's about to strike noon."

Rae was pulled from her thoughts. "What happens at noon?"

But Aubrey was already heading over to where a crowd had started to gather. Built into the side of an old tower were two enormous clock faces stacked one above the other with a tiny gold sun rotating around one of them.

Rae and Clara caught up to Aubrey, and the three of them stood in a row, Rae peeking at Aubrey out of the corner of her eye. She was still wearing the T-shirt she'd had on the night before, and her ponytail was a mess. It was nearly one AM when Rae and Clara had found her at the bar and led her back to the hostel, and it was nearly four AM when she finally agreed to try to get some sleep. Before then, she'd told them a little about the fight she'd had with Jonah. She told them what he'd said about Leah and about New York. But she didn't mention anything about him leaving. Or why she'd ended up at that bar.

Honestly, it pissed Rae off a little. She kept wondering what would have happened if Aubrey had never called. If she and Clara had stayed in the shadows of those buildings a little bit longer, arms around each other, breathing each other in.

The hour chimed, and Rae shaded her eyes and lifted her head. A mechanical skeleton emerged from inside the clock and pulled a cord to make a bell ring.

"Well," she said. "This is some pretty weird shit."

Aubrey made a small noise that might have been a laugh. (Rae decided to believe it was a laugh.) Mechanical figures moved across the clock in a procession. Saints and apostles, their faces contorted in anguish. Tourists clicked their cameras. And then the bells stopped chiming; the crowd dispersed.

"Damn," Rae said. "I'm so unbelievably glad we don't live in medieval times."

They headed away from the square, Rae and Clara keeping up their end of the conversation and trying to act like everything was normal, Aubrey definitely not doing the same. They crossed the Charles Bridge, and Rae snapped some pictures of its dozens of statues: a lot more saints, dudes in robes, a decent number of despondent expressions.

Rae stopped in front of one. "I mean, look at these guys. They're standing on a cage full of screaming people."

Clara stopped, too. "I think back then you were either the guy standing *on* a cage full of screaming people or the guy *inside* a cage full of screaming people."

"Reminds me of middle school." Rae took a picture of the

statue and then another of Clara, who leaned into the lens, smiling. Rae could see herself reflected in Clara's sunglasses. They both paused for a second, and Rae knew they were thinking the exact same thing: What would it be like if they could get a little bit closer? What would they do if they were alone?

"Aubs!" Clara said, like she'd just remembered she was there. "Come be in the next one." But Aubrey shook her head and gazed absently at the strange, pearly-gray water.

Rae shrugged. "I guess we should keep going."

They were headed for the Vyšehrad, a fortress built over the Vltava River. They had to climb a hill to get there, and when they arrived, they were sweaty and exhausted. Clara flopped onto a bench. "This place is"—*inhale*—"cool"—*exhale*—"isn't it?"

The fortress was a series of sprawling ruins hovering over the city. It was overgrown with greenery and cut through with pathways that teemed with dog walkers and joggers. Beyond that, Prague's red roofs looked hazy, almost indistinct in the golden afternoon light.

"Okay." Clara stood up from the bench. "I need to pee."

"But we just sat down," Rae said.

"Exactly. We had so much coffee this morning, and we haven't stopped anywhere for *hours*. I'll be right back."

"Don't get lost," Rae called as Clara disappeared around a bend on the path. She hated seeing her go, even for a little while. But she needed to get over that. Soon *she* would be the one leaving. She would be the one on a plane landing in Australia.

That harsh dose of reality made last night seem unreachable, as far away as an image in an old photograph. She pushed her feet through the gravel. "So," she said to Aubrey. "Is it true that people in Prague used to throw each other out of windows?"

"The Defenestrations of Prague," Aubrey said. "Yeah, that's true."

"*Defenestration*," Rae said. "I love that word. I can't believe there's a word for tossing someone out a window."

"I think, back then," Aubrey said, "you were either the guy throwing someone from a window or the guy being thrown."

Rae smirked. So Aubrey wasn't totally checked out after all.

A bird sang in the branches above them, and Rae let her head roll back. The sky was blotted with purple smog, and the sun made kaleidoscopic patterns behind the trees.

"I'm sorry I missed last night," Aubrey said. "Will you show me the pictures you took?"

Rae dropped her head. "I didn't take any."

"Oh." Aubrey drew her legs onto the bench and went quiet for a minute. "Rae?" she said eventually.

"Yup?"

"I want to tell you something. About yesterday. I want you to know, you shouldn't blame Jonah for going. It was seriously all my fault."

"Aubs, *no way*. Listen. As someone who has dumped and been dumped, I promise you, his reaction is completely on him. He didn't have to be so dramatic."

Aubrey rubbed at a birthmark on her knee that Rae had never noticed before. "That's what I'm trying to say, though. He couldn't help being dramatic. What I did...it was pretty unforgivable."

Rae ground her toes into the gravel again. "What exactly did you do, Aubrey?"

Aubrey took a deep breath. And for a second, Rae was certain she was going to get an answer. Until Aubrey's expression filled with terror. She looked the way she had when Jonah tried to convince her to try out for the musical. She looked like she was about to have a panic attack. "I—I can't," she said. "I'm sorry, but I can't talk about this."

"Okay," Rae said, but she felt annoyance flare up inside her again. So, Aubrey wasn't telling her something. Big news. Rae had figured that out yesterday. She still didn't know whether Gabe had been involved in the whole Jonah-getting-the-fuck-out-of-here thing. Or why Gabe had gone out by himself early that morning. Maybe Aubrey was waiting for Rae to ask about him directly. Or maybe she really did need to keep this to herself for a while, deal with her own secrets and heartbreak. But, if that was true, Rae wished she would at least *pretend* to think about someone other than herself. Rae wanted to say, *Last night was one of the best nights of my life. I had the most perfect kiss I've ever had, and you don't even care where I went or what I did. You haven't even asked.*

"It was a serious dick move," she said instead. "Jonah leaving like that. I mean, if he'd stayed, he could have talked things over with you. He would have realized that this doesn't have to be *The. End.* You know?"

"Of course it's *The. End*," Aubrey said. "We can't come back from something like this."

"But maybe you can," Rae said. "You're still moving to the same city, right? Going to college makes relationships complicated, I get it. But that doesn't mean you have to cut each other off completely."

Now Aubrey was the one who looked annoyed. She snorted. "That's pretty rich coming from you."

"What exactly do you mean by that?"

"Never mind." Aubrey shook her head.

Rae clenched her teeth as a woman walked her dogs past them. A scruffy terrier sniffed the pebbles around Rae's feet, and she rubbed the top of its nose, letting it *wuff* into her hand.

After the woman left, Aubrey said, "The thing is, I can't really explain any of this to you. You've never been in a serious relationship."

Rae blew a curl out of her eye and slouched against the bench. They were both silent now, watching the city below. A transparent sliver of moon appeared in the sky, and Rae latched on to that first hint of evening. She let it carry her back to last night and an alleyway behind a moonlit church. She let it remind her that this day would eventually end, and that, at some point soon, she might be kissing Clara again.

19

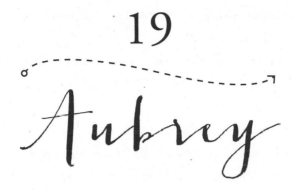

Aubrey

Thursday, July 7, to Friday, July 8
PRAGUE to FLORENCE via VIENNA

Aubrey!" A hand was shaking her arm; Rae's voice was in her ear. "Aubrey, you have to wake up."

But Aubrey couldn't. She was stuck inside a dream, walking next to abandoned railroad tracks. The ground was covered in green moss and other plants that twined around the metal. Aubrey could have sworn her friends were right beside her a moment ago, but they weren't anymore. She tried to listen out for them, but all she heard was a distant train whistle. The ground began to rumble. She felt it even as she drifted toward consciousness.

"*Aubrey.*" Rae was more insistent now. "Are you listening? We overslept. We're going to miss our train."

Aubrey sat up with a jolt. "Is this a joke?"

"No! Get up now!"

"But I set my phone alarm," Aubrey said.

"I turned it off," Rae said. "I heard it and I turned it off, *okay*? I screwed up!"

It was their last evening in Prague, and they were supposed to catch a sleeper train to Vienna just after midnight. In the morning, they would take another train to Florence. Aubrey's parents had insisted on booking them an extra night in their hostel in Prague to give them somewhere to stay until they left for the station. So Aubrey had crawled into bed at six PM after setting her alarm for ten.

But now it was nearly eleven thirty. Clara was on the floor, cramming knotted phone chargers and sandals into her bag. Aubrey yanked off her pajama bottoms and tried to pull on her denim shorts, but she fell to the side, banging her leg on the wooden bed frame.

"Fuck!" She was this close to bursting into tears. And not only because they would probably miss their train. But because Jonah was still gone, and she and Gabe had been avoiding each other since that stupid night at the bar, and Rae was being so cold with her—she had been ever since they went to the Vyšehrad.

Rae shoved a sweatshirt in her direction. "We have to go *now*."

Gabe was waiting for them on the hostel's front steps, gripping the straps of his heavy backpack. His shirt had song lyrics printed on it, but it was too dark out for Aubrey to read them. They stood as far away from each other as they could.

"Don't slow down!" Rae jumped off the stoop. "There's no time to slow down!"

They sprinted up the narrow alley from their hostel to a boulevard teeming with fluorescent-lit clothing stores and fast-food restaurants before turning into a park behind the station. There were fewer streetlights here, and the trees were cast in a strange purple glow.

With five minutes to spare, they raced through the station entrance, stopping briefly in the hall to figure out where their platform was. Aubrey's veins thudded with adrenaline, so she stared up at the high-domed ceiling, trying to calm herself down. Nearby, a gold clock chimed the hour. The tiled floor echoed with people's footsteps. This was the last thing she would see in Prague; she tried to make it count.

"Platform six!" Gabe shouted. Aubrey's lungs burned as they raced down a final corridor toward their train. Rae and Clara fell onto one of the small beds in their cabin, and Gabe landed on the other. A third bed was fastened to the wall above Gabe's head.

"How"—Gabe gasped—"how *the hell* did we pull that off?"

"I don't know," Rae said, "but I officially hate running now. Wait. Nope. I've always hated running."

"This place is so vintage!" Clara said. "It makes me wish I was wearing gloves with pearl buttons and carrying a hatbox."

The train wrenched out of the station, and Aubrey swayed in the doorway.

"Oh!" Rae said. "Do you think someone on this train will get murdered?"

"Um." Clara pushed Rae's shoulder. "I hope not."

"But then we could solve the mystery," Rae said. "What's more vintage than an old-fashioned train murder mystery?"

"That's not really what I was going for," Clara said, but she relaxed against Rae's shoulder. Rae pressed her lips together, blushing down at her lap.

Aubrey stayed frozen in the doorway. She wanted to bring up the phone conversation she'd had with Rae the night before the trip started. About *Strangers on a Train* and *Murder on the Orient Express*. But Rae and Clara were paying such close attention to each other. It kind of felt like they were excluding her. "We could have missed it, though," she said. "We could have missed our train and been stuck in Prague all night."

Rae's features hardened. "But we didn't."

"We shouldn't have slept through the alarm, though," Aubrey said. "We convinced our parents we were responsible enough to handle being here. We need to start acting that way."

"We made the train, dude," Rae said. "You can officially chill about it."

The train twitched; Aubrey held on to the sides of the door. "Why do you sound so annoyed at me?" she asked.

Rae crossed her arms. "I'm not annoyed."

"Well, you're acting like it. You have been since yesterday."

"Okay," Rae spat. "Maybe I am a *teeny, tiny bit* frustrated by the way you keep making this trip all about *you*."

"You know what?" Gabe clapped his hands together. "I'm starving. We should get dinner. Low blood sugar at midnight? Never a good thing."

"Agreed!" Clara's eyes flitted nervously between Rae and Aubrey.

"What do you mean I'm *making this trip all about me?*" Aubrey asked.

"It's pretty simple." Rae sat forward. "You want to eat dinner at some fancy-ass restaurant in Paris? We do it. You want to go to museums in Amsterdam? We leave a party and try to find you some. And even though you were incredibly painful about it the whole time, Clara and I still went out of our way to take you everywhere you wanted to go in Prague."

"Oh yeah." Aubrey rolled her eyes. "Because you had so many other ideas. The only trip you even care about is your precious one to Australia. You don't give a fuck about being here."

The train was moving faster now. They couldn't see anything in the window except their pale, eerie reflections. "That's such bullshit!" Rae said. "And also, it's completely different. I'm moving there."

"Believe me, we know!" Aubrey said. "And we know you can't wait to ditch us for your wild new life and the wild new friends you'll have there. You'll probably tell them all about how quaint and boring we were. *Once, my friend Aubrey lost her shit because we almost missed a train. Ha ha ha, she was so high-maintenance. Anyway, let's make art and drink an entire bottle of gin!*"

"Jesus, Aubrey. Where are you even getting this from?"

"From you! From your new hair and your tattoo and— and everything! From the way you get so aloof whenever I talk to you about college. You're transforming into this brand-new person, and she's secretive and she's mean, and *I don't like her.*"

"Now I get it," Rae snarled. "You can't stand the fact that I'm changing. That soon, my whole existence won't revolve around you anymore. Well, big news, Aubs—it *already* doesn't. It never has!"

Clara jumped up, her arms extended as if she were trying to physically keep them apart. "That's it. Both of you. Back away right now."

Her voice yanked Aubrey from her rage. "We're not anywhere near each other," she said.

"This is a small compartment," Clara said. "We're all near each other."

"Nothing we can do about that." Rae crossed her arms even tighter.

"Actually, there is." Clara picked up Rae's bag from the floor. "We've got two cabins, and there are four people in this room. We should split up."

"I can't stay with Gabe!" Aubrey said, instantly freaking out. She couldn't even trust herself in the same bar as this guy. Who knew what she would do *sleeping in the same room*?

The tips of Gabe's ears went red. He coughed into his hand. "I'll . . . you know, I'll go wherever."

"Fine," Clara said. "Aubrey, you stay here with me, and Rae, you go with Gabe."

Rae's mouth formed a small *o* of surprise. "But he's a boy!"

"And you're a lesbian," Clara said. "I think you can both control yourselves for one night."

Shock and awe flashed over Rae's face, but she didn't argue. She slung her bag over her shoulder and left the room. Gabe hovered in the door for a moment longer, looking sheepish. "Well," he said. "Good night?" And then he slunk into the hall.

The cabin felt much larger now.

"I'll sleep here." Clara pointed at the bed she'd been sitting on with Rae.

Aubrey sat on her bed and unfolded the fleecy blanket beside her pillow. Her mattress was thin but firm, and everything shook with the movement of the train. "Thanks for doing that," she said to Clara.

"You're welcome." Clara wrapped her long red hair into a knot on the top of her head.

Aubrey took out her phone and sent a quick text to her parents, telling them she was safely on her way to Vienna. She also said that she was tired and that she would call them tomorrow. She'd avoided talking to them ever since Jonah had left. She knew they'd have to find out about it eventually, but she wanted to prolong that moment as long as she could. Their panic would only make hers much, much worse.

Clara changed into plaid pajama shorts and a tank top. She took her toothbrush into the bathroom and came back again, sitting on the edge of her bed, hands braced on her knees. "Okay, here's the thing," she said. "I talked to Jonah."

Aubrey hugged the blanket against her chest. "*Jonah?* When? What did he say?" Blood was pounding in her ears. *Had he mentioned anything to her about Gabe?*

"He texted me the other day," Clara said. "He thought we'd be worried about him, and he wanted to let us know he's fine."

"Did he tell you what he's doing? I mean, is he still using his Eurail pass? Or did he go back to London?" All of Aubrey's anxious energy bubbled to the surface. "And has he said anything to his parents yet? Because they haven't told my parents, and they definitely would have if they knew. Unless he told them not to. Did he mention if he told them not to?"

Clara shook her head. "He didn't give me any details."

"Oh." Aubrey was disappointed but also relieved. Her kiss with Gabe was still a secret—for now at least.

Clara turned off her bedside light and lay down, and Aubrey did the same. She imagined that, right now, they were passing a row of houses and that someone was sitting by their window, watching this train streak by. She closed her eyes and pretended she was that person. She was the one watching the train trail off into the distance, listening to the sound of it as it disappeared.

"Aubrey?" Clara said.

"Yeah?" Aubrey opened her eyes.

"I'm sorry about tonight—and also, I understand why you couldn't really talk to us about what happened with Jonah. It must be extra hard, because we're all in this together and we're all Jonah's friends, too. I wouldn't know how to handle it, either."

Through a crack in the curtains, a flash of light glided over Clara's bed and then Aubrey's.

"Thanks," Aubrey said with a sigh. "This has been such a weird week."

"I know."

There were a few seconds of silence. Aubrey was grateful that Clara understood. Clara was a little more sensitive than Rae. A little more romantic. Sometimes Aubrey thought they had the same fears about going off to college—they were both nervous to plunge into so much change. Aubrey stretched out her legs; her feet touched the cool plastic beneath the window. Lights kept drifting in, wafting over their beds like ghosts.

"But, Aubrey?"

"Yeah?"

"Whatever else you do, don't treat Rae like that *ever* again."

20

Rae

Friday, July 8
PRAGUE to FLORENCE via VIENNA

Gabe went to the dining car to get food, but Rae was too wound up to eat. She walked up and down the strip of carpet between her bed and Gabe's, listening to the train creak and shudder. She plugged in her phone charger and drafted a few texts to Clara—*hey, what a night, huh??; are you sleeping? don't answer if you're sleeping. I mean, obviously you wouldn't, but...; quick! knock twice on the wall when you get this message!*—but she didn't send any of them. They hadn't had a chance to talk about the kiss yet, so everything she wrote sounded way too casual or *way* too awkward.

Her phone rang. She dove for it.

"I haven't heard your voice in ages!" Lucy said.

"Mom." Rae slumped onto her bed. "It's been a week. And I text you all the time."

"Yes, but I like hearing my only daughter's voice, thank you very much. Plus, I wanted to make sure you'd actually caught your train."

"Am I seriously *that* untrustworthy?"

"Rae, darling, you're eighteen. Of course you're untrustworthy. So, tell me everything. Where are you right now? What can you see?"

"I'm on a train. I can see an electrical socket."

"Sounds fancy."

"The fanciest." Rae detached her water bottle from the side of her bag and took a long swig. The train went around a bend, and her body swung to the side. For a second, she remembered her fight with Aubrey and felt awful. How could she have lost her temper so quickly? How could she have said all that stuff about Aubrey being selfish?

The next second, she remembered what Aubrey had said first—*You're transforming into this brand-new person, and she's secretive and she's mean, and I don't like her*—and Rae got pissed all over again.

"You haven't sent me any pictures," her mom said. "I want to see it all—the hostels, the dodgy bars. Don't leave anything out."

"I'll send you some now."

"Great! I'll get them printed and you can take them with you to Australia."

"Uh-huh," Rae said. But she didn't want to talk about Australia right now. Her brain felt cloudy, and her life felt so complicated. What would happen with Clara when she left? What would happen with Aubrey? It was a lot to wrap her head around. "What are you doing?" she asked, changing the subject. "Where's Iorek?"

"Sitting next to me. We're in the studio."

Rae lay back on her pillow. "It's kind of late to be working."

"Actually, I've been thinking about you. I had this idea for a piece about travel. Maybe a collage? Something about what we imagine a place will be versus what it's like when we actually get there. Your pictures might inspire me, kid."

"Mom," Rae said, "you need to sleep."

"I sleep! And there's this wonderful innovation—it's called caffeine. You should try it sometime."

Rae's stomach churned. Was this what her mom would be like next year? Staying up all night, throwing herself into work, clearly drinking *a lot* of coffee. And what would Rae be like without *her*? Even now—even during this five-minute phone conversation—she felt hollow with homesickness. She wanted to eat microwaved noodles at her kitchen table and hang out in the studio with Iorek, drawing in her sketchbook. She wished she could forget her fight with Aubrey, and the fact that Clara was one room away but Rae still couldn't talk to her, and the fact that next year was rushing toward her at an unrelenting speed, never slowing down, never taking a break.

"Rae?" her mom said. "You still here?"

"Yeah." Rae rubbed her eyelids. "I'm here."

"Did you get those messages I sent you about Sydney? With the pictures of Bondi Beach? It's got this art deco architecture, and there's a pool right there, floating in the middle of the ocean. Check your e-mail and see."

"I'll do it later."

"Okay. Well, pass the phone to Aubrey for a second. I want to say hi."

"Mom. Everyone here's asleep."

Her mom paused for a moment. "Okay, kid. But you know"—her voice went a little quieter—"it's normal if this trip isn't going exactly the way you'd hoped. Traveling with friends can be tough. I went with this girl, Annabelle, to Budapest back in '98, and I thought it would be so much fun. But we drove each other up the wall."

Rae fidgeted with the corner of her pillow. The train chugged around her like a heartbeat. She wanted to believe that her mom was right—that all this tension was just a side effect of traveling together, of being in all the same places and never getting a moment apart. But the problem was, she'd never needed a moment apart from Aubrey before. Maybe this was about who she and Aubrey were becoming. Maybe they were turning into people who wouldn't stay best friends.

"I don't think I can stay awake," she said. "Can I call you when I get to Florence?"

They said good night and hung up. Rae turned on the tiny

reading light above her bed, took the bangles off her wrist, and opened up her sketchbook. There were a few images from Prague she wanted to get down while they felt fresh—the Astronomical Clock and the Charles Bridge and the view from the Vyšehrad. She dragged her pencil across the paper, but her mind kept skipping back to other things—to a square at night, a church, and a girl.

She turned the page and drew the girl instead. A girl standing between buildings so out of focus, they could have been clouds. But she was completely solid. The fabric of her dress fell to her knees, and her collarbone touched the hollow of her neck. The corner of her mouth was pulled into a slight curve—

Gabe opened the door; Rae snapped her sketchbook shut.

"You should seriously go out there." Gabe hopped onto his own bed. He was holding a bag of M&Ms and a soda. "The people in a train dining car at two in the morning are wild. I think this one girl was a musician. And there was a guy in a wrinkled business suit sitting all by himself, just drinking coffee and reading Ernest Hemingway. What do you think his story was?"

"He's a misogynist?" Rae offered.

"That's one possibility." Gabe put his hands behind his head. His expression was dreamy but awake—like he wanted to sleep, but his mind was busy going over so many other things. "Do you think this is what happens as we get older?" he asked. "We start seeing adults more like people. We start wondering what they did in their life and how they got to where they are."

"I think we just become adults, too," Rae said. "And then we realize we're all equally fucked-up."

Gabe sat up and put his feet on the ground. "I've made a decision. What do you think about literature?"

"Like, in general?"

"Like, as a major. For me. I've never really considered it before, but—I don't know. Books are almost like songs, aren't they? You can read one a hundred times, but every time you get something different from it."

"Um," Rae said, "sure?"

Gabe scratched at his chin. Rae wondered if this whole literature thing had anything to do with Aubrey—she was, after all, their resident English major. But whatever. Rae had no desire to ask him about Aubrey or her major or how the hell any of that related to him.

"I might not sleep yet, if that's okay?" he said. "I feel like listening to music."

"Go ahead." Rae kicked off her flip-flops. "I'm not tired, either."

He uncoiled his headphones and fished through his stuff for a book with a shiny cover he must have bought in Prague. Rae heard the tinny sounds of a guitar and drums—the opening riff of a Joy Division song—coming from his phone. She heard him push around his pillow and prop himself against the wall behind him.

Rae opened her sketchbook again and turned the page. The picture she'd been working on before didn't seem right anymore, so she started something new. Two girls on a train, sleeping in separate rooms. A thin wall ran between them, but the perspective was from above so you could see them both. One girl's hair coiled over her sheets as she slept; the other girl sat up with her stuff all around her, a pen and paper in her hand. Graphite stained Rae's fingers as she worked. Her wrist ached, but she didn't stop.

Rae had fallen asleep.

Her head was crunched against the vibrating wall; her sketchbook had fallen to the floor. She woke to the sound of the curtains swishing open. Gabe was perched at the edge of his bed, looking at something outside.

"Whatissit?" Rae mumbled. "Are we there?"

"Oh, sorry." He looked over at her. "I was trying to be quiet."

She pushed her bangs out of her eyes and picked up her sketchbook. When she sat back up, she could see what Gabe was looking at: the sunrise. Patchwork fields painted red and orange. A moving landscape bathed in gold.

"Rad," she said, her voice croaky.

"Here." He handed her a paper cup with a black plastic

lid. "I've already had two of these. We're going to need a lot to get through today."

She took a few sips of the hot black coffee, her gaze trained on a flock of birds that hovered over the fields. Their forms were distant and smudged, like pencil marks against the sky. Rae stretched out her wrist, which hurt even more than it had the night before. Plus, her neck was stiff, and she knew she had to sit all day on another train from Vienna to Florence. It would be hours until she could have an actual shower and feel normal again.

"She'll be okay," Gabe asked suddenly, "won't she?"

"Who?" Rae yawned. "Aubrey?"

Gabe nodded.

"Of course she will," Rae said. "This is just her first major heartbreak. She's having the necessary meltdown."

"I guess so." Gabe rubbed his palm over his face and turned back to the window. But now, Rae couldn't stop staring at him. He looked like he'd slept even less than she had—the sheets were crumpled at the bottom of his bed, and his shoulders were tense, eyes alert. She gripped her coffee as it hit her that she knew what was happening to Gabe—she knew because the exact same thing was happening to her. It had been happening to her all week. All *year*.

Here they were at six AM, restless and staring at the sunrise over a place they'd never been before. They were both so awake—and they were both so in love.

21

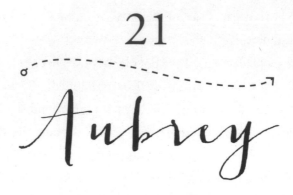

Aubrey

Friday, July 8
FLORENCE

Home sweet home," Clara said.

Aubrey put her bag down. Their apartment in Florence had high ceilings with exposed rafters, worn hardwood floors, and a beige couch covered in faded pastel cushions. It was early evening, and after two long train rides, Aubrey's eyelids felt like cement. She ran her fingers along the back of the couch while Clara and Rae unlocked the shutters. Muted light striped the floor; pigeons outside beat their wings.

"Better, right?" Clara dusted off her hands. "Less depressing?"

"Totally," Rae said.

In the light, Aubrey began to notice other small details

of the apartment: the bits of folded newspaper beneath the dining table's legs, the miniature washing machine squeezed into the equally miniature kitchen, and the old board games shoved beneath a chipped-glass coffee table. There was a cracked vase filled with wilted lavender blossoms on one of the windowsills. Dust motes bobbed through the air.

The room was eerie and cavernous, as silent as a held breath. It made Aubrey think of an old countryside church she'd visited with her parents when they'd first moved to England. She remembered standing in the dark aisle of it, noticing the trees that moved behind stained-glass windows, feeling hushed and somber and still.

She felt that way now.

Although maybe that was because Jonah wasn't with them.

The apartment had originally been his idea. He'd texted the listing to her at three AM one night with a series of question and exclamation marks. She'd woken up and messaged him back right away with *OMG PERFECT!* The apartment itself was run-down enough that, split between the five of them, it wasn't too expensive. And renting it meant they wouldn't be stuck in hostels for the rest of the trip. It meant they had three whole nights to live in their own place—to make their own food, hang up their own laundry, and practice living like grown-ups.

"I'm going to take a shower," Gabe said. He took his stuff up to the low-ceilinged second floor, where there were two bedrooms and a bathroom. Aubrey walked toward the windows. She saw laundry lines strung between buildings and someone watering flower boxes on the balcony across the way. But she felt so removed from it all. Like she was living above it, only skimming the surface.

"I'm going out," she said, turning to her friends.

Clara and Rae were kneeling on the ground, picking through the pieces of an old Monopoly set. "Where to?" Clara asked.

"Not sure. The Duomo's near here and the Uffizi Gallery. I don't want to wait till tomorrow. I want to see something tonight." She tucked one of the apartment's heavy keys into her pocket and paused a beat before opening the door, waiting to see if they would offer to come with her.

But they didn't. Clara took out a metal game piece and placed it on the ground, and Rae did the same. There was something about how they were bent toward each other, the way they were both so focused on the exact same thing—it was like when kids play a game that doesn't make any sense to adults. It was like they were speaking to each other in code.

Aubrey grabbed her wallet and phone. She opened the door.

The area around the Duomo was a tourist haven: souvenir stands and gelato stalls, cute cafés with outdoor tables, everyone wearing sneakers and wraparound sunglasses. And in the center of it all was the Duomo, a cathedral with a spherical, rust-colored top, like a sun caught in perpetual daybreak.

It was pretty. But also boring. *Why had she come here all by herself?*

She ordered an espresso at the closest café and took a seat at a table outside. At the table beside her was a family: two teenagers— a boy and a girl—and their parents. They had strong Scottish accents, and the teenagers were arguing while their parents wordlessly shared a lemonade. One year ago, that could have been Aubrey and Chris and their parents. It occurred to her that, in her entire life, she'd never been this isolated before—no family, no friends. Even Rae wanted nothing to do with her now. She was floating alone, without a safety net.

And *that*, she realized, was why she'd chosen Columbia— not just because it was the school of her dreams or because of its great English-lit program or any of the other reasons she'd always given people. She'd chosen it because of Jonah. Because if she was going to leap into the unknown, she wanted to do it with someone who could at least hold her hand.

Okay, okay, she thought. *Make a list, Aubrey. Make a list of things you can control.*

She tasted her espresso, which was strong and bitter. She imagined being in her bedroom at home, with her desk and her bed and her floral curtains. She imagined sitting on the floor and going through all the books she'd decided to bring to college—*Pride and Prejudice* and *I Capture the Castle* and her copy of *The Chamber of Secrets*, full of the notes she and Rae had written to each other when they were twelve. There were other books—ones about belonging, about leaving, about falling in love. The books she'd chosen to sit on the shelves in her dorm. The books that would keep her company.

Her pulse began to slow; the café seemed to grow quiet.

Gabe pulled out the chair across from her and sat down.

"Gabe!" Aubrey nearly knocked over her espresso. "What are you doing here?"

"Sitting," he said. His hair was slicked back, like he'd rushed over right after his shower. Like he'd tried to find her as quickly as he could. He picked up a sugar packet and spun it on the table.

"*Sitting?*" she said. "As in, you followed me here and now you're sitting, because—because why?"

The daughter of the family at the next table was watching them with interest. But when Aubrey caught her eye, the girl went back to scanning the crowd, her expression sliding into boredom.

"I heard you telling Clara and Rae you were coming here," he said.

"And you decided to check on me?"

"I decided to come, too." He leaned into the center of the table. "You said it yourself, Bryce. There's a lot to see around here."

A waiter carried a few plates of tomato pasta by Aubrey's

head. She tugged at the sides of her cottony shorts. She wished she'd taken the time to shower and change as well. She wished she didn't feel like she'd been traveling all day. "This place is pretty crowded," she said.

"We could leave?" A dimple twitched on the left side of his mouth. "If you want?"

They pushed their chairs back at the exact same time, and, without saying a word, picked a direction and decided to follow it. A moped shot past them and swerved around a corner. They crossed a bridge as the dusky evening crept toward night. Here, the crowds began to fade away and their surroundings slowly transformed. Houses gave way to stretches of stone walls with cypress trees growing behind them. The sound of church bells drifted on the breeze; the cobblestone road was bumpy and uneven. They were walking uphill, which made Aubrey's muscles strain. But she wouldn't stop. Gabe took long strides, and she did her best to match them, using each one to leave behind Rae and Jonah and every stupid fight she'd had on every stupid train since she'd left London. She walked until she was completely out of breath, until a few houses began to reappear, all of them painted a bleached yellow. Over the wall running beside them, she saw a miniature Florence laid out below. Red-roofed building after red-roofed building.

"Wow," she exhaled.

"It's so—" Gabe said.

"Far away." She rubbed the side of her face on the shoulder

of her shirt. The city seemed impossibly small, like she could reach out and touch the tops of the buildings. Like the evening haze was steam she could wipe away with her fingers.

"You know"—Gabe panted—"I think I kind of remember Florence. I must have come here with my parents when we lived in Madrid. When I was, like, four or something."

"What do you remember?"

"Mostly Zaida convincing me we should sneak away from our parents. When they found us again, I was crying, but Z played it cool. She told them they should have been more responsible."

Aubrey felt the corner of her mouth lift. She could imagine tiny Gabe stranded in a crowd of people, gripping his older sister's hand. But it was also weird to think of him being so young. And even weirder to think that, in a different part of the world, she'd been that young, too. Fourteen years ago, none of her friends had even moved to London yet. They hadn't known that all their lives were about to collide.

"Do you think you'll ever live there again?" she asked. "In Spain?"

"My mom would love that," Gabe said. "She's pretty worried that she and my dad didn't take us back there enough. We went for a few summers, and once when my *abuelo* died, but it always felt really strange. I'd spend every afternoon in my *abuela*'s house, which was kind of familiar but in ways I couldn't place. My relatives kept telling me and Z how American we were now."

"But your sister decided to go back," Aubrey said. "She's there now."

"Sure. But just to study abroad. That doesn't really count. Anyway, after a couple years at Barnard, Z's in love with New York. She wants to get her master's in urban planning, move into a brownstone, and stay there forever. Barcelona definitely isn't home. Neither of us even speaks Catalan."

"I'm jealous of her. I wish I was as certain about what I wanted."

"You are."

She turned to face him. "You want to know the truth? I have no clue anymore. Everything I planned had *something* to do with somebody else—this trip was about the future Rae and I used to talk about, New York was about the one I had with Jonah. My life doesn't make sense now."

"Your life isn't supposed to make sense at eighteen."

"But I hate that!"

"Me too!" He grinned. "I was just trying to make you feel better."

A small car wheezed up the narrow road, crowding them against one of the houses. Aubrey examined its red front door and sheer curtains, its windowsill with a lavender-painted radio and a pineapple sitting on it. She still felt tired but in a good way. In the way she used to feel when she would run in the woods behind her old house in Connecticut, eventually collapsing on the grass of her backyard. In the way she used to feel when she would swim in the ocean on family trips to Maine, the heaviness of the water pressing down on her. "What do you think?" she asked. "Should we start figuring out our lives?"

"Right now?"

"We'll start simple." She pointed behind her. "Do you want to live in that house?"

"Hold up. Explain to me how picking *a house* is the simple place to start?"

"Because. You can work your way from there: house, job, family, blah, blah, blah."

He moved slightly closer to get a better look. "I guess I could be into it. These hills would be fun to bike around. And I'm especially feeling that pineapple."

"If I never live somewhere with a pineapple in the window," Aubrey said, "I won't be living at all."

He laughed, and Aubrey's mood lightened—it was the first time in days she'd made someone laugh. "Do you want to see what's up there?" she asked, gesturing at a set of stone stairs built between two small gardens.

They climbed farther above the city. It was nearly dark and everything around them was calm. Aubrey was almost convinced that she and Gabe were entirely alone, that the rest of the city had somehow been abandoned.

They emerged onto a small courtyard surrounded by houses. There was a fountain in the center with a stone lion carved into its base, and outdoor chairs and potted plants were arranged by each of the front doors. A few children's bikes leaned against one another. A tiger-striped cat slept, curled across the cracked ground.

Aubrey sat on the top step and lay back. Her hair was damp with sweat, and her limbs felt even weaker now.

Gabe sat next to her. "That—was not a fun climb."

"Shhh," Aubrey said. "Listen to how quiet everything is. I bet the people who live here don't want tourists walking around."

"I get it. We want it to be a surprise when we stroll through their front doors later."

"So we can hang out in their living rooms."

"And possibly their kitchens."

There were no streetlights here, only a few lamp-lit windows and the streaky summer sky. Aubrey had always liked this time of the evening, when it was still just bright enough to make out the shapes of clouds. Someone must have been cooking, because the rich smell of basil, garlic, and tomatoes wafted from a slightly open door. It mixed with the mineral scent of bubbling water in the fountain.

"I liked your idea." Gabe lay down, too, folding his hands over his stomach.

"Which one?"

"About my major. About studying English. I didn't sleep much last night, so I did some research on my phone, found all the requirements."

Aubrey propped herself up on her elbows. "You do realize I was kidding about us figuring out our lives right now?"

The sleeping cat woke up and began padding toward them, eyes bright with curiosity.

Gabe propped himself up as well. "You know what I found out? Reed offers classes in poetry. And that made me think of this interview I read with Leonard Cohen once. The way he talked about writing lyrics, it was like he was talking about writing poetry. You were totally right, Bryce. Music minus the instruments. It's perfect."

"Wow," she said. "First the pineapple house, now your major. I'm on a roll."

"Yeah." He breathed out a laugh. "You can honestly plan anything you want for me. You're pretty decent at it."

"Okay." She lay down again, got settled. "Radio."

"Radio?"

"You have a great voice." She blushed up at the sky. "It's not showy or anything—not, like, a voice meant for the stage."

"Thanks?" he said.

"*But* it's low and kind of soothing. It makes everything you say sound convincing. Next year, you should work at your college radio station."

"How hipster of me," he said. "Okay. And you should work at your school newspaper. Tell them you want to review museum exhibits and openings and stuff. That way you can go to as many of them as you want for free."

"Oh my God." She swatted his arm. "That's genuinely brilliant."

"Well." She could hear the grin in his voice. "I owed you one."

The cat slunk between them, and Gabe reached out to stroke one of its ears. The fountain gurgled and the distant city hummed. The uncertainty Aubrey had felt earlier began to ease. She had this image—a small, barely tangible one—of what she could be doing next year. Of who she could turn out to be.

"Tell me something else," she said.

"About what?"

"About New York. About what I'll be doing there."

The cat's tail swished against her arm. When she turned her head to the side, she saw that Gabe's features were creased, like he was concentrating on something above the clouds. "Okay," he said. "But consider this practice for my radio show. You need to close your eyes so I can set the scene."

She closed her eyes. A minute or so passed.

"A dorm room," he said eventually. "New York City. It's—nice. I mean, I know it's a dorm, but you decorate it. You have piles of library books everywhere, and you never turn them in late—mostly because the library is where you spend all your time."

"I'm such a nerd," she said.

"Bryce." His voice was mock-stern. "You can't interrupt my radio show. And your eyes are open."

She squeezed them shut again as the cat curled up by

her ear and began to purr. The stones beneath her were still sun-warmed.

"Okay," he said. "You take a bunch of classes, but you also go somewhere new every weekend. You take the Staten Island Ferry, and stand by the railing outside, even when it's fall and it's windy. Just so you can watch the Statue of Liberty go by—plus the ticket's free, Bryce, don't forget that part. Sometimes you do this kind of stuff with friends, but sometimes you do it by yourself."

Every word he said made it come to life even more—the streets of New York, a boat on the Hudson, the sidewalk forming under her feet one step at a time.

"When it's winter," he said, "you don't go out as much because of the snow. But in spring, you eat outside on the library steps with everyone else. It makes you think about right now—about these steps we're sitting on and how all the stuff you do in New York isn't so different from the stuff you did with us. It makes you think about how connected it all is." He paused. "Is this getting boring? Can you still see it?"

"Yes," she said, her eyes shut so tightly it made the light burst around her. "I can see it."

22

Rae lined up the tarnished Monopoly pieces along the pockmarked wooden floor. The room rang with the sound of Aubrey closing the door, but Rae didn't bother looking up or even acknowledging that she was gone. Clara was watching her, probably wondering what she was thinking and why she hadn't tried to make up with Aubrey.

But the truth was pretty simple: Rae was still pissed off. And the more she thought about it, the more pissed off she got. Aubrey had spent the whole summer talking about her-and-Jonah or her-and-Gabe or her-and-all-the-things-about-New-York-she-was-afraid-of. She'd talked about her plans and what she wanted out of this trip, but she'd never cared if any of that matched what Rae wanted.

A year ago, that might not have bugged Rae so much, but maybe what Aubrey had said on the train was true—maybe Rae was changing. Maybe they were growing apart.

And now, on top of all that, Rae knew that Gabe was in love with Aubrey. And—holy shit! What was she supposed to do with information like that? Was she supposed to keep it a secret? She had so many secrets now that they were impossible to keep track of. It felt like they were crushing her.

"Rae?" Clara's voice made everything go still.

Rae's eyes met hers.

Gabe's footsteps squeaked on the stairs, and Clara looked to the side. Rae picked up a Monopoly top hat, pressing it until she felt an indent in her forefinger and thumb.

"That was fast," Clara said to Gabe.

His hair was dripping wet, and his shirt was rumpled around his stomach, like he'd just pulled it on. "Yeah," he said. "I'm all about—water conservation. Saving the planet. Stuff like that."

"Okay," she said, clearly confused. "Are you going somewhere?"

He paused by the front door. "I thought I might walk around. You know. Get a feel for the area."

"Sure," Rae said flatly. "Walking is good." She put the top hat down and picked up a tiny metal dog. The door opened and shut again. But Clara was still right there, hair piled on top of her head, twisting a heart-shaped ring around her index finger. It dawned on Rae that there was no one else here. She and Clara were finally alone.

"Do you want to get food?" Clara asked.

"Now?" Rae asked. "Together?"

"Now," Clara said. "Together."

"Cool." Rae stood up, legs shaky. "I'll just—let me get changed first."

Upstairs in the bedroom, she quietly panicked. She didn't know what to wear. She didn't know how to look like the type of person Clara would go on a date with. (If this even was a date. Which maybe it wasn't. But then again, maybe it was!) *Okay, okay, Rae, you've been on dates before. You are totally good at dates.* She settled on a jersey dress with a strappy back she'd been too self-conscious to wear before and fussed with her short hair until it curled around her chin in a way that was, thankfully, cute. Usually, the feeling of makeup on her face creeped her out, but she decided on some eye shadow and flavored lip gloss. Just in case.

Back downstairs, Clara had put away the board games and was sitting on the back of the couch. Rae resisted the urge to tug and fidget with the thin material of her dress. She felt raw and nervous, her blood buzzing in her veins. "Okay," she said. "You—um—ready?"

Clara stepped forward and took Rae's hand, their fingers sliding and fitting together. "Yes," Clara said. "I'm ready."

Rae's impressions of Florence at night were a blur.

She managed to register a line of restaurants, buildings with sandy exteriors, and postcard racks crowding the sidewalks. With each step she and Clara took, all she could think was *this is a date, this is a date, this is a date*. Her heart beat in her palm. Even walking was giving her motion sickness.

"So," she said. "Is there somewhere you want to go?"

"I have an idea," Clara said.

"Great!" Rae said. *As long as you don't let go of my hand*, she thought. *As long as I don't somehow realize I'm still asleep on a train from Prague to Vienna and this is all a dream.*

They stopped for pistachio and hazelnut gelato, and then Clara led them to a rose garden that curled along a hillside with visitors lying on the grass, gazing down at the city. A few bronze sculptures were dotted around the lawns. They must have been part of some modern-art exhibit—a few were shaped like cubes, others like arcs that appeared to dip in and out of the ground.

Clara dropped her beat-up purse beside one of the arcs and climbed on top of it.

"Should you be doing that?" Rae asked.

Clara got settled. "Sitting here?"

"Yeah. What if we get in trouble?"

"Aubrey?" Clara scanned the area. "Where are you? Why does your voice sound exactly like Rae's?"

"Very funny."

"I thought so." Clara tucked a loose piece of her hair into one of her bobby pins. "Look around. If we weren't supposed to climb them, a sign would say *don't climb the sculptures.* Anyway, since when do you care this much about rules? You used to skip European History all the time, because you said Mr. Carson was too sympathetic to patriarchal systems of government."

Rae adjusted the straps of her dress. "Guess I can't argue with that."

She clambered up to join Clara, feeling the cold, mottled bronze against the backs of her thighs when she sat down. She had to brace her feet against the side to stop herself from slipping off, but the view made all the discomfort worthwhile: She saw the Duomo and craggy apartment tops and church spires. This had to be her favorite thing ever—looking onto something that was so much bigger than she was, getting a small sense of how expansive the world could be. She'd felt that way sitting on the beach in Georgia when she was a kid. And hanging out in the back of her mom's antique shop, looking at pictures of Australia's coastlines in these old guidebooks Lucy had collected.

Clara tugged at the ring on her index finger. "You don't feel weird, do you?"

"No," Rae said. And then, "Wait. Do you?"

Clara shook her head. "Not even a little bit."

"Great. I'm glad." But she wondered why Clara wasn't holding her hand anymore. Would it be awkward if she took hers instead? Farther down the hill, a couple lay on a picnic blanket, whispering in each other's ears.

"Rae," Clara said. "Did—did you really think I was straight? Until I told you about Leah?"

Rae began to skid down the arc. She pressed her palms against it to keep herself from falling. "Honestly? I did. I mean, you never said so *explicitly*, but I guess I assumed." She pushed some curls away from her forehead and felt frustrated by how heteronormative she kept being. She really, *really* didn't want to fuck this up. "But it doesn't matter what I thought," she added. "I guess I was just a little surprised that you never told me you liked girls. Obviously, you didn't have to. But if anyone would have understood, it would have been me."

"I didn't think there was anything to tell," Clara said. "When that whole thing with Leah happened, I didn't know if it meant I was a lesbian or bi or pansexual or what. All I knew was that I liked kissing boys, and I liked kissing her, too."

"So she just kissed you? Out of nowhere?"

Clara squinted at the sunset. "She came backstage to the costume room one day when I was fixing hemlines. I thought she must have been bored with rehearsal or something, but instead, she told me how obvious it was that I was into her. And then, somehow, we were making out."

"Romantic," Rae said.

"Shut up." Clara shoved Rae's shoulder, making Rae lose her balance again. Clara grabbed her arm, pulling her back up.

"Thanks," Rae said.

"You're welcome."

She was still holding Rae, and they were sitting so much closer now, hip bones touching. Rae inhaled, and the evening air smelled like roses. She exhaled and said, "But you never dated her?"

"We kissed a couple of times, but that was it. We never even talked about it afterward. I tried once, but Leah got super evasive. She told me I was being clingy."

"Wow. I always knew I didn't like her, but it turns out I actually hate her."

Clara shook her head. "You shouldn't."

"Yeah, I should. She treated you like crap, which means that she is, by definition, crap. In fact, do you have her number? I'll call her right now and tell her exactly how crap she is."

"But this kind of thing happens all the time." Clara twisted her ring around her finger again. Her dress was green with small red polka dots. It matched the scene perfectly. "You hook up with someone, but you're not in love with them. You don't even have a crush on them. I can't be mad at Leah for doing to me what I've done to other people."

"Seriously," Rae said. "You are *nothing* like Leah."

"Maybe not. But sometimes a kiss doesn't mean anything. It's just a kiss. And that's another reason I wanted to talk to you." She sat up straighter. And Rae's throat began to close up. *Please, oh, please*, she thought. *Please don't say it was just a kiss with me.*

"I know I was flirting with you in Amsterdam," Clara

said, "and I *know* I kissed you first in Prague, so if this isn't a big deal to you, I completely understand. But you should know something: It is a big deal to me. The reason I kissed you is that I like you, Rae. I like you so much."

The wind shifted and played across them. Rae felt like the whole garden was whirling. In the past year, she had dreamed of this exact moment so many times. She'd imagined the places they would stand and the tone of Clara's voice and the way their hands and lips might touch. Rae had felt the thrill of believing—even for one second—that this was possible. But she'd never imagined how nervous she would be, or the flowers that would be growing all around them, or the way they would both sit teetering on this ridiculous sculpture. And she never could have guessed how, even when it was happening, it would still feel like a fantasy. Like maybe even this garden wasn't real. Like maybe this was all just a story Rae was telling herself.

"Clara," she said. "I like you so much it makes my stomach hurt. I've liked you for so long, but I didn't know what to do about it, which is a first for me, because I've known how to handle a crush since, like, middle school. The only reason I didn't kiss you is because I was scared of screwing things up. I wasn't sure you would want to kiss me back."

Clara's face went a deep shade of crimson. "You liked me for so long?"

"Yes." Rae gripped the sculpture and focused on the branches above, on their slender green leaves and blooming roses. "Ever since last summer, when we'd hang out all the time. I hated waking up in the morning and knowing we had to go different places. I hated thinking about what would happen when Aubrey and Jonah and Gabe came back and I didn't have you to myself anymore."

Clara's knee rested against Rae's. "That summer was the first time I was one-hundred-percent certain I liked girls. It made me wonder about all the girls I could have been kissing."

"*All* the girls?" Rae asked. She wanted to sound confident, but she knew she didn't. She could feel herself unraveling.

"No," Clara said softly. "Not *all*."

Her pinkie finger moved to the fabric of Rae's dress. Rae noticed the dark plum nail polish she'd applied that morning on the train from Vienna. She heard Clara's breath, quiet and persistent beneath the sounds of the garden and the city and the night. They leaned into each other, their lips only inches apart. Clara touched Rae's face, and Rae touched Clara's— and they tumbled right off the sculpture, landing in a heap.

Clara burst out laughing. "That was totally your fault!"

"Was not!" Rae brushed dirt from her arms. But those had *definitely* not been her best moves.

"It really was," Clara said. And then they were finally kissing again, dizzying and fast. Rae's hands touched Clara's neck, arms, waist. Clara pulled Rae to her, their bodies lining up, eyelashes brushing each other's cheeks. They stopped for a moment, hearts pounding, to catch their breath.

Grass was tangled in Clara's red hair, and the evening light blushed deep behind her. She rested her hand against

Rae's cheek before kissing her again. And Rae didn't care if this was against the rules or if they were about to get yelled at or even kicked out of the park.

Because at that moment, no one else was there. The garden had grown out to cover the world, and they were alone.

23

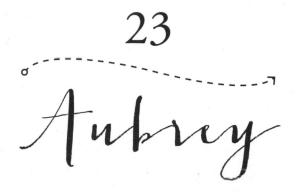

Aubrey

Sunday, July 10
FLORENCE to ROME

It was early morning, and Aubrey and Gabe were on their way to Rome.

They were only going for the day, so they'd caught a train that left just before seven AM. It rattled quietly through patchwork fields and villages, its windows shimmering with condensation. Aubrey had brought a Virginia Woolf book with her from one of her course's summer reading lists, but the words kept rolling past her eyes, moving as quickly as the scenery outside. So she watched that instead: the orange and red farmhouses, the peaceful clouds, the hills that crested and dipped along the skyline.

Gabe sat beside her, sharing her armrest and tapping his

foot as he listened to music. Out of the corner of her eye, Aubrey saw a glimpse of his EVIL DEAD T-shirt and his mouth moving silently to a song she couldn't hear.

She thought back to yesterday, to the two of them wandering through Florence for hours. Not talking about Rae or Jonah or even college anymore. Just throwing themselves into the list of churches and museums Aubrey had wanted to see, staying out past midnight, until they were so tired Aubrey's mind finally went silent and dreamy. She'd woken up at five this morning to meet him again, but she'd done her best to make sure Clara and Rae didn't wake up with her. She hadn't wanted to ask if they felt like coming, too.

Gabe pushed back his headphones. "Did you bring any music?"

She shook her head. "I forgot."

He twisted one half of the headphones so she could cup it against her ear and turned up the volume. He was listening to Phoenix, a band he used to play for her freshman year when they spent all that time together painting sets. At the sound of the heavy plunking piano and drums, Aubrey could remember exactly how she'd felt on those early-fall afternoons. Hours of painting gray buildings and a steely sky, making mistakes and not even caring, because she wasn't an artist and had never wanted to be. She remembered how the music had made the afternoons seem too short, like they were songs themselves, each one ending before she wished it would.

"Is this okay?" Gabe asked. "I figured you still liked them."

Aubrey swept her thumb over the pages of her book and said, "This song is one of my favorites."

He eased back in his seat and pressed a button on his phone. The song began to play again.

"This doesn't feel right." Gabe stood on the train station platform, hands lifted and palms tipped up. "Is this temperature even natural?"

"I think my face is on fire." Aubrey's sunglasses turned the searing morning light to amber. The heat crawled into her pores, making her wish she'd brought a compact mirror with her. There was *no way* she didn't look sweaty and puffy right now.

They headed out of the station into a tangle of glinting streets full of tour groups and cars spewing exhaust. People fanned themselves with maps, and vendors stood by open coolers, selling tiny plastic bottles of water for five euros apiece. As they waded away from the station, Aubrey's vision went foggy. She couldn't keep track of all the street signs.

"Are you sure this is the right direction?" she asked Gabe.

They'd planned on seeing the Trevi Fountain first, which, according to Google Maps, was a twenty-minute walk from the station.

"I think so," he said.

"You *think* so?" A group of people wearing matching COLE FAMILY REUNION! T-shirts took over the sidewalk, separating them. Aubrey tried to shout over their heads, *"You mean you don't know for sure?"* Dark clouds rolled across the sky, blocking the sun. Aubrey was fiddling with her phone, pulling up a map, when a woman wearing bright-green sneakers knocked into her shoulder. Aubrey's phone clattered to the sidewalk, and she lunged for it at the exact moment a tall guy wearing expensive sunglasses did. Her knees skidded on the pavement, but her hand touched it first. "Don't even think about it," she snapped. "This is mine."

The guy raised an eyebrow but didn't argue with her. He strolled away, while Aubrey scrambled to her feet, rushing back over to Gabe. "Did you see that?" she asked.

"See what?"

"That guy!" She pointed behind her as they both kept walking. "He tried to steal my phone. I dropped it, and he totally went to grab it."

"Are you sure? Maybe he was just trying to be chivalrous."

"Are you kidding me? Rome is a big tourist city, and big tourist cities are *full* of pickpockets. Besides, even if he was trying to be chivalrous, I don't need some guy picking my phone up for me. My weak girl arms can handle it, thanks."

Gabe looked amused. "If he'd taken your phone, we could have chased him down together. And I know a lot of Italian swear words."

"How *chivalrous* of you."

He obviously thought she was overreacting. He was treating her the way her friends always did—like she was Aubrey, the girl who panicked. The girl who saw a potential catastrophe in everything. She wished things could feel as simple and effortless as they'd felt yesterday.

They were at a red light, waiting to cross the street. Motorbikes gunned their engines. People crowded around them, smelling of sunscreen and sweat, carrying shopping bags with flashy designer logos. Maybe Aubrey shouldn't have come here. Maybe being with Gabe like this—in a new city where no one even knew they were—was a huge mistake.

What if something happened to them? What if they *did* lose their phones? Or their train tickets or their money? What if they couldn't get back to Florence and no one knew where to look for them?

"Aubrey?" Gabe sounded concerned. "You don't look great. Are you still thinking about your phone?"

"No," she said. "Let's just keep going, okay?"

But that was definitely the wrong thing to do. She shouldn't be running around Rome with her ex-boyfriend's best friend. She shouldn't be having fun and acting spontaneous while Jonah was out there somewhere, probably still hopping trains, probably angry and alone.

Go back to the station, she thought. *Tell Gabe you need to turn around and get the next train out of here.*

The sky cracked with thunder. A girl to the side of Aubrey

squealed and covered her head with her hands. Rain from a heavy summer storm began to pelt down on the cars. Lightning flashed in the gloomy sky.

The light turned green, and everyone scattered. Gabe and Aubrey gripped hands and took off across the road. They ran in the direction Gabe had been leading them, toward the Trevi Fountain, where carved stone gods seemed to emerge from the billowing mist. Water cascaded down their sides and drummed against the fountain's surface, while Aubrey and Gabe stood in front of it, holding hands.

"Wow," Aubrey breathed, rain trailing down her forehead and getting caught in her eyelashes.

"Yeah." Gabe squeezed her hand. "Next stop?"

They took off again, running through the storm that covered the city like a glistening, metallic sheet. It veiled small alleys and churches and made the back of Gabe's shirt grow darker and darker. Tucked into one of those alleys, Aubrey spotted a glowing OPEN sign hanging in the window of a storefront.

She tugged him inside.

The door closed; the sounds of Rome disappeared.

Gabe shoved his wet hair aside and scanned the aisles of a record store. "This wasn't exactly on the itinerary," he said.

"Screw the itinerary," Aubrey said.

The walls of the store were painted a pale, buttery yellow and decorated with framed album covers. There were no other customers, but a girl sat behind the counter, wearing a lacy vintage dress and flipping through a magazine. There was a record player next to her, and now that the storm was muted, Aubrey could hear Otis Redding crackling through a set of speakers.

"Should we look around?" Gabe asked.

Aubrey realized they were still holding hands. All the remaining warmth in her body flooded to her fingertips. She stepped away from him, felt their palms break apart. "Yeah. We should see what they have."

Her shoes squelched as they went to stand on opposite sides of the same aisle and began hunting through the records. Images flickered past Aubrey's eyes: big hair and neon logos and black-and-white photographs.

"What are you in the mood for?" Gabe asked. "Country? Heavy metal? Techno?"

"All of the above." Aubrey stopped flipping for a moment. "Actually, let's go for something really cheesy. What about that song everyone cried over at prom?"

"The Ellie Goulding one?" Gabe said. "I don't think people were actually crying over the *song*. It probably had more to do with the fact that they were wasted."

"Cynic."

"You're telling me you don't think they were wasted?"

"No, they absolutely were. But that's not the only reason to cry at prom. It's an emotional time."

"Correct me if I'm wrong," he said, "but I don't remember *you* crying. Or getting wasted."

Aubrey ran her fingers over the plastic-wrapped edge of a record. It was bizarre, thinking about prom. It had only been a couple months ago, but it could have easily been years. Jonah had been Aubrey's date, Gabe had gone with this cute junior girl from his chemistry class, and Clara had brought—and then ditched—a boy she was semi-friends with. Rae had worn a tuxedo and said her date was the patriarchy, but she'd killed him, so now she had no date. And then, a couple of hours later, she'd made out with Emily St. James.

Aubrey remembered taking pictures with everyone before the dance, riding the tube all dressed up, and falling asleep on a pile of sleeping bags in Jonah's living room late at night, her hair still stiff with hair spray.

"I wasn't sad then," she said. "We were still doing the musical. We still had the whole summer and all of this to look forward to. We hadn't even graduated yet." She tapped an alphabetical marker between albums. "Plus, prom is pretty ridiculous, right? It's just a bunch of teenagers getting drunk and crying to Ellie Goulding."

Gabe cracked up. Wind pressed at the edges of the door frame, the storm groaning outside. "Okay." He lifted another album, this one with a picture of Bob Dylan in profile, a hat pulled over his eyes, his scarf curling to one side. Aubrey had seen it in Gabe's house before. "You know how certain songs can make you think of one place or moment or something?"

he asked. "I don't remember much about living in Madrid, but whenever I hear "One More Cup of Coffee," I start thinking about all this random stuff from back then."

"Like what?"

"Like—lying on the floor while my parents made dinner. And looking up at this peach wallpaper we had in the kitchen. My sister would usually be in the corner practicing cartwheels, and everything smelled like chlorine, because my dad liked to listen to this album in the summer, and that's when we'd go to the pool all the time."

Aubrey pulled at a strand of her wet, wavy hair. "You should write that down. So you won't forget it."

Their hands were still poised above the records, but neither of them was looking down anymore.

"Now tell me one of yours," he said.

"One of my what?"

"One of those songs. The kind that makes you think of stuff you didn't even know you remembered."

"Okay, I guess I have a couple. Give me a minute." She riffled through her memories. Of the Beatles songs her parents would play on road trips to Maine, of the Lady Gaga ones she would belt out with her friends in Connecticut. "There are tons," she said.

"Name a few."

She scanned the records in front of her. "Well, P. J. Harvey reminds me of your house. And Phoenix totally brings me back to freshman year. And—Tegan and Sara and Sleater-

Kinney always make me think of Rae." Mentioning Rae should have upset her, but it didn't. She felt like she was piecing something together, something important. "They're like time capsules, aren't they? You could put them all in a row and listen to them one after the other. And if you did it with your eyes closed, maybe it would feel like being home again."

The music scratched and skipped, and the girl closed her magazine and stood up to change the record. There was a beat of static, and then something new began to play—a woman's voice, low and full of yearning, accompanied by a twangy acoustic guitar. Aubrey tried to make out a few of the lines. She wanted to remember it later.

Quietly—so quietly, Aubrey almost didn't hear him over the music—Gabe said, "I didn't mean it."

Aubrey blinked at him. "Mean what?"

He flicked the same album back and forth. "All that stuff I said in Prague. How I made it sound like I regretted kissing you. Because, Bryce, the thing is, I really don't."

The bell above the front door jingled. A man shook out an umbrella and stamped out his shoes before walking to the world-music section. Through the open door, Aubrey could see rain popping and sparking on the sidewalk. When it closed again, the music sounded so much louder. She could hear the lyrics now—they were about sitting at a kitchen table with someone, drinking coffee, and talking about their day. How easy it was to be with that one person.

Aubrey looked up at a rusted air-conditioning vent. Gabe was waiting for her to respond. But whatever was happening between them—*if* something was happening at all—she needed time to figure it out. She needed time for things to feel like they did in the song. Simple. Easy.

He moved down a few steps and she followed, leaning forward. Drops of water fell from her hair and hit the cellophane on a record. "Later," she said. "I want to talk about this, but— not yet. Not right now. Later."

Understanding washed over his features. His voice was a murmur, as soft as the rain sounded from here. "Okay," he said. "Later."

The song warbled, stopped, and changed. Their eyes locked, and then dropped back to the records.

24

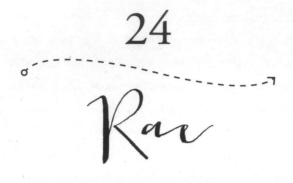

Rae

Sunday, July 10
FLORENCE

Clara took a step back and crossed her arms, hugging her sketchbook.

"What do you think of this one?" she asked Rae.

"I think it's one of the most famous paintings in the world," Rae said.

"Psh. Everything here is famous. What do you *really* think of it? And you're about to be an art major, so you have to say something smart. Say it with a British accent!"

"Hard pass. I suck at a British accent."

They were spending the morning in the Uffizi Gallery, walking down its long marble corridors and staring at paintings of myths and angels and *lots* of naked bodies. Right now, they were looking at a Botticelli. *The Birth of Venus.* A goddess stood on a shell floating on the ocean, her long red hair wrapped around her and roses drifting down. The painting was massive; it was vivid, bright, and blue.

"I think," Rae said, "it's beautiful."

But she kept glancing to the side instead, taking in Clara's furrowed brow and the small red buttons on the waist of her skirt. She watched the goose bumps form on Clara's arms in the air-conditioned chill and the way she scuffed her shoes on the glossy floor. Because Clara wasn't a fantasy. Or some perfect painted image. She was real, and that was even better. She was the girl who'd kissed Rae in a rose garden above the city and a few other places since. She was the girl standing with Rae now, turning every image on the wall flat and gray.

Clara leaned in. "What do you think Gabe and Aubrey are doing later?"

"No clue," Rae said. But the thought of Aubrey made her briefly cringe—she'd been trying to avoid it as much as she could.

"They didn't come back till late last night," Clara said.

"Not that we can talk."

Clara blushed. "That's true." They'd arrived back at the apartment only a few minutes before Aubrey and Gabe did. For most of yesterday, they'd scoured the city for places to be alone. And in the evening, they'd sat on the front steps of an old building, showing each other pages from their sketchbooks, things they'd worked hard on but had always kept to themselves. When they walked home, they took their time, stopping to kiss on bridges and on narrow streets between apartment buildings.

"I was just thinking," Clara said, "it's our last night here. We should commemorate it somehow. We should throw a surprise party."

"A surprise party for who?"

"For Aubrey and Gabe. For all of us."

"Is it really a party if only four people go?"

"Of course it is!" A guided tour assembled in front of the painting, and a woman in a navy-blue suit addressed the group. Clara spoke quietly. "I'm really good at this stuff. Rose and I used to plan parties for my parents' anniversaries before she went to college. They were themed and everything."

"I know you're good," Rae said, "but I don't have a great history with parties. You think it's going to be completely harmless, because everyone there is really into Broadway musicals, but then someone brings a bottle of tequila, and someone else suggests a *Phantom of the Opera* sing-along, and before you know it, you're standing on Lisa Tomiyama's coffee table fake-opera-singing to a bunch of theater geeks."

Clara bit her lip. "You have to admit, though, that was a fun night."

"Best of my life," Rae said drily.

A woman holding a map of the gallery edged up beside

them, fixing her glasses on her nose and craning her neck to listen to the tour guide. Rae played with the spiral in her sketchbook. She and Clara had decided to come to the Uffizi so they could draw, but she hadn't wanted to copy any of the art itself. She'd spent her time sketching the people around her instead, the ones who looked tired and bored or serious and intent. All of them revolving around one unchanging piece of art.

"I like it." Clara touched the corner of the page. It was a picture of a little boy staring up at the Botticelli.

Embarrassed, Rae shielded it with her hand. "I've been staring at it for too long. I kind of hate it now."

"All of your drawings seem so alive," Clara said. "Your photographs, too. That's why I love them all so much."

The woman with the map gave them a pointed look.

"This is a big gallery." Clara took Rae's hand. "We should see as much of it as we can."

They found themselves in an impossibly long hallway with a black-and-white floor and a row of tall windows running down one side. White stone statues stood balanced on heavy pedestals, and the air felt even colder here. Rae shivered in her tank top and shorts.

"Isn't it weird how empty it is?" Clara asked. Their footsteps echoed. "Doesn't it make you feel like we've stumbled into someone's house?"

"This would be a super-weird house," Rae said. "You'd need a map just to find the bathroom."

"And it would be extra creepy at night. All those depressing medieval dudes staring at you from portraits."

"God, we're sophisticated. We're, like, experts on classical art."

"Yeah." Clara sighed. "Our teachers would be so proud." She sat on a bench in front of a window and reached down to rub her calves. "If we walk too much, the day will go by faster. We need to slow down."

"Good plan." Rae joined her on the bench. It did feel oddly quiet here. She pulled out the map they'd picked up at the entrance. "Look at how many rooms there are. We could spend the entire day going from wing to wing."

"And then we can head home," Clara said, "and plan for the party."

Rae closed the map. "Okay, what is with this whole party thing? You seem pretty determined to have one."

"Like I said, it's our last day in Italy. It might be nice to do something with—all of us." She tapped her heels against the ground.

"Uh-huh," Rae said as it finally clicked together. "*All of us* as in me and Aubrey in the same room. Are you trying to get us to talk to each other again?"

A few kids stampeded down the hallway, their exhausted parents warning them to slow down. "I guess it *is* a little strange." Clara watched them pass. "The two of you haven't said anything to each other since we left Prague. Has this ever happened before?"

"Nope," Rae said.

Clara looked alarmed. "And you don't think that's a bad thing?"

"Well. Not necessarily. Aubrey and I can be pretty co-dependent. Maybe we need a break."

Clara's eyes widened further. "But what if you leave in a few days and you're still not talking to her? What will you do then?"

Rae wasn't sure what to say. It wasn't like she wanted to leave things this way forever. But she didn't want to have a Big, Important Conversation with Aubrey, either. If she and Aubrey made up, her time in Florence wouldn't be about her and Clara anymore. Once again, it would be about Aubrey and all her plans. Or maybe worse—if Aubrey found out about Rae and Clara, she might be hurt that Rae had kept such a big secret from her.

And Rae couldn't take that.

She wanted to concentrate on Clara. On the sheen of purple glitter along her cheekbones, on her shoulders tinted red from the sun. Rae couldn't imagine ever saying good-bye to her.

So she pictured this instead: They would go back to London together. They would hang out for as many days as they wanted and take the tube to each other's houses and watch movies and work on their art in Lucy's studio.

Clara turned to look out the window now, and Rae could tell she was slipping into herself. Down the hall, a clock chimed. A statue's long shadow reached across both of them. And even though Rae wanted to avoid any mention of Aubrey, she also didn't want Clara to be so concerned about her. She wanted every second of today to be perfect.

"Okay," Rae said. "We should do it. We should throw a party."

"Really?" Clara seemed elated. "You think so?"

"Sure. It is our last night here, right? We can't waste it."

"We'll get food and drinks after we're done here," Clara said. "Oh, and what do you think about streamers?" Rae's face must have changed, because Clara added, "Fine, no streamers. But I promise you, this will be fun."

Rae took Clara's hand and held it between both of hers, telling herself that, *yes, they still had time. They had whole hours, days, and nights left together.* "Of course it will."

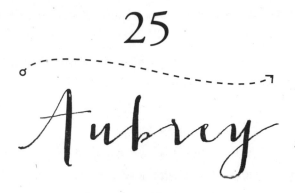

25
Aubrey

Sunday, July 10
ROME to FLORENCE

Rome seemed better after the rain.

The air was less stifling, the streets were less cluttered. Aubrey's stomach was weightless and buoyant, like she'd ridden a Ferris wheel to the very top. Like she was suspended in those few, bright moments before she had to glide back down to earth. She and Gabe navigated their way to ancient ruins and fountains. They cut down alleys where teenagers played games of soccer and people stopped to splash their hands at coppery *nasoni*. They followed the map on Aubrey's phone—a dotted line that led from the Trevi Fountain to the Tiber River to the Colosseum.

In the evening, they searched near the station for somewhere to eat.

"Pizza!" Aubrey said as they joined a line snaking down the sidewalk. "This is definitely the right choice."

"I can't exactly see straight," Gabe said. "Is it possible to be so hungry you get kind of drunk?"

"Here." Aubrey took her water bottle from her bag and handed it to him. "You're probably dehydrated."

He grinned woozily. "My hero."

She took a bow. When they reached the front of the line, they saw a glass case full of enormous square pizzas. Aubrey ordered a slice covered in mushrooms and garlic, while Gabe got his with Parma ham and mozzarella. He chatted to the guy behind the counter, saying things in Spanish that the guy answered in Italian, their languages close enough that they could piece together a conversation. Gabe made him laugh, full-bellied and delighted as he handed over two paper bags.

After the heat of the day, the evening felt cool and light. Passing buses and cars whipped down the street, kicking up a breeze that swirled down the sidewalk. People came outside to rest on benches or eat in restaurants with the doors thrown open and lively music playing. "I love this place at night," Aubrey said. Gabe bit off a mouthful of pizza. "*Christthisisamazing*. Bryce, have you tried this yet? It's fucking amazing."

"It's pizza," Aubrey said. "Of course it is." But when she

took a bite, she had to cover her mouth to stop herself from gasping. The crust was crispy and a bit charred, and the cheese was molten and spicy with garlic. Even the mushrooms were hot and buttery and more incredible than any mushrooms she'd ever tasted in her life.

In the station, they found a place to sit and finish eating. Announcements floated toward the high ceiling, and suitcases rumbled past, sounding like ocean waves. Aubrey could see blisters forming by the straps of her sandals, but she couldn't feel them yet. On the departure board, platform numbers and train times clicked over and over.

"Doesn't this feel different?" Aubrey asked. "It's like nowhere else we've been."

"Different how?" Gabe swallowed his last bite of crust.

"Maybe because we didn't plan on coming here, so it feels like a secret. Like it's all this extra time we're not supposed to have."

"Technically, it is a secret. We didn't tell anyone where we were going."

"Which was probably pretty stupid."

"Very stupid," he agreed. But she could tell by his expression that he didn't mean it. And she didn't really mean it, either. If she had the chance, she wouldn't undo anything about today. She wouldn't change one part of it.

"Look," Gabe said, lightly tapping her wrist. "Our train is up."

The lights in their carriage were dim when they boarded,

and strips of reflective orange stickers guided them to their row. Aubrey took a seat by the window, and Gabe sat on the aisle. They both stared forward, arms crossed. Aubrey was extra aware of how small a space this really was.

A staticky announcement came over the speakers. "What did they say?" Aubrey asked when it was over.

Gabe rubbed the side of his neck. "I couldn't understand all of it, but I think it had something to do with conserving electricity? And that's why they turned off the lights?"

Aubrey pushed her shoes against the metal footrest in front of her. "That explains it."

Through the window, she saw a group of people disembarking from another train. They looked sleepy and grateful to have arrived, and Aubrey felt jealous that they had all this time in Rome ahead of them. She wanted that, too—time before she had to go to Barcelona and London and New York. Time with Gabe that felt like this—stolen, private—before she had to figure out what was really going on between them.

She knew she liked him—*of course* she liked him; he was one of her best friends. She liked his droll sense of humor and the dimples in his cheeks and his fussy, constantly tousled hair. She liked him for coming over that one time just to show her how to change the flat tire on her bike. She liked him for the nights he texted her before she fell asleep and the free periods he came to study beside her in the library.

He was her only friend who felt okay with silence the

way she did. The two of them had spent so many quiet hours together, not saying much but not feeling weird about it, either. Just listening, thinking, keeping each other company.

"We could turn on the reading light," Gabe suggested. They both reached above at the same time, their fingertips meeting.

"Sorry," Gabe said.

"No big deal." Aubrey pulled her hand back and held it with her other.

The train moved lightly away from the platform, as if it had been nudged. This was usually the part when Aubrey liked to look outside, but she was still facing Gabe. She was still thinking about everything that had happened today. She'd told herself for so long that she liked him as a friend, but now she saw it differently: She'd never kissed a friend the way she'd kissed Gabe. She'd never thought so hard about the small gap between a friend's seat and hers, the few inches that stopped them from touching.

The train began to hit its stride. The reading light was still off.

"What changed?" she asked.

Gabe blinked. "Well, we were in Rome about five seconds ago, and now we're not."

"No." Aubrey tried not to hold her breath. "In the record store, you said you didn't regret kissing me. But after the end of the play, you acted like I didn't even exist. And when I asked if we could be friends, you said no."

Gabe frowned at the armrest. "I shouldn't have said that."

"But you did. And you meant it, didn't you?"

The sound of the train was constant, and Aubrey was glad to have it. It felt like it was supporting them, giving their conversation momentum.

"I did mean it." Gabe's eyes were still pointed down. "Until I talked to Rae."

"*Rae?* What does Rae have to do with anything? And when did you talk to her?"

"In Amsterdam. She told me I needed to grow some ovaries and stop being so shitty to you. And she might have mentioned something about how . . . you used to like me."

Aubrey's body tensed. "Rae told you that?"

"It was an accident. I swear, she didn't mean to."

"It's okay," Aubrey said, but she was still trying to sort through all this. *Rae and Gabe had talked? Rae was the reason Gabe had stopped pushing Aubrey away?* "I actually assumed you knew that already," she said. "I figured I was painfully obvious."

"I had no idea. I thought it was only me—who liked you."

The door to their carriage opened and a train conductor came up the aisle. Aubrey realized she was gripping the armrest. Gabe dug through his pockets for their tickets. She noticed that the fabric of his T-shirt still smelled like rain, and there were red, sun-kissed marks beneath his eyes. If she kissed him now, she was pretty sure the kiss would taste like salt.

The conductor stopped at their seats. Aubrey was reeling.

She couldn't deny it—that desire she'd felt before, that need to be close to Gabe. It was stronger than ever. She could see it for what it really was, now that she wasn't hiding in her lists of places to go, now that she wasn't letting a day of buildings and fountains and roads drown it out.

Those things were gone, and what she was left with was this: She liked Gabe. She had since the moment she met him.

The conductor left. Gabe turned toward her again. "So. You were telling me how much you liked me?"

Aubrey hid her face with her hands. "This is *so* humiliating."

"Bryce." His voice was warm. "It isn't."

She peeked at him through her fingers. A passing light illuminated his arm and then his cheek. Aubrey imagined brushing her fingers everywhere the light touched him.

"Freshman year," she said. "During the play. I had...*a crush* on you. I loved painting those stupid sets with you even if I was really crap at the painting part."

"Yeah," he said. "I had fun, too."

She shook her head. "It was more than that. Every day, I hoped we would take the train home together. And when we didn't, I'd spend the whole time wondering what it would be like if you asked me out. Or if, instead of painting, we made out one day. There. Is this humiliating enough yet?"

"Still no." His eyes were teasing. And Aubrey wondered if he was thinking the same thing she was—of pushing up the armrest, of losing that last, small barrier that lay between them. She ached for it, but she knew she needed to hold off. They'd thrown themselves at each other three times now. This time, they needed to talk.

"Is there anything you feel like telling me?" she asked.

"I already did. I wanted to kiss you one month ago and also two days ago and also four years ago. Sometimes I tried not to want it, and sometimes I thought I was vaguely successful at that, but then we'd hang out alone again, and I'd realize I was bullshitting myself."

Aubrey felt a tingle down her back. "But you got so weird sophomore year."

Gabe softly bumped his head back against his seat. "I had no idea how you felt. I got weird because I was trying to get over you."

"But *why*? I wasn't even dating Jonah then."

"But he already liked you, I could tell. And I really thought you liked him, too."

Aubrey couldn't believe it. The beginning of sophomore year, she'd noticed that Jonah was cute; she'd even told Rae that she could understand why other girls liked him. But *she* hadn't liked him. Not like that. Not until months later. "What on earth gave you that idea?" she asked.

"Well, for starters, he's Jonah. It's an objective fact that he's a decently attractive guy. Plus, whenever I was eating lunch with him or hanging out with him at rehearsals, you'd usually find a reason to come hang out."

"And you never thought that had something to do with you?"

He sighed and looked up to the ceiling. "I was tall and gangly and I liked listening to music more than I liked actual human interaction. Plus, I wore those bright-yellow sneakers all the time. Remember those? Z said they made me look like I was skiing in space."

"Oh yeah." Aubrey giggled. "They were pretty bad."

His head dipped back toward hers. The train hiccuped, and Aubrey's stomach did, too. "You were extremely pretty," he said, "and smart and you knew everything about London. You honestly seemed way out of my league."

Aubrey kept hold of the armrest. "Everything you're saying about me is how I felt about you. I mean, you'd lived in *two* other countries before England. And you're so passionate about all the things that interest you—all those eighties music videos you showed me, and the interviews with songwriters you sent me, and those stupid parks in Oregon you're so desperate to visit. You get invested in things and you make them sound fascinating. That's why every time we hung out—every time we texted, or we sat around your house, or you played me some new song we'd listen to again and again—I was falling for you. I didn't realize it at the time, but I do now. I'm certain of it."

"Aubrey—" he said, but she didn't want to talk anymore. She didn't think she could.

She ran her thumb along his lips, and he went still. Her hand moved to the back of his neck, her rib cage pressed to the armrest. This time, she didn't want to rush. His hand found her elbow and they waited there, Aubrey's eyes tracing the line of his jaw and the shape of his mouth before their lips finally touched. The backs of his fingers slid down to the side of her shirt. Aubrey bumped up the armrest with her knee, and he helped her push it all the way back. They drew together, Aubrey's breathing going shallow. She thought that this was a kiss like a whispered secret. It was a kiss of gray-blue paint and darkened theaters and the needle on a record player scratching out a wistful song. It was a kiss pulled from all the moments they'd both tried to overlook but couldn't. Her mouth opened; his palm flattened against the skin of her back. But still, they kissed as slowly as they could. Even as the train kept picking up speed, kept going forward, kept cutting a light through all that darkness ahead of them.

26

Sunday, July 10
FLORENCE

This apartment isn't exactly…" Rae paused.

"Clean?" Clara finished for her.

They were standing at the bottom of the stairs, the bags of food they'd just bought heaped on the dining room table. Last night, they'd made pasta for dinner, and the unwashed pots and plates still littered the kitchen counters. A layer of dust covered everything.

Clara clapped her hands together. "I'll get the vacuum."

"We have a vacuum?" Rae asked.

"We must!" Clara opened the door to the closet behind the stairs. "Grown-ups always own vacuums."

Rae went into the kitchen and filled the sink with soap

and water. The air in the room was stale, so she climbed onto the counter and opened a small window high above the cupboards. It framed a square of dark blue sky, a single stone tower etched across it.

Rae stopped to stare at it, listening to the hum of the evening as it poured inside. She thought this would make a cool picture—the kind her mom would like—so she went to find her camera. Its strap settled around her neck, its familiar weight resting against her chest. She climbed the counter again and snapped a picture of cracked white paint on the wooden window frame, of an old tower with wispy clouds curling above it. Rae liked that it was an image of Florence only she could see. A tiny corner of the city that, right now, belonged only to her.

She scrubbed the dishes, the warm suds covering her hands and arms. She'd never given it much thought before, but she wondered if this was what it would feel like having an apartment of her own someday. A studio, probably, with her mom's paintings on the walls and a sofa bed and high windows that overlooked a city. Maybe in Melbourne. Or maybe somewhere else. Any of the hundreds of places she could picture herself living. She would open the windows while doing the dishes. She would hang her laundry out on a small balcony and fold up her sofa bed to have friends over at night. They would drink and talk and hang out till the early hours of the morning. Actually, it was kind of nice to think about. It made adulthood seem almost okay.

A bell chimed outside, bringing Rae back to the present.

She dried her hands on the bottom of her T-shirt and went into the living room. Everything had been transformed. The main lights were off and candles, glimmering in candleholders, rested on every surface. A green brocade tablecloth had been placed over the dining table, with wineglasses and bowls of chips and plates of cheese and crackers arranged across it. It was all set out so neatly, like Clara had obsessed over getting it just right.

"Come look at this." Clara sat on the floor by the couch. She'd unpinned her hair so it fell in waves, and she wore a dress Rae remembered her making last summer—cherry-printed fabric and straps that tied as bows. She was pulling old cassette tapes out of a bunch of shoeboxes and placing them in separate piles. "I found these in the closet with the vacuum," she said. "Aren't they great?"

"They're cool." Rae sat down, too, although she wasn't really thinking about tapes. She was thinking about the way Clara bent forward to read the names of songs to herself. She was thinking about her deep red lipstick and the bows on her shoulders and how carefully she was organizing each pile. Rae wondered what it would be like if they weren't eighteen. If they were five or six years older, and their lives were a little more stable, a little more still. Maybe they would be moving in somewhere together, sorting through boxes of their own stuff and making lists of supplies they needed to buy. A colander, a duster, a chest of drawers—things Rae had never realized until now she would eventually need to own.

"We'll let Gabe decide what to play first," Clara said. "He'll love that."

"What can we listen to them on, though?" Rae picked up a pile of the cassettes and was surprised by how clunky they were. "These are approximately a hundred years old."

"Hold on." Clara disappeared behind the couch and emerged again with an ancient boom box in her arms. "Voilà!"

"*Whoa*," Rae said. "That thing looks prehistoric as fuck. There's no way in hell it works."

"Only one way to find out." Clara plugged it in and pressed a few buttons. The tape clicked over and big-band music began to play—the kind that had to be from the 1930s or something. A woman sang in French, and Rae thought she recognized the song as one she and Lucy had heard during a trip to France. Or maybe Gabe had played it for Aubrey once and then Aubrey had played it for Rae. Whatever it was, Rae loved it. It was exactly what she felt like listening to right now.

Clara came back over. "See? Doesn't this feel like a party?"

"For sure." Rae pulled the camera off her neck. "Want to see some of the pictures I've taken?" They scrolled through images of the apartment and Prague and Amsterdam. There was the one of Clara standing on the Charles Bridge, Rae's reflection in her sunglasses. There was the one of the two of them in the hostel in Amsterdam, Clara's hair like red smoke, Rae twisting away from the camera. Both of them looking disheveled and sleep-deprived and happy.

"You have to send me these." Clara leaned closer to the screen.

"Yup," Rae said, but she didn't want to scroll back any further. It was too overwhelming to think of how much had happened in such a short span of time. That picture in Amsterdam had been taken less than a week ago, but Clara hadn't known how Rae felt about her then. And when she'd told Rae that she wished the five of them were going to college together, Rae had been sure she didn't want the same thing. She'd been determined to move far away, determined to start over.

But now that was the last thing she wanted.

She wanted *this*. She wanted rooms that felt like her own and a desk where she could sit every day and draw alongside someone. Her wide-open future—all the unknown places she'd imagined herself exploring—now seemed small in comparison. So much smaller than making breakfast with Clara every morning and sleeping under the same sheets with her every night.

"Cupcakes." She abruptly switched her camera off. "You still want to make them, right?"

Clara must have been a little thrown, but she didn't show it. She pulled her hair to the nape of her neck. "I'll get everything out."

They walked into the kitchen, where Clara took mixing bowls and vanilla extract and flour from the cupboards. Rae hoped Clara knew how to bake, because *she* definitely didn't. She and Lucy loved buying intricate cakes from famous London bakeries, but they couldn't even throw together a brownie mix without ruining it. And they both majorly sucked at cooking. When Rae went to college, she'd probably live off bowls of cold cereal and toasted bagels.

"Is something wrong?" Clara asked tentatively. "You seem a little distant."

Rae shook her head. "I was just thinking about bagels."

Clara closed a cupboard door. "I thought maybe it had something to do with our conversation earlier? About you and Aubrey? Do you know what you'll say when you see her tonight?"

"Honestly," Rae said, "I don't really care."

"But how can you not care?" Clara dropped a bag of flour on the counter, making Rae jump. Clara seemed upset now.

"I don't know." Rae picked up a corkscrew from the counter and flipped it nervously in her hands. "She just hasn't been on my mind."

"So you don't care that you're about to leave her?" Clara said. "Or that you're going to Australia and never coming back?"

"I'll come back. Someday. I mean, probably."

"But what if she's not there when you do? What if her parents have moved to the States and she has no reason to visit England ever again? Doesn't that bother you? Are you already so completely detached from her?"

A few drops of water fell from the faucet into the still-full sink. Rae kept twisting the corkscrew. "Clara," she said, "are you definitely talking about me and Aubrey right now?"

Clara's face reddened. "Yes."

"You're talking about me leaving. And what happens to my relationship—with Aubrey?"

Clara backed up against the fridge. "It's taken you *two days* to forget about your best friend," she said. Rae could hear the sadness in her voice. "How long will it take you to forget about me?"

Rae's stomach plunged.

She turned and put the corkscrew back in a drawer. What was she supposed to do now? Forgetting Clara had always been the point. It had been one of the perks of going to school so far away—that her memory of Clara would finally fade, that she could finally figure out a way to move on. But that idea seemed so ridiculous now—moving on seemed beyond impossible.

"We should bake," Rae said, "or the cupcakes won't be done in time." She ripped open a bag of sugar so forcefully that she knocked it over. Sugar drenched the counter and overflowed to the floor. Rae watched it stream toward the fridge and beneath the oven, obscuring the faint pattern of green vines on the tiles. She stood frozen as the bag finally emptied and fluttered to the ground.

And then she started to sob.

Her chest heaved. Hot tears splashed down her cheeks.

Clara's arms wrapped around her shoulders, and Rae smelled her orange-raspberry scent. "Rae," she said. "It's okay. I don't want stupid cupcakes that badly."

"It's not—" Rae stammered. "It's not the cu-cupcakes. And it's not Aubrey. It's—I don't want to go to Melbourne!" She continued to cry. More than she'd ever cried about anything else. Maybe more than she'd ever cried *period*.

In the other room, the tape was still playing. Candles were lit and the food was set out, ready for the party. Rae slid to the floor, and Clara went with her. They were both sitting in a pile of sugar.

"Of course you want to go," Clara said. "You want adventure. You want change."

"But *Australia*?" Rae said. "What the fuck was I thinking? New York would be adventure and change. California would be adventure and change. I mean, it's college! The whole freaking thing is adventure and change!"

Clara rubbed circles on Rae's back. "So try Melbourne for a year. If you hate it, you can always transfer."

"But if I try it, that means I have to go. I don't want to leave and have to *find myself* or whatever. I don't want any of that. I want—I want to stay with you."

Clara pulled back to look at her. Rae clamped her mouth shut. That was *definitely* the dumbest thing she could have said. "I'm sorry." She shrugged away, the granules of sugar itching against her legs. The motor in the refrigerator hissed and hummed. "That was weird. I know you have to go to LA.

You *should* go to LA. Visit your sister at Stanford, do your art-school thing. And when you meet some talented sculptor guy—or talented sculptor girl—I promise you, I'll be happy for—"

"Rae." Clara placed one hand on the ground and the other on Rae's knee. Her gaze was intent. "You are aware that I'm already in love with you, right?"

Rae leaned against the cabinet beneath the sink. The blue oven clock blinked across from them. Clara's hand was still pressed to the sugar on the ground, her lips parted, like she wanted to keep talking. But Rae decided to talk first.

"Clara," she said, "I hope it's pretty obvious that I'm in love with you, too."

The time on the clock changed just as they kissed.

It was still one of the first kisses they'd had, but for some reason, it didn't feel new anymore.

Because this was Clara.

Clara, who'd slept over at Rae's house countless times, bowls of popcorn on the floor, mugs half filled with tea and open DVD cases on the coffee table. Clara, who'd skipped class with her sophomore year because it was snowing outside and they wanted to walk to a coffee shop for hot chocolate. Clara, who'd knitted a scarf for her eighteenth birthday and waited by her locker first thing in the morning to give it to her. Clara, who she loved. Clara, who loved her back.

They lay down. Clara kissed Rae's neck and each one of her shoulders. Rae closed her eyes and felt their kisses grow deeper. Their legs laced together. The sugar was everywhere beneath them, like snow, like the sand on the beach in Paris. Rae stretched one hand across the tiles and imagined that the vines were real. They grew all over the room, twining around pipes, creeping toward the ceiling. And Clara and Rae were lost in the middle of it all, safe for a little while longer.

The front door opened.

Clara rolled off Rae, and Rae sat up, desperately brushing sugar from her dress and bracing herself for all the questions Aubrey and Gabe would *definitely* have. But when she stood up, her first sentence got lodged in her throat. She didn't say anything at all. Because it wasn't Aubrey and Gabe standing in the entranceway.

It was Jonah.

27

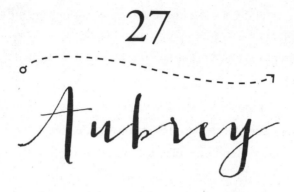

Aubrey

Monday, July 11
ROME to FLORENCE

Aubrey didn't realize their train had reached Florence until the light came on above her.

She and Gabe were still kissing, and everything felt like it was moving so fast. There was another announcement and the sound of doors breathing open.

Gabe sat back sheepishly. His mouth and cheeks were red. Their carriage was so bright that Aubrey could see a coffee stain by her feet and the rude word someone had written on the back of her tray table. She touched her own lips and felt how swollen they were. She didn't know what would happen next—maybe they would argue. Or stop speaking to each other. She and Gabe had never kissed without arguing or giving each other the silent treatment afterward.

"We're here." Gabe slipped his hand into hers. "Let's go home?"

They tiptoed through the streets of Florence. It was way past midnight, and the busy strip of clubs and bars led into long, quieter stretches, where the streetlights glowed but every window was dark. In those areas, they kissed again. Gabe was taller than Aubrey, so sometimes they struggled to work out the logistics. She took the top step of a building stoop while he took the bottom. He picked her up but lost his balance and they both fell against a trash can.

"Look what you did, Bryce," he whispered, and she kissed him to shut him up. They backed against a pair of green shutters, her hands crushing through his hair, his skimming the waistband of her shorts.

She hoped it took them hours to get to the apartment.

But, too soon, they made it. They climbed echoing concrete stairs to the second floor. Gabe whispered, "Do you have the key?"

"I think I left it in Rome." She turned around. "Guess we'll have to go back."

"Guess so." He reached into her bag and took the key out for her.

She laughed as they approached their door. Music was playing on the other side, which meant Clara and Rae were home. But Aubrey wasn't disappointed. She felt the way she had yesterday—heady with exhaustion, ready for sleep. Except tonight, she knew she would sleep lightly. And she would dream the whole time about trains that whispered their way through the night.

Gabe brushed her ponytail aside and kissed the back of her neck. The door was already unlocked, Aubrey pushed it open, and...

She couldn't take it all in at once. Snacks and wineglasses and a dark-green tablecloth. A boom box set up in the corner with cassette tapes and shoeboxes beside it. Candles everywhere. And Clara and Rae standing by the kitchen, looking petrified.

Looking at Jonah, who stood right across from them, still carrying his backpack.

Aubrey couldn't move. She felt like a statue. *What the hell is Jonah doing here?*

"Aubrey," he said.

"Jonah." Aubrey bit her lips together.

No one else said anything. They all just watched one another like they were trying to figure out how they'd gotten here. Was it obvious that Aubrey and Gabe had spent the whole evening making out? Aubrey was pretty sure her face gave the game away. Everyone could probably tell that she still felt Gabe's touch on her skin. Like a sunburn, or an afterglow.

"Surprise!" Clara threw up her arms. No one reacted, so she dropped them. "It's... um... a surprise party."

Aubrey swiveled toward her. "You and Jonah *planned* this?"

"No!" Clara and Jonah said at the same time, but Aubrey wasn't convinced. Clara had said on the sleeper train that Jonah had texted her. Maybe Clara had talked him into coming back. Maybe they'd come up with this whole elaborate scheme to get him and Aubrey in the same room for—for a surprise party?

Rae dusted something that looked like glitter off her arms. "We've got food. And wine. I, for one, will be having some wine."

"Yeah." Gabe jerked his chin up. "I'll take some, too."

They gathered around the table, filling up glasses and small plates. It was nearly one in the morning, and the candles and music made Aubrey feel delirious. Like she was at a dinner-party scene in some gothic story. Like she was waiting for a dark and awful truth to be revealed. Clara was the only one even remotely dressed for a party. Rae was still wearing her usual grungy clothes, but it looked like she'd borrowed some of Clara's red lipstick. Which made no sense. Rae *never* wore lipstick.

They each took a seat at the table.

"Jonah." Clara picked at the food on her plate. "Wow. I can't believe you're back."

"I know," he said. "Sorry I didn't tell you earlier. But Aubrey and I booked the apartment together, so I had this e-mail from the landlord with the building's key code in it. And the door was unlocked." He bit into a cheese cracker.

Gabe drank his wine at an alarming rate.

"So." Rae shifted in her chair. "How was—like—Europe?"

"Europe?" he asked. "As in the entire continent?"

"Yeah, you've still got your Eurail pass, right? I assume you've been traveling around."

"Which is completely unfair." Clara jumped in. "Girls can't go backpacking alone without everyone telling them how *dangerous* it is. Sexism is such trash."

"Actually," Jonah said, "I didn't go anywhere new."

"Oh?" Rae said. "What did you do, then? Bum around on trains or something?"

"No," he said. "I pretty much just hung out with Leah."

Everyone went silent. Aubrey grabbed the wine bottle from the middle of the table and poured as much into her glass as would fit. She'd had red wine with her parents before, small glasses at Christmas and New Year's, but it tasted different in large gulps. More like syrup.

"You did?" Clara said.

"I took the first train I saw going back to Amsterdam. I didn't know if I'd stick around or what, but when I called Leah, she said I could crash at her place."

"Hmm." Clara cut an urgent look at Rae, who crammed three potato chips into her mouth at once. Aubrey could see them calculating, trying to figure out how to respond. They both knew her big fight with Jonah had been partially about Leah. But they didn't know what had happened after that. They didn't know about her kiss with Gabe or about Rome or about the fact that, a few short minutes ago, she hadn't really minded that Jonah was gone. That she didn't even care he'd been to see Leah.

Not really, anyway.

Rae finished chewing. "And you just stayed there? In Amsterdam?"

Jonah shrugged. "I saw Leah's show a few times. And we went out to some bars with the people she's been working with. They're all professional actors. It was pretty rad."

"Oh man," Rae said. "That sounds . . . rad."

"Definitely," Gabe said. Beneath the table, Aubrey felt his feet move forward, the ends of his shoes touching the ends of hers. Her muscles relaxed. She pressed his shoes back.

"What about you guys?" Jonah asked. "How was Prague?"

"It was fun," Clara said. "Very . . . European!"

"We walked around," Rae said. "Saw a weird clock and shit."

Jonah snorted. "And that's *all* you two did?"

Abruptly, Rae pushed her chair back and stood up. "Hey, isn't this a party? Why aren't we doing party things?"

"Eating is a party thing." Aubrey broke one of her crackers in half.

"No, she's right." Clara stood, too. "We're not supposed to sit around all night."

"I want to keep talking, though," Jonah said, his eyes moving quickly to Aubrey and then away again. "Why don't we play a game?"

"Dude," Rae said. "That's a *terrible* idea."

"No, no, it's good—I promise." He picked up a bottle of

wine from the center of the table. "And it's a really easy one. Leah and I played it every night."

"Like I said." Rae stared at him hard. "A *really terrible* idea."

Jonah ignored her, and Aubrey got the distinct feeling he was set on doing this. Maybe he was trying to make her jealous. That didn't seem like Jonah, but then again, this whole night was beyond strange. Anything was possible. "Let's sit on the floor," he said. "This feels too formal."

He headed into the living room, and since no one seemed to know what else to do, they followed. They sat in a circle on the rug, Gabe sifting through a pile of nearby cassettes and Rae chewing her thumbnail. All the windows and shutters were open. The candles had started to burn low, flames shaking in the breeze that wafted inside.

The apartment was a little bit cold and sort of spooky at night. Every time one of them moved, the hardwood floors rasped and whimpered. For the first time all day, Aubrey wished she had a sweater.

"Okay." Jonah placed the wine in the center of the circle. "This game is called Truth or Drink."

"Gee." Rae tapped at her chin. "I wonder how you play that?"

Jonah grinned. "Told you it was easy. So, everyone takes a turn. You ask the person next to you a question—any question you want—and they either answer truthfully or they take a drink."

Clara smoothed her skirt around her knees. "What direction should we go in?"

Gabe got up, taking a cassette with him to the boom box. Aubrey watched him slip from candlelit glow to candlelit glow.

"It doesn't matter," Jonah said. "Whichever way you want. Why don't you start?"

Clara was sitting between Jonah and Rae. She glanced at each of them, considering thoughtfully before angling herself toward Rae. "Okay," she said. "My question for you is this: Out of me, Jonah, and Gabe, who would you marry, who would you screw, and who would you kill?"

"Oh Christ!" Rae said. "I hate that question!"

Clara's expression went sly. "You can always take a drink."

"Ugh, you win." Rae looped one of the tassels on the rug around her index finger. "I guess I'd screw Gabe, because— I don't know—he thinks 'Dig Me Out' is the best Sleater-Kinney song. Which means I'd have to kill Jonah and marry . . . *you I guess.*"

Clara dropped her head, but Aubrey could see her beaming.

"*Thanks,*" Jonah said.

"Sorry." Rae looked at him over Clara. "Guess you're the disposable one here."

All the air seemed to leave the room. Rae must have realized what she'd said, because she made a face and scrubbed her curls away from her forehead. Jonah focused intently on the contents of his glass. Gabe pressed play on the boom box, and the song that floated out was the same one he and Aubrey had listened to in the record shop that afternoon. It was like oxygen. It was a quiet message he was sending only to her. Something to make her feel okay.

"Anyway," Rae said. "My turn."

Gabe came back and took his place next to Aubrey again. He didn't smile or even look in her direction, but when he placed his hand on the ground next to her, she knew what it meant. He was saying everything would be fine; he was reminding her that he was there.

"Aubrey," Rae said, "I guess I'm supposed to ask you. So—um—where did you guys go today?"

But Aubrey wasn't really paying attention. She was listening to the song. She was remembering the rainy streets of Rome and the colors of all those albums that had been laid out in front of her. "Rome," she said.

"*Rome?*" Clara said. "Hold on a second. What were you doing in *Rome?*"

"Just—" Aubrey hitched up one shoulder. "Seeing it."

"You never told us you were going there." Clara sounded genuinely baffled.

"I know. And I get that we should have, but it's not like you and Rae said anything about what you were doing today."

"Ha," Jonah said. "Do you really want details?"

The candle closest to her burned out, smoke unwinding from its wick. Aubrey sipped more wine. "Why would I not want details?"

"Because." Jonah leaned back on his hands. "How much do you really want to know about them making out?"

Aubrey was sure she must have misheard.

Or maybe Jonah was making some joke she didn't understand.

Rae groaned, collapsing onto the floor. "I *knew* this game was a bad idea."

"We need more wine!" Clara leaped up to grab another bottle.

Gabe whistled under his breath. "This is definitely not how I expected tonight would go."

It wasn't how Aubrey had expected it would go, either. In fact, nothing about this day—or this week or this entire mess of a summer—was what Aubrey had planned it to be. She looked at Rae. *"You and Clara kissed?"*

"I don't know." Rae was still lying down. "Are you asking me as part of the game?"

"Jesus! Is that seriously what matters right now?" But when Rae didn't answer, Aubrey got flustered. "Fine, whatever! I'm asking you as part of the stupid game. Truth or Drink, Rae: *Did you and Clara kiss?"*

Rae sat up and picked some wax off the floor at the edge of the rug. Then she took her glass of wine and downed it in one swallow.

Aubrey's skin prickled. "Oh my God. Why are you being such a bitch right now?"

"Not sure. Why are you calling me a word that I *hate*?"

Jonah seemed dumbstruck. "Since when do you guys talk to each other like this?"

"*Since you left,*" they said together.

"Which was when?" he asked. "Thirty years ago?"

"It might as well have been," Aubrey muttered. She knew she sounded angry, but she couldn't help it. She was worn thin. Her mouth was sticky with alcohol and her head pounded from heat and dehydration. The song from the record store was still playing, but Aubrey could barely hear it now. Her ears had started to ring.

"You know what?" Gabe said. "We've got to get up early tomorrow. Why don't we go to bed? We're all way too tired for this."

"I'm not tired," Aubrey said. But she was. She was so tired she felt a little drunk. And Gabe was right—they needed to stop and sleep this off. But she really didn't want to. They were all here now. They might as well start being honest with one another. "We should finish the game," she said.

"Sorry, Aubs," Jonah said. "The game's over."

"No, it isn't." Aubrey picked up the open bottle Clara had just brought over and thrust it toward Jonah. "Truth or Drink, Jonah: What were you *really* doing in Amsterdam? Did you go there to make out with Leah?"

"*Aubrey,*" Clara hissed.

Aubrey's arm was still extended, hand still gripping the bottle's neck. She and Jonah were looking at each other, fully, for the first time since he'd come back. "That's why you wanted to play this game, right?" she said. "You wanted me to ask that question. You wanted to find out how much it bothered me. How *desperate* I was to know."

"You're making me sound like a psychopath."

"I know you, Jonah. And I asked you a question, so you have to respond."

Jonah crossed his arms. "Okay. We kissed. But I don't see why you care so much when you've clearly been doing the same with Gabe all day."

Aubrey dropped the bottle. Dark liquid pooled like blood, seeping into the rug.

Rae and Clara shot up and ran into the kitchen to grab paper towels. Aubrey stood, too. The wine had splashed onto her clothes. It dripped from her knees.

"I'll help," she said, tears clouding her eyes.

But Clara and Rae were already wiping it up. Gabe took a few paper towels and did the same. There was no way they'd be able to get the stain out. The landlord would contact them, and Aubrey would have to pay for a new rug, and since she didn't have enough money, her parents would have to lend it to her. Everyone would think she was so irresponsible.

The night air swept through the room, snuffing out more candles. The leaves on the plant in the corner quivered. The five of them were still there, still in a circle, but they were doing their best to avoid one another. Except for Clara and Rae, who, Aubrey noticed, were crouched close together. So close it was like they were trying to block everyone else out. They were taking care of each other.

And suddenly, Aubrey understood why Rae looked like she was wearing lipstick.

"Wait," Clara said after a moment, sitting up on her knees. "Jonah. What did you mean about Aubrey and Gabe?"

"Didn't she tell you guys?" Jonah asked. "They kissed on the train in Berlin. Right before I left."

"Berlin?" Rae directed this at Aubrey.

"And in Prague," Aubrey said.

"And somewhere between Rome and Florence." Gabe sighed. "Since we're being so truthful all of a sudden."

Jonah massaged the sides of his head. He seemed drained now, like the day was catching up with him. Like he needed to sleep. "Leah told me I should come back," he said. "She told me I should let you know that— it's okay what happened. I mean, it wasn't the best fucking moment of my life or anything, but it makes sense. Us breaking up. We probably wouldn't have lasted anyway, right?"

Aubrey felt the room tipping out from under her. Jonah hadn't come here to pick a fight or make her feel guilty. He was here because he was fine with what had happened. Because he was already over it. It made her feel relieved and unnerved and *so* confused. She couldn't believe what was happening right here—in this dim room on this dim night. She couldn't believe that the strings that held them together were snapping apart. She and Jonah were officially over. She and Rae were barely being civil to each other.

The five of them didn't fit together anymore.

She took a paper towel and started wiping at the carpet. "I'm so sorry about the mess," she said. "Please let me clean it before I go."

"Go where?" Rae said.

"Bryce?" Gabe said. And in his voice, she heard the questions he was really asking. *Are you okay? What can I do to make this better?* He was solid and real and as comforting as the music he'd always played for her.

But Aubrey knew the truth now—just because something was comforting didn't mean it was forever.

28

Monday, July 11
FLORENCE

*A*ubrey!" Rae walked in as Aubrey grabbed an armful of clothes and threw them on her bed. Her backpack lay open across the pillows.

Rae didn't know why her brain picked now, of all moments, to realize this, but Aubrey must have bought the bag especially for this trip. It was bright and sturdy and clearly brand-new. Unlike Rae's, which she'd dragged around for years. Rae could picture it now: Aubrey at a store, trying out new backpacks; Aubrey sitting at her computer, looking up which ones were the most comfortable and the best for train travel. She really had put so many hours of thought and work into this trip.

Rae closed the door. "Aubrey," she said again, "stop. What are you doing?"

"I'm leaving." Aubrey tossed an olive-green tank top onto her clothes heap.

"It's two in the morning. There aren't any trains leaving now."

"So I'll go to the station and wait until there is one."

Rae held up both hands. "Remember the last night we were in London? When you said you were worried about being axe-murdered? Doesn't spending all night in an abandoned train station seem like a pretty decent way of making that happen?"

Aubrey looked under the bed, pulling out a few pairs of socks and underwear. "I'm not going to get murdered. That wasn't an actual worry."

"Dude, of course it was. And now I'm worried about it for you. Plus, you can't just leave like this. You can't pull a Jonah on us."

"I'm not pulling a Jonah. I'm not going to make out with Leah in Amsterdam."

Rae pretended to gag. "That is *so* not an image I wanted in my head."

Aubrey yanked at the zipper on her bag. Rae had to think fast. It was obvious she and Aubrey weren't on great terms, but that didn't mean Rae thought she should *leave*. Leaving was so extreme. And impulsive. It wasn't what Aubrey deserved after everything she'd done to get them all here.

Rae's eye snagged on the nightstand, where Aubrey's passport sat by a bottle of Clara's perfume. She grabbed it and held it over her head. "There!" she said. "You can't go anywhere without this."

"Rae." Aubrey scowled. "Stop being a child."

"I'm not." Rae stretched her arm farther, keeping the passport out of Aubrey's reach. "I just want to talk to you for a minute."

Aubrey let go of the zipper and crossed her arms. "Fine. Let's talk."

Rae shifted the passport behind her and backed up against the door, just in case. "What's this all about? Is it because of Jonah and Leah?"

"Of course not." Aubrey nudged a flip-flop across the floor with her toe. "I don't give a crap about Leah."

"But Jonah must have something to do with this. Are you mad at him for leaving? Or for coming back? Or is it like a Venn diagram of those two things? Come on, Aubs. Talk me through it." Her hands were starting to go numb from being squished behind her, but there was no way she was giving in. Seeing Aubrey getting ready to run off had freaked her out. It had made her wonder if tonight was the last chance they would have to get their relationship right.

"I'm upset about Jonah," Aubrey admitted. "He doesn't want to be my boyfriend anymore, which is good news, because I don't want to be his girlfriend, either. But that basically means we've been lying to each other for months. Everyone's been lying to everyone. Including you."

Rae exhaled through her nose. "What did I do?"

"You didn't tell me about Clara."

"Oh." Rae's arms slackened a little. "Yeah, I did do that."

Aubrey rubbed her eyes with the heels of her hands. "You're in love with one of our best friends, and you kept that from me for how long? Days? Months? *Years?*"

"Um. I never said anything about being 'in love' with her."

"But you are."

"How on earth do you know that?!"

"Because. You're my best friend. I know how you act around girls you like, and I know how you act around girls you *really* like, and you never acted either of those ways around Clara. Which means you must really, *reeeeallly* like her."

Rae squirmed. It wasn't news that Aubrey understood her better than anyone else did, but it was still disturbing to think she'd seen through Rae so easily. Especially since this felt so incredibly private. "I don't know." Rae scrambled to change the subject. "Is this because you're in love with Gabe?"

Aubrey sat on the bed, crossed her arms over her legs, and put her head down on top of them. The light from another apartment building bent through the shutters and over her body.

"Holy shit," Rae said. "Is that a yes? Are you saying we fell in love at the same time?"

"I'm not saying anything." Aubrey's voice was muffled.

"Holy shit!" Rae said again. "This is like if our periods synced. But *so* much weirder."

"I just want to go home. I miss my room and my parents and my stuff. I hate tiny bottles of shampoo, and I really hate these beds."

Rae wondered if the wine was starting to get to her, or if this bizarre long day was finally wearing them both down. She pushed herself off the door and sat with Aubrey. "This whole Clara-and-me thing, it's—kind of weird to talk about. And it's still new. Nothing even happened till Prague."

"But you had a thing for her." Aubrey lifted her head, her hair falling from her ponytail. There were red wine splatters all over her shirt. "You must have. It explains why you never mentioned liking anyone this year. And why you were so dismissive of everyone you kissed."

"I guess." Rae rapped the passport against her thigh. "But people are allowed to keep a few secrets. It's what humans do."

"I don't. Not with you, anyway. I've told you every embarrassing thing that's ever happened to me. I told you about stress-crying in the middle of my calculus final. And back in June, when the musical ended, I told you about kissing Gabe."

Rae felt a brief surge of irritation. "Yeah. And you told me *all* about you guys going to Rome together. *And* about making out in Berlin. You didn't spare me any detail."

"That's different!" Aubrey cried. "I wanted to tell you those things, but I—I couldn't. We haven't even been speaking. And I was confused. I didn't understand why Gabe and I kept kissing."

"Because you're into him."

"Yeah." Aubrey dropped her head to her knees again. "Thanks."

Rae ran her hand over the shaved patch at the back of her head. This wasn't going as well as she'd hoped.

"I'm so unbelievably sick of change," Aubrey said. "I hate that it's happening all at once."

"It isn't," Rae said. "You used to wear *Adventure Time* T-shirts every week and watch *High School Musical* obsessively. You don't do that anymore."

"That's not what I mean." Aubrey stood up, the floorboards murmuring. "That's just growing up. It's gradual. I tried to feel ready for graduation. And I tried to feel ready for this summer—I genuinely wanted my life to get so much bigger than it was. But I thought, when that happened, we'd be in it together."

"Well, that's ridiculous. We can't be each other's security blankets forever."

"Which you made extra sure of. By choosing to go to Australia."

"Well, where did you want me to go?" Rae couldn't hide her exasperation. "New York?"

"Yes!" Aubrey said. "Of course I did!"

Rae shut up. *What the hell?* Aubrey had never said anything like that to her before. They'd never—*never*—talked about going to college together.

"It was what we planned." Aubrey played with the ponytail

holder around her wrist. "When we watched those old movies that Lucy likes. We talked about riding sleeper trains all over Europe and getting an apartment somewhere so we could be roommates. We were going to spend every summer in a different country."

"But we were kids! We also talked about living in Antarctica and rescuing penguins."

"Yeah." Aubrey's voice was almost pleading. "But that doesn't mean it was *all* bullshit. Does it?"

Rae feigned an interest in the painting on the wall: the silent, unmoving fields, the sun frozen at midday. *Of course* it was bullshit. It had always been bullshit. Something fun to think about, something fun to dream about, but not something that was supposed to be real.

The last time they'd talked like that, they'd been twelve, maybe thirteen. And they were eighteen now.

Eighteen was when Rae was supposed to give up high school and her friends and her whole life in London. It was when she was supposed to bulldoze over everything and dive headfirst into whatever came next. Exactly the way her mom had.

But she wasn't stupid—she'd always known that would be tough. So she'd tried to harden herself to the fear, tried to tell herself she didn't feel it so much.

Rae thumbed through Aubrey's passport. It was strange, because now she could see that Aubrey and Clara were pretty similar in one way. They both didn't want to lose everything

269

they had now. They both didn't want to throw away their home and all the important memories they'd collected over the last few years. Clara had changed Rae's mind about so many things. She'd made Rae understand that she wanted to hold on, too—to those small, wonderful hopes she had for her future, to all the moments she'd found with Clara.

But, for some reason, Rae hadn't been trying to keep Aubrey in the same way. She'd been doing exactly what Aubrey had accused her of doing—pushing her aside, closing her out. And at the same time, she'd been pulling Clara closer.

Because she wasn't ready to let go of Clara yet.

But, maybe, she was ready to let go of Aubrey.

"Don't worry," Aubrey said. "I'm not going to leave now." But her voice sounded cold and flat.

Rae could only nod and stand up. She put Aubrey's passport on the bed and left the room, closing the door and listening to it click—putting even more walls between them.

29

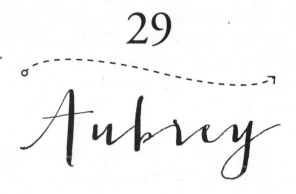

Aubrey

Monday, July 11
FLORENCE to BARCELONA

On the way to Barcelona, Aubrey sat in a separate carriage from everyone else, reading the same Virginia Woolf book she'd taken with her to Rome.

It was the middle of a long day of travel. Fourteen hours and five tight connections in order to get them from Italy to France to Spain. The train she was on now trundled through the South of France, a misty summer storm leaving streaks of water on the windows. Aubrey balled up her sweatshirt and used it as a pillow. Across the aisle from her, a mom placed plastic animals on her tray table and told a story about them to her toddler. The toddler sipped a juice box, listening closely.

Aubrey turned a page in her copy of *The Waves*. She'd

reached the part where the characters were on a train, too. Six of them, all leaving school. The narrator moved between their thoughts, shifting from fear to hope to ambivalence. Six different people. A track dividing six completely different ways.

A food cart rolled past, and Aubrey emerged from the story. Like she was waking up from the depths of sleep. Like the curtain had fallen at the end of a play.

She ordered a warm cup of tea and sipped it as she watched the rain. And while she did, she thought about Gabe and Rae. She thought about this morning, how, as they'd left the apartment, she'd avoided saying a word to Gabe. How she'd been too embarrassed to talk about last night. Or about Rome, which seemed so far away now.

And she thought about how certain she was that she and Rae weren't going to be friends like they had been before: attached at the hip; threaded together, so that when one moved, the other followed.

But maybe this was what needed to happen.

Since she'd never figured out how to be alone before, she would figure it out now. She would spend today with this tea and this window and the quiet company of this book. Books were better than friends anyway, because a book had never kissed a girl in Prague and then become all elusive and cagey about it. A book had never gotten bored of her or decided to move to the other side of the world from her or done mysterious things that Aubrey would inevitably find out about through social media—like hang out on a beach in Melbourne with a brand-new, hipster clique or get spur-of-the-moment tattoos and haircuts.

Aubrey's legs started to cramp. She got up and took her book, picking her way toward the back of the train. After the final carriage, she reached a door that opened onto a small vestibule with long glass panels looking over the tracks—the shadows of trees were spread across them, and a gray stripe of gravel ran beneath. Aubrey stood by the window. The whole scene kept changing in front of her, the tracks falling out from under her feet.

"Aubrey?" a voice said behind her.

She turned and saw Jonah walking toward the open door.

"Jonah," she said, "what are you doing here?"

"You know." He shrugged and seemed a little uneasy, but he came over to join her anyway. "I didn't feel like sitting. And hey, look at this. We found a cool view."

"Yeah," she said apprehensively. "I guess we did."

They watched the scenery pass by for a moment, his reflection next to hers. His hair was sun-bleached, and his clothes were dark. He looked different somehow—a little bit wilder, a little bit looser. It hadn't even been a week since he'd left, but he seemed almost older, too. Like he was one step closer to becoming the person he would someday be.

"Last night was pretty awkward," he said to the window.

"You could say that."

"And that wine," he said. "That wine was really bad."

273

Aubrey glimpsed at him. "How could you tell?"

"Technically, I don't know shit about wine. But yikes. That stuff tasted like a Cherry Coke that got drunk."

"Good point." The sunlight winked in the metal of the tracks; Aubrey tried to count the rushing trees.

"All right." He let out a breath. "So. Do you want to talk or what?"

"I don't know. Do you?"

He crammed his hands into his pockets. "I want to clear the air, yeah. And I want you to know I'm not *with* Leah now. We hung out, and she was cool about me staying with her, but I don't know where things will go from here."

"Jonah. You can be with anyone you want."

"I know. But still."

They stopped talking. Aubrey crossed her arms over her book and looked down. She and Jonah had never really dealt with long silences before—Jonah had always filled them even when Aubrey couldn't. She stared at the tan forming on top of her feet and at her shoes reflected in the glass. And beyond that, at the train tracks that continued to move beneath them. A seemingly endless string.

"Breaking up really sucks," she said.

"Yeah," he said. "It does."

She turned to the side to look at him. "Does everyone hate me now? Is that what they're saying when I'm not around?"

"No." He turned toward her, too. "Does everyone hate me? For leaving?"

"They were just confused. Well, Clara and Rae were confused. I don't think they expected us to break up, like, ever."

"*Ever?*"

"I know, right?" She pressed her elbow against the glass. "But I don't think I'd pictured it, either. I thought if it did happen, it would be sometime in the far, distant future. I thought we'd be so mature that maybe it wouldn't hurt as much. But I guess that was pretty ridiculous."

"No," he said. "It wasn't ridiculous."

Aubrey nodded. It was funny how even now—even after everything that had happened—she felt okay being around him. She was still comfortable sharing the same space as him.

"I guess you're pretty mad at me," she said. "And Gabe. Are you really mad at Gabe? You don't hate him now, do you?"

"I wouldn't say *hate*. I just—I don't know. I'll get over it." His eyes fell to the book in her arms. "What are you reading?"

"*The Waves*," she said eagerly. "By Virginia Woolf. Have you read it?"

"That's more your area than mine, Aubs." But he took it from her anyway. It was a paperback, a used copy she'd found at a bookstore near Lucy's antique shop. The cover was a photograph of waves cresting and foaming. The title ran across it in white.

"It's really perfect," Aubrey said. "It's about this group of friends who all go to school together when they're kids, but then they get older, and they start leading these really different lives. But I think the point is supposed to be that they're still connected in some way. Even when they don't talk to each other for years. Even when they're in completely different parts of the world."

Jonah opened the first page. "Sounds like an Aubrey book to me."

Aubrey bit her bottom lip. The train swayed a little, making it look like the tracks swayed, too. But Aubrey didn't lose her footing. She was here with Jonah, and, in some ways, things still felt the same. He was still cute and sincere and a little bit unkempt. She was still anxious and worried and overthinking everything. And they both still knew each other. They still held so many pieces of each other's lives. He gave her the book back, and she hugged it to her chest.

"Why did you come back?" she asked, her voice barely a whisper.

"This was our trip," he said. "I couldn't miss out on it. Not all of it, anyway."

Aubrey looked back outside and realized it wasn't raining any longer.

"And I don't hate Gabe," he said. "We'll probably even hang out again. Not right away, but you never know. Maybe we'll play some video games over winter break. Hash it out with simulated death."

"My parents are going to be so unhappy when I tell them we broke up. My mom will definitely still invite you to our Christmas party, though."

"Cool. But, Aubs. Your mom does remember I'm Jewish, right?"

"Yeah." Aubrey sighed. "I should probably remind her of that."

They both turned to face the window again, watching the view like they were watching a movie. Images on a screen. All that reflected light.

Aubrey squeezed her book even tighter. Standing so close to the window, it was almost like they'd let go of the train Like they were sailing this fast all by themselves. She wanted to stay there for hours as the scenery ran away behind them. Reminding her that they were here, they were here, they were here—and then they were gone.

30

Monday, July 11
BARCELONA

Y ou have to bring your camera," Clara said.

They'd arrived at their hostel in Barcelona just after nine PM, and Gabe's sister had already invited them to hang out at her apartment near the university. Rae and Clara were getting ready to go. Clara stood by the full-length mirror, winging her eyeliner, as Rae put on ChapStick and slung her camera bag across her neck. She glanced across the room to where Aubrey sat on her bed, reading *The Waves*. Behind her, the door to the balcony was open, framing Aubrey with a backdrop of buildings—all their red façades and long windows. She hadn't said much since they'd met up again at the

Barcelona Sants train station over an hour ago, but she hadn't tried to run home to London, either.

Rae decided to take that as a win.

"See you later," she said to Aubrey from the door.

"Yeah." Aubrey didn't look up from her book. "Later."

Rae and Clara headed out into the warm Barcelona night. The city was a burst of colors—reds, greens, and yellows. Everything shaded in rich, blazing hues—the gurgling fountains and the cafés advertising tapas and the palm trees planted along the roads. The air felt heavy and tropical, like it does before a thunderstorm. Rae could smell the sea nearby.

As they neared the university, Clara said, "I have this really great idea," and she tugged Rae through a set of heavy oak doors. Rae found herself in an entranceway with a shiny floor and bulletin boards covered in rumpled flyers. The ceiling arched above her, and to her side a boy sat on a bench looking over notes and bobbing his head to the music in his headphones.

"Is this a cultural landmark or something?" Rae asked. "Or—oh! Is it Hogwarts?"

"Could be," Clara said. "But it's also a college. I wanted to see what it's like to be in one of these."

"It reminds me of high school. But, like, bigger."

Clara knotted their hands together. "Just act like you belong."

They started exploring the hallways. Most of the lights had been turned off, and most of the students must have gone home by now, because there weren't many other people around. When a janitor pushed a cart of cleaning supplies past them, Rae half expected him to say something—to ask who they were or demand to see their student IDs. But he barely even glanced their way. Maybe they really did look like students. Maybe they looked like they actually belonged.

At the end of one hall, they stumbled into an empty courtyard. Covered passageways lined its peripheries, and a few chairs with desks attached to them—the same kind Rae had sat in for years at LAS—were stacked in the corners. But in the lawn at the center was a tree, its branches fanned out and filled with bright-orange fruit. Even covered in shadows, Rae could see how vividly green the leaves were. How the orange fruit glowed.

Clara put her purse next to a desk and went to stand by the tree. She had on the same silver dress she'd worn their first night in Paris, but her hair was styled differently now, tied into a low, loose knot. Her shoes were the purple sequined ballet flats she'd had on the day they traveled to Prague. "Do you think this is what it will feel like to be in Melbourne?" she asked.

"Not exactly." Rae took the lens cap off her camera and took a picture of the arches in the passageways. "Considering it's a different city."

"Yeah. You're probably right."

Rae walked across the courtyard while Clara fidgeted with the sides of her dress. "But maybe it could be like this," she said. "If—I were with you."

Rae stopped. "If you were with me?"

"As long as you want that? As long as you don't mind if I come visit?"

"Yes!" Rae's heart swelled. "Wait—I mean, *no*, I don't mind. And yes, I really want that."

"You do?"

"Of course I do! But you remember it's Australia, right? It's about a million miles from California."

Clara's face filled with affection. "I think I could probably get a flight there. Also, I have long summer breaks."

"Which are winters in Australia."

"I like winter." Clara kicked some grass at Rae's feet. "I like hot chocolate and radiators. I'll even bring gloves."

Rae plucked at one of her curls. "Seriously, though. You don't have to. If you meet someone else. If you realize you've made a rash decision, I'll totally get it."

"Rae." Clara circled her fingers lightly around Rae's wrist. Here, in this abandoned place, the only sounds she could hear were cicadas and the swish of leaves. But also, she could see so many moments coming to life: Clara waiting to meet her at an airport in Australia and then coming to campus with her. The two of them sharing Rae's tiny dorm bed. And Rae would fly to see her in California, too. They'd lie on the beach together until late at night. They'd wander boardwalks and eat dinner outside. These weren't concrete plans or anything, but they still felt possible. They felt true.

Rae pushed her camera to one side, and she and Clara slipped together. They kissed beneath an orange-green tree in the middle of a magical city, and everything seemed so right. It seemed like there were so many options now. So many minutes and days spread out in front of her. So many opportunities to find her way back to the people she cared about.

She pulled away from the kiss. "Oh no!" she said.

"*Oh no?*" Clara scrunched up her nose. "What exactly is *oh no* right now?"

"Not you." Rae shook her head. "I just thought about Aubrey."

Clara moved farther back.

"Not like that!" Rae said. "And this is seriously the worst timing ever, but—I remembered her sitting in that sad room all by herself."

"Yeah," Clara said.

Rae's thoughts were going a million miles a minute. She felt weightless, a little bit with hope and a little bit with fear. But mostly she felt stupid over how she'd been treating Aubrey—she couldn't believe she'd thought that they had to fall apart. "You were so right, Clara," she said. "You were *so* right when you said I needed to talk to her. And when you said I might regret leaving things like this. I thought I was cool with it, but I guess I'm really not."

Clara grinned. "I love being right."

And when they kissed again, Clara pulled her back against the tree. Rae's pulse raced. She thought about all the kisses just like this one, about how this one wouldn't be the last. She tasted Clara's lip gloss; she felt the night and her whole world expand; she heard—something *scritch* behind her. A door being thrown open, voices giggling, feet stamping.

A class had just gotten out.

"Maybe we should go." Clara rubbed her mouth with the back of her hand. Together, she and Rae ran through the hallways, their laughter echoing as they fell out the door and back into the night.

Clara kissed her again and Rae felt like they were spinning. Or maybe Barcelona was spinning around them. A reverse merry-go-round. The kiss ended, but Rae felt lit up. Tonight was electric, and she was alive.

"Go back," Clara said, her breath against Rae's cheek. "Invite her out. And then come find me."

As soon as she reached their hostel room door, though, Rae felt a lot less certain.

Aubrey wouldn't want to talk to her. Rae was going to walk in there, and Aubrey was going to ignore her, and that was going to be really freaking uncomfortable. Maybe Rae should just leave, go find Clara instead.

She walked a few steps away from the door before she

remembered how she'd felt when she'd talked to Clara. Like everything was beginning, not ending. Like her life was blooming, not shrinking. She didn't have to give up on her friendship with Aubrey. She wasn't going to let herself.

She came back, turned the handle, and walked in on Aubrey... putting on sandals.

"Oh." Rae paused. "Are you going out?"

"We just got to Barcelona," Aubrey said. "Did you think I was going to stay inside all night?"

Yes, Rae thought. "No," she said. "But I guess I figured you wouldn't want to go alone."

"I can handle myself." Aubrey was wearing her glasses instead of contacts, which she only did when she'd been reading for hours. And Rae recognized her super-short white shorts and V-neck blue shirt as an outfit they'd picked out together at H&M.

"Clara's at Gabe's sister's apartment," Rae said. "That's why I'm here. You should come with."

Aubrey hesitated. "No thanks. I can't."

"You *can't?*"

"I guess I *can*, but I don't want to. I've been dying to see what the city looks like at night." She placed her wallet in her purse.

"In that case..." Rae paused, deliberating. "Is it all right if I come, too?"

A look flickered over Aubrey's face—Rae couldn't tell

for sure, but she thought it might have been relief. "Yeah," Aubrey said. "It's all right with me."

The city seemed awake now, even more so than it had when Rae had left with Clara. Every table at every restaurant was full. Every shop was open and all the streets flowed with traffic. It felt like everyone was out, like everyone had somewhere to be.

Aubrey took them in the opposite direction from the university, walking quickly. "You seem to know where you're going," Rae said.

"I look at a lot of maps. Have you really not figured that out about me yet?"

"And you're a confident walker," Rae said. "That's an important skill to have in New York. Walk confidently, hold your purse by your side, carry your key in your hand when you go home alone at night."

"Are these things Lucy told you?"

"Oh please. Lucy's oblivious. I learned it from *Forensic Files*."

"Helpful." Aubrey smirked. They turned onto a long avenue with dozens of glitzy storefronts twinkling in the dark. It reminded Rae of the Champs-Élysées on their first night in Paris. And of the canals she, Aubrey, and Gabe had walked along in Amsterdam. And of the square she and Clara had stumbled onto in Prague. It had the same energy, the same liveliness. Rae felt the same way she had in each of those other places—like the night had barely begun.

A group of women wearing expensive-looking clothes came out of a bar, filling the night with the heady smell of perfume. Rae and Aubrey separated as they veered around them. When they came back together again, Aubrey said, "Jonah and I talked today."

"When?" Rae said. "Just now?"

"A few hours ago. Somewhere in the South of France."

"Damn." Rae messed with the settings on her camera. "What did you say?"

"Not much. But we're definitely broken up now. I mean, we were definitely broken up before, but—it feels more final now. If that's even possible."

"It is," Rae said. "I think. So, you're okay with it?"

They stopped at a red light. The boulevard reached ahead of them, seemingly for miles, before bumping into a series of hills at the horizon.

"I am," Aubrey said. "I think." Their conversation was less stilted than Rae had thought it would be. And the fact that they were talking at all had to be a positive thing. Plus, she couldn't ignore this atmosphere, the way it crackled and hummed, the way it made her think of all the nights they'd spent hanging out in London, picking up smoothies in Covent Garden and crossing Waterloo Bridge just to gaze at the skyline, just to feel awestruck by the city they lived in.

They crossed the street, but Rae slowed down a little. "Aubs," she said. "Smile."

Rae captured her mid-turn and grinning. "Cute," she said.

"Wait," Aubrey said. She pointed to the background of the picture, right behind where she'd been standing. "What's that?" They both looked up at the needle-thin spires rising between blocky buildings. Aubrey cast Rae a quick look, and they picked up their pace, diving around streetlights and trash cans, racing like kids through a playground obstacle course.

When they finally reached it, Rae's first instinct was to take a picture. She *had* to take a picture of something like this. But she couldn't make herself move. The church took over her entire field of vision. Its spires were illuminated, extending toward the sky like arms. Up close, it looked as if the whole thing were made of muscle and sinew. The carvings that covered its body seemed to ripple with motion. It wasn't frozen. It wasn't capturing some long lost moment from the far-off past.

It was alive. It was breathing.

"It's so..." Aubrey staggered.

"Tall," Rae finished for her. And now she did take a picture. "What should we do? Can we go inside?"

"It has to be closed by now. But we can still stare at it, I guess."

They wandered around it until they found a bench by a tourist stall, where they sat, still mesmerized. Rae thought again of everything she'd seen this week: the Louvre in Paris, the canals in Amsterdam, the Astronomical Clock in Prague, and the Botticelli paintings in Florence. Of all those things, she couldn't believe Clara wasn't here for this one.

"It's the Sagrada Família." Aubrey pulled up the Wikipedia entry on her phone to show Rae. "This has to be the most famous church in Spain. Maybe even Europe."

Rae lowered her camera. "Europe is really all about churches, isn't it? That's my main takeaway from this trip. Churches, old art, trains."

Aubrey looped the strap of her purse around her index finger. "Do you mind if I ask you something?"

"About Europe?"

"No." Aubrey let go of the purse strap. "I guess I'm still thinking about Jonah. And how not-devastated I am that we broke up. Honestly, talking to him on the train today, I could tell we *both* felt lighter now that we're over. Is that seriously messed up? I mean, is there something wrong with me?"

"Of course there isn't," Rae said gently. "There were signs that you and Jonah weren't on the happily-ever-after path. You did *kiss* Gabe a few weeks ago. And also a few days ago. And yesterday—"

"Anyway." Aubrey's face went a dark shade of red. "That's not going to happen with you and Clara, is it? You two aren't breaking up anytime soon?"

"No," Rae said, "we're not."

Aubrey dropped her gaze to her purse. "You could have told me, you know. That you liked her."

"I know." Rae placed her camera on the other side of her so she could move closer to Aubrey. "And a part of me really wanted to. If the idea of telling *anyone* hadn't freaked me the fuck out, I would have totally told you."

"So, tell me now. And start with the fact that I wasn't wrong, was I? You are in love with her."

Rae peeled a loose splinter of wood off the bench and flicked it at Aubrey's leg. "*Yes.* Which is so weird, because my original plan was to stop thinking about her once I left. But that's definitely not it anymore. It feels like there could be a future for us."

"That's seriously big," Aubrey said.

Now Rae felt herself blush. "She's already talking about visiting Melbourne, and I could go to California during one of my breaks. I have this very specific image of the two of us hanging out under some palm trees. Although, honestly, that's probably because I don't know anything about California."

Aubrey laughed, but she still sounded shy.

"Are you sure you want to talk about this?" Rae tried to gauge her reaction. "Is it too weird for you?"

Aubrey flicked the splinter back at Rae. "You really think *this* is the weirdest thing that's happened to me since we left London?"

Rae fell back against the bench, shoulders quaking with laughter. "Oh my God! Has *anything* about this trip been normal?"

"How about when I got drunk and tried to set up Clara and Gabe?"

"Oh, that was super normal." Rae hiccuped. "But not as normal as Gabe coming with me to get a haircut."

"Or when Jonah showed up in Florence."

"And when Clara and I decorated the entire apartment! And Clara yelled, '*Surprise!*'"

They were both laughing now. Rae gasped for breath, leaning back against the bench to trace the tops of the spires with her eyes. "Just think," she said. "We've got all of tonight and a whole other day of this trip left to go. Who knows what weird stuff will happen next?"

"Yeah." Aubrey pushed her glasses up her nose. "I guess that depends on whether I can steer clear of certain people or not."

"And by 'certain people,' you mean Gabe?"

"He didn't—say anything about me today? On the train?"

Rae tilted her head one way and then the other. "Nah," she said. "But he was pretty quiet. What's going on with you guys?"

"Nothing," Aubrey said. "Or—I don't know. I just needed some space."

"You could call him now, though. Tell him, *Sorry, Rae and I took a detour to some enormous church, but we're on our way over.*"

Aubrey seemed to withdraw again. "I can't do that."

"It's easy, I swear. I'll even dial his number for you."

The Sagrada Familia grew brighter and brighter, becoming a beacon as the city sank toward night. Even at this hour, the air was still humid; it smelled of hot sidewalks and the sea.

"There's no point," Aubrey said. "You said it yourself. We can't be each other's security blankets forever. When I was talking to Jonah earlier, I understood what you meant by that. I realized you were right."

"I wasn't right." Rae thwacked Aubrey's arm.

"*Ouch*," Aubrey said. "Jesus, do you realize how strong you are?"

"I might be small, but I'm scrappy as hell," Rae said. "And listen. Because this is important. Although I do love the idea of being right basically all the time, in this particular case, I was wrong. *Incredibly* wrong. You're allowed to leave home and stay in touch with your friends at the same time. That's the whole reason I'm here. Because I've been a dickhead to you recently."

Aubrey was still rubbing her arm. "I get why you were mad at me, though. Everything felt like it was spinning out of control, and I handled it really badly."

"But I made it worse because you could tell I was keeping shit from you. Which I was. You totally called it."

Aubrey's eyes were cautious. "Does this mean you want to keep in touch? Even after you go to Australia?"

"Of course I do." This time, Rae took both of Aubrey's hands. "I'm going to be traveling with *my mother* till January. I'll need to talk to you frequently. Possibly every day."

"Yeah, but then you'll start school."

"Exactly! And since you won't be spending your entire New York life with Jonah, I expect you to get your ass up in the middle of the night and Skype me whenever I feel like it."

"Tyrant." Aubrey smiled a little. The sky was dark now, but lights around the church turned the stone yellow and orange. Like the leftover glow from a sunset.

Rae's phone started to ring, and she let go of Aubrey's hands to check it. It was Clara, but she didn't answer right away.

"I guess she must be wondering where you are," Aubrey said.

"Yeah," Rae said.

Aubrey adjusted her purse in her lap. "Do you know how to get to Zaida's apartment?"

"Nope. But I'll figure it out." The phone stopped ringing, and Rae typed Clara a text, letting her know she'd be there soon.

"I doubt it's complicated," Aubrey said. "Just look it up on Google Maps."

Rae concentrated on the church for a moment, like she was trying to read something in its elaborate carvings. "You know what, though? I suck at directions. Remember that time we had to meet at the British Museum for a field trip and I got lost? I ended up at that random McDonald's instead."

"You didn't 'get lost.' You pretended you did so you could go get a McFlurry."

"Still." Rae placed her phone on the bench between them. "I'm bad at maps. Absolute garbage."

Aubrey sighed through her nose, but she took the phone anyway and opened up a map. "Lucky for you," she said, "I'm really effing great at them."

31

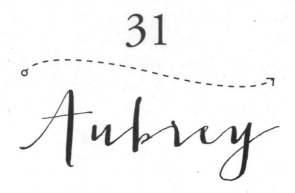

Aubrey

Monday, July 11
BARCELONA

Aubrey was sweating.

Maybe because it was hot outside. Or maybe because the streets were jam-packed—young people in skimpy summer clothes escaping their humid apartments, carrying drinks, and milling around the sidewalk with friends.

Aubrey and Rae were by the university now, and according to Rae's phone, the apartment was only a few minutes away. Aubrey wished she'd thought to put her contacts back in. She wished she'd brought a hairbrush or some deodorant in her purse.

"This must be it," Rae said. They'd reached a building with an arched stained-glass window above the front door.

Aubrey checked the number beside it. "Yeah," she said. "Must be."

Rae pressed a button, and the intercom buzzed. But Aubrey was staring up at all the windows, trying to guess which one Gabe was behind, trying to imagine what he was doing right this second—if he was wondering who had just buzzed up, if he was staring at his phone and asking himself why she hadn't texted yet.

Or maybe he'd forgotten all about her. Maybe he didn't care where she was.

"Dude." Rae held the door open for her. "You look so pale. You're not going to faint or anything, are you?"

"No." Aubrey stepped inside. The door shut behind her, and the street noise extinguished like a snuffed-out candle. "At least, I don't think so."

It was dark in the lobby, and their eyes took a few seconds to adjust. Low lightbulbs droned above. There was a blue, black, and orange mosaic printed on the floor and burnished gold mailboxes built into the walls. In front of them, Aubrey saw an old-fashioned elevator, its copper gears coated in dust. Rae touched the grated door. "This looks kind of—antique."

"You mean death-trappy," Aubrey said. "We should take the stairs."

They looped around landing after landing, past walls with a pattern of roses and vines on them, vines that seemed to grow after Aubrey and Rae.

"Did Clara say who was here?" Aubrey asked.

"No. But she told me we should come over fast."

"They must be bored," Aubrey said. "It's probably just Jonah, Clara, and Gabe sitting with Zaida and her roommates. They probably don't have anything to say to each other." Her head felt like it was swimming. Every floor brought her a little closer to Gabe—a little closer to seeing him again, a little closer to being in the exact same room.

"We'll need to liven things up," Rae said. "We'll have to be the entertainment." One floor above them, a couple emerged from an apartment, speaking to each other in a mix of Spanish and English. Hipster rock music poured out after them, the song ringing all the way down the stairwell. Rae lifted an eyebrow at Aubrey. "Then again, maybe not."

The apartment itself was brighter and a lot louder than the rest of the building. The furnishings were simple but nice: a coral couch with a quilt thrown over its back, a beat-up leather armchair with a few split seams along the sides, and old movie posters hanging on the walls. But beyond that, the only thing Aubrey saw were *people*. They overwhelmed every inch of the room. They flicked cigarette ash out the window and huddled near the iPhone dock debating music choices.

Clara emerged from behind a boy wearing a Salvador Dalí T-shirt. "Aubrey! Rae!" She held a plastic tumbler over her head. "Zaida threw us a party!"

"I can see that," Aubrey said.

"Three parties in one week." Rae took the tumbler from Clara and had a drink. "Not bad for a bunch of theater nerds."

Aubrey worried one end of her glasses. She tried to take stock of everyone in the apartment and noticed Jonah in a far corner, talking to a girl with a flower crown in her hair. When he caught sight of Aubrey, he lifted one hand in a static wave. She lifted her hand, too. They probably wouldn't talk tonight, but still. It felt important to acknowledge him.

"You came with Rae!" Clara said in Aubrey's ear.

"She talked me into it," Aubrey said.

Clara radiated delight. Rae said something to her that Aubrey couldn't make out, and Clara whispered something back. Now that Aubrey could see them like this, she was amazed it had never occurred to her that they should be together. Had she really never noticed how much Rae *smiled* when Clara was around?

"Hey!" Clara shouted at someone behind Aubrey. "Look who I found!"

Instantly, Aubrey's insides turned over; her hands went cold. The entire party seemed to muffle, like Aubrey was hearing it from the other side of a wall. He was here. He was only a few inches away from her.

"Glad you made it," Zaida said, joining their circle.

Zaida.

Not Gabe.

"Hi," Aubrey said. The pressure inside her fizzled to nothing. "This is a great party."

"Thanks." Zaida sipped from her beer bottle. She wore an orange maxi dress and long, dangly gold earrings. Although she was shorter than Gabe, she definitely looked like she was related to him. She had the same heart-shaped face and the same dimples when she smiled. "Honestly though," she said, "I have no idea who half these people are. My roommates have too many friends."

A guy jumped onto the couch, pumping both his fists in the air. "We're going to get more alcohol!" he shouted, and the room erupted in cheers.

"Roommate?" Rae asked.

"Roommate's boyfriend," Zaida said. "But yeah, basically a roommate at this point."

The crowd flowed around them. Aubrey felt like there were marbles tipping and scattering in her stomach. *Ask her*, she thought. *Just ask Zaida where Gabe is.*

"So, where's Gabe?" Clara asked.

Thank God, Aubrey thought. Who was she kidding? She would never have been able to do it herself.

"He's probably on the roof," Zaida said.

"*The roof?*" Aubrey said. "Why would he be there? Isn't it dangerous?"

"There's a garden up there." Zaida yawned and flicked her hair, making her earrings shimmer. "My little brother can fake being an extrovert when he has to, but the kid needs his alone time."

Rae's gaze locked with Aubrey's.

"So," Zaida said, "do you want a drink?"

"No!" Aubrey cried. And then she dialed it down a notch.

"Um. No thanks. I just, I need to go. For a minute. I think I dropped my phone on the stairs."

She turned and darted back into the hallway, where she stood beneath a light fixture and wondered how the hell to get to the roof. Music vibrated through the hall. "Up," she said out loud to herself. "Duh, Aubrey. Roofs are up." She thumped up the stairs to the top floor. The ceiling was low here, and there were no apartment doors, only a single metal one wedged partially open with a heavy book. Aubrey held her hand up to the door's gap.

She could feel the air outside.

Footsteps headed toward her, and Aubrey got out of the way as a girl and two guys shoved through the door. One of the guys had a cigarette behind his ear. The girl accidentally stepped out of her flip-flops and paused to slide them back on, calling after the guys to wait. Even after they'd left, Aubrey could hear their voices drifting all the way to the lobby. She turned back around, and the door was still wide open.

Because Gabe was holding it.

Oxygen filled her lungs. A gust of wind blew right past them, pushing her hair into her eyes. She held it back with one hand.

"What are you doing here?" they asked at the same time.

She flushed. He did, too.

"Zaida told me about the roof," she said. "She mentioned there was a garden?"

"Yeah, see for yourself." Gabe moved out of the way so she

could come outside with him. They climbed one more set of stairs together, and when they reached the top, Aubrey found herself surrounded by ceramic pots, all of them overgrown with small trees and purple flowers and vines that climbed over low walls circling the edges. Twinkle lights had been strung through some of the trees, and a crescent moon hovered in the sky, gossamer clouds slipping across it.

This didn't seem real. It didn't seem like a place that could exist among so many buildings and boulevards. Aubrey felt like she'd fallen through a portal. Like they were somewhere no one else would be able to find them.

"Why didn't your sister have the party up here?" she asked, stunned.

Gabe sat down on a blue-and-white lounger. "It's an exposed concrete square six floors above the ground. Probably not the best place for people to get drunk."

"Fair point." Aubrey walked over to one of the walls. She could see the iridescent city below in every direction—its busy skyline and speeding headlights, its miniature café umbrellas and dark, distant hills. The sound of passing cars and music kept carrying up toward them.

"It feels like the whole city is throwing the same party," she said. "Do you think it's always like this here?"

"It's a nice night and the middle of summer," he said. "People are enjoying it."

Aubrey maneuvered between the plants to sit on the lounger across from his. The plastic strips bit into her legs.

Gabe had his hands linked between his knees. His shirt was neon pink, and his shorts were dark, striated denim.

"You look extra hipster tonight," she said.

"I am dressed for a party."

"Which you convinced your sister to throw for us."

"Well." He shrugged. "I pulled the few strings I have."

She sat forward. "Your sister and all your best friends are downstairs. Everyone in Barcelona is out having the time of their lives, and you're avoiding all of it."

"Bryce." He sat forward as well. "What are you doing here?"

"Gabe," she said, "I . . ." And here it was: the part where she wanted to bail. The part where she wanted to start a new conversation so she wouldn't have to find out where they would go from here. So she wouldn't have to say how she felt and risk her heart on someone who was leaving so soon.

But even though she was scared, she also knew she had to do this. It should have felt precarious, sitting like this, balancing on a platform above a city that was a blanket of lights. But for once, Aubrey felt steady. She felt certain. "I'm here to see you," she said.

His expression was unreadable. Whatever he thought of her, she couldn't figure it out. "Don't worry," he said. "I already understand."

"Wait. Understand what?"

"What you're about to tell me. About how I can't get in your way."

Now it was her turn to be baffled. "Gabe. What are you talking about?"

His shoulders hunched. "It's obvious, isn't it? I can't get in the way of you moving on from Jonah. I can't get in the way of you going to New York and starting your *life*. I refuse to be that guy, okay? You clearly want time to deal with the stuff that's been happening, and I'm not going to be some shitty dude who demands you give all your attention to me."

A breeze picked up, carrying with it the scent of flowers. "Is that why you didn't talk to me today?" she asked.

"You wanted me to leave you alone. I could tell."

She sat on the very edge of the lounger. "No, that's not it. I did need some time, but not because I wanted to get away from you. I was just—*terrified*. Of how this summer is going to end soon. Of how close I am to losing you and Rae and— everything. I'd never thought of my life without all of you in it. I'd done everything I could not to have to face that."

"But you're facing it now?"

"I think so," she said. "I'm trying, anyway. And this is what I'm starting to realize: Maybe I can't have things exactly the way they are now, but I can still have them. I can go to Columbia and I can still talk to Rae. I can still talk to you." Her courage fumbled. She focused above her, on the shape of the moon. "Especially you."

A beat of silence. "Why especially me?"

"Because. I think I'm in love with you."

Gabe went quiet again. So quiet that she could hear his

inhales and exhales. So quiet that she thought maybe, this time, she'd lost him for sure.

And then he crossed the distance separating their chairs, and he kissed her.

They stood together, the sudden breeze growing stronger. It snagged at their hair and their clothes. Aubrey was on her tiptoes to reach his mouth; he ducked down to meet hers. And in that moment, with the noisy city beneath them, it really did feel like the entire world was celebrating. Like the atmosphere fizzed with champagne. When they finally broke apart, she was shaking.

"Is that an *I love you* back?" she asked. "I just want to be clear. For the record. For—historical purposes."

"It was an *I love you* back." He kissed the corner of her lips. "It was a *this could be the start of something, right?*" He trailed his fingers down her back, sending a line of sparks down her spine.

Making understanding wash through her.

Making everything clear.

Maybe she was about to lose a hundred things—things she was always going to lose, things she couldn't help. But she was gaining a thousand more—things she couldn't even begin to guess.

And she didn't want to guess yet. The possibilities were there, and they were all she needed. They were enough.

"This could be the start of something." She pulled his mouth to hers again. "Right."

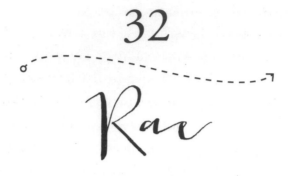

32

Rae

Wednesday, July 13
BARCELONA to LONDON

Their plane back to London was delayed.
Again.

"Another hour." Gabe returned from the flight desk, flopping into his chair beside Aubrey.

"It's nearly ten o'clock," Clara whimpered. "How did it get so late?"

"Don't know," Jonah said. "Because that's how time works?" He'd gone to the magazine stand across the departure lounge a few minutes ago and brought back sodas and bags of potato chips. He tossed a bag at Clara. She caught it and pulled it open.

Aubrey was the only one not paying attention. She was

reading the end of *The Waves*, completely rapt. Rae's sketchbook was propped against her bent legs, and she was drawing each of them in turn—Clara curled up in her seat, one of her two braids undone; Gabe looking around, interested in everything going on nearby; Jonah eating chips; Aubrey reading.

In a few hours, when they finally landed in London, it would be after midnight. Lucy would be waiting at Heathrow to drive Rae home, and when they reached the house, Iorek would dance around the kitchen while Lucy made peppermint tea. She would chastise Rae for not even mentioning getting her hair cut. She would ask to look through all her photographs and sketches. She would ask her how she felt now that the trip was over.

And Rae would say she felt exactly the same and completely different.

There was no other way to describe it.

Aubrey looked up from her book, eyes brimming with tears. "That was the best book I've ever read," she said.

"Oh no." Clara yawned, pressing her cheek to Rae's shoulder. "Is it sad? Does someone die at the end?"

"I don't really know." Aubrey sniffled. "It might be about how we're all going to die eventually?"

"Bummer," Jonah said. His phone chimed, and he wiped chip crumbs from his hands before checking it.

"Poor Bryce," Gabe said. He placed his arm on the armrest between them so it lined up exactly with hers. Rae watched them, searching for a clue as to what had happened at Zaida's party two nights ago. Aubrey had said they were okay again, but clearly there was more to it than that. They didn't hold hands or kiss—not in front of the rest of them, at least—but something was connecting them in a way they hadn't been connected before. They seemed drawn together even when they weren't physically close.

"I know what will cheer you up," Rae said and closed her sketchbook. "Aubs. Come with me."

Together, they passed long banks of empty seats and stopped at the huge windows that looked onto the tarmac. Sleek airplanes waited in the dark, poised for flight.

"This is what's going to cheer me up?" Aubrey asked. "Looking at planes?"

"We're in an airport," Rae said. "I've only got so much to work with."

Aubrey's mouth flicked upward. "Well, when you put it that way."

There weren't many flights boarding just then, and the terminal felt vacant and kind of sparse. Rae liked how still everything seemed, how the only people around drank coffee or typed quietly on their laptops. How, here, even time felt like it was moving a little slower. Through the glass, she saw a plane take off, heard a *whoosh* as it lifted into the air. It was all so different from what she'd become used to—the unending clatter of trains, the nearness of their coming and going.

"I'd never flown anywhere until I moved to London,"

Aubrey said, staring at the plane's blinking lights as it climbed higher and higher. "Did I ever tell you that?"

"Seriously?" Rae said. "Me neither."

"You hadn't?" Aubrey pulled away from the window.

"Nope. Lucy and I used to drive everywhere. She pretends she's fine with it, but she actually *hates* flying."

"My parents thought I would hate it, too," Aubrey said, "since I was such a nervous kid. But I kept reading so many books about London and seeing so many movies that were set there. I couldn't wait to find out if it would live up."

Rae scrutinized her best friend's features. "Can I tell you a secret?"

"Obviously."

"I was totally afraid. I cried the whole way from Atlanta to London."

Aubrey's face split into a smile. "That's not possible! *How* were you more scared of something than I was?"

Rae twisted one of the metal buttons on her denim jacket. "Life's full of unanswerable questions, I guess."

They both faced the window as another plane got ready to take off. The denim jacket was one Rae had borrowed from Clara, and she'd painted her nails the same purple as Clara's as well—although she'd chipped half the polish off already. "Okay," she said. "Your turn to tell me a secret. What's the deal with you and Gabe now?"

"There's no deal." Aubrey put her hands on the glass. "I'm

leaving in a few weeks. So we're going to spend those weeks together."

"A few *weeks*? Is that it?"

"For now, anyway. And that's not exactly nothing."

Rae hugged her jacket around herself. "I've got less than a day, I guess."

Aubrey's gaze tracked a curling line that moved across the sky. "Let's hang out tomorrow. We'll go to Borough Market and get free samples from all the food stalls. Then we'll get buzzed on strong coffee and sit on the lawn outside the Tate Modern until the absolute last second we can. You, me, and Clara."

"That," Rae said, "sounds awesome."

"It does, right?" Aubrey seemed hopeful now, but Rae felt kind of sad. She tried to memorize the feeling of standing right there. She wanted to make sure that when she thought of this night later, she would think of her and Aubrey.

Blending into each other. Part of the same thing.

Eventually, Clara's voice called them over. "Our flight's about to board. We might actually leave this time."

Clara was holding Rae's sketchbook, and she was wearing one of Rae's shirts—an oversize button-up with the sleeves cut off that Rae had bought at a charity shop junior year. "Will you show me what you were working on?" Clara asked.

"Yeah," Rae said. "But fair warning: It's still pretty rough." She and Clara bowed over the sketchbook as Rae flipped through the pictures she'd drawn over the nearly two weeks they'd been gone—the first one was of the Seine, a river of glittering black ink that sliced through the center of the page, Clara sitting on its bank, her hair whipping around her face. Rae got to the pictures she'd drawn on that frenzied sleepless night in Amsterdam: one of the five of them sprawled out on the train from Paris; one of the houseboat party and teenagers dancing on a deck; one of Aubrey and Gabe by a canal, their bodies fluid with conversation, as fluid as the water they were balanced beside.

The last picture was drawn in ink—Rae hadn't wanted to start with pencil; she'd wanted it to feel permanent.

It was Aubrey, Gabe, Clara, and Jonah. Waiting for a plane.

The woman at their gate picked up a phone and made an announcement. She told them to get their boarding passes and passports ready. There was a stir in the departure lounge as people began to gather their things.

"Here we go, kids." Jonah slid his phone into his back pocket. "Real life begins right now."

"This has been real life," Clara said defensively.

"Fine," Jonah said. "Real Life: Part Two."

Gabe took Aubrey's paperback and put it neatly in his bag for her. She looked cold, so he gave her his hoodie, and she pulled the sleeves down over her hands. They didn't make eye contact, and they weren't speaking right then, but Rae could almost hear the quiet words they weren't saying, the plans they were silently making for all the upcoming days they'd have together.

Next to her, Clara had gone back to examining the picture. "You didn't add yourself," she said.

"Huh?" Rae said.

"This sketch. It's of all of us. But you should be in it, too. Maybe you can draw another from a picture." She took Rae's camera bag and waved down their friends. "No one's allowed to leave yet!"

Aubrey groaned. "But it's so late. And we all look sleepy."

"That doesn't matter," Clara said. "These are our last minutes in Barcelona. We need an honest representation of how they happened." She herded them into a group by the line of people boarding the plane. Clara held the camera out in front of them.

"This will never work," Jonah said.

"Can you even tell if we're all in it?" Gabe asked.

"It's totally fine if I'm not!" Aubrey said.

"Guys," Rae said, "Clara will make this rad, trust me."

"Thank you." Clara kissed Rae's cheek. And Rae closed her eyes. And as she did, the flash went off in front of her, a bright purple-blue starburst. Everyone yelped and complained.

Another announcement came from their gate. A final call for boarding. Aubrey, Gabe, and Jonah made their way into the line, but Clara and Rae lingered for one more moment.

"We should check the picture," Clara said. "Make sure it looks all right."

"Let's post it online right now," Rae said. "Aubrey will love us."

But Jonah was right—it hadn't worked at all. Rae's eyes were closed, and Clara's face was a pale smudge as she kissed her cheek. Jonah was sticking out his tongue, and Gabe and Aubrey weren't looking at the camera, because they were looking at each other.

It almost seemed like an illusion. The five of them in this completely new arrangement. Standing together in a way that, when this trip began, they never could have dreamed of. But also, it made perfect sense.

Completely different.

Exactly the same.

"Rae?" Clara whispered. Their hands clasped. "It's time to go."

"Okay," Rae said, but she kissed Clara one last time. It was a kiss to make her grounded, a kiss to make her still. A kiss to let her swallow every last fragile second of this day and this trip. Rae felt those seconds filling her lungs. She felt each one freezing, like a photograph she could take out and look at later.

The kiss ended, and color blotched Clara's cheeks. "We should go," she said. "Are you ready?"

Rae squeezed Clara's hand in return. "Yeah," she said. "I'm ready now."

ACKNOWLEDGMENTS

Writing this novel was a little bit like interrailing through Europe. Sometimes it was all beautiful views and gelato in the sunshine. Other times? It was more like losing my passport and sobbing in random train stations. I'm lucky to have been surrounded by so many people who helped me draw the lines that would eventually connect this story.

Molly Ker Hawn: You are a superstar and superhero. It's impossible to overstate how grateful I am to have you in my corner, so I'll just say this—I could bake you a million chocolate chip shortbreads as a gesture of thanks and still owe you a million more.

Pam Gruber: Your humor, heart, and guiding hand kept this book on track even when I feared it was going off the rails. (Sorry for all the train metaphors!) Thank you for the wit and wisdom you brought to Aubrey and Rae's story and for never losing faith that it would come together in the end.

This cross-continental gal hit the jackpot when she found her home at Little, Brown Books for Young Readers in the US and UK. Bouquets of roses to these members of Team USA: Farrin Jacobs, Megan Tingley, Victoria Stapleton, Hannah Milton, Stef Hoffman, Jessica Shoffel, Danielle Yadao, Karina Granda, and Jen Graham. And to Tina McIntyre, who has supported me through every iteration of my publishing career. Bouquets of roses as well to these members of Team UK: Kate Agar, Stephanie Allen, Laure Pernette, Emily Thomas, and Sophie Burdess.

Thank you to everyone at The Bent Agency, and to all the foreign co-agents and publishers who bring stories to readers around the world.

My innumerable thanks also to the librarians, booksellers, and book bloggers who work so tirelessly to champion novels and find them homes.

Thank you to the wonderful YA community for making me feel so welcome this past year. I can't name you all, but I can at least try: Alwyn Hamilton, Stephanie Kate Strohm, Martin Stewart, Jennifer E. Smith, Becky Albertalli, Alison Cherry, Katherine Webber, Carlie Sorosiak, Elizabeth Eulberg, Stephanie Garber, Emily Bain Murphy, Cat Clarke, Rebecca Barrow, Harriet Reuter Hapgood, Alexia Casale, Birdie Milano, Meira Drazin, and Ali Standish. Not to mention the awesome, badass Writing Weasels: Kat Ellis, Dawn Kurtagich, Fox Benwell, Marieke Nijkamp, Jenn Faughnan (Jenniely), David Purse, Ronni Davis, Tatum Flynn, Emma Jackson, and Simon Clark.

To Mom, Dad, Jessica, Cecil (and Malfi! and Ally!): I

can't thank you enough for putting up with me when I was in the Existential Crisis phase(s) of drafting this book. Here's to all that swimming pool therapy and a hurricane wedding.

Thank you, Julie Haack, for being a best friend and a home all wrapped in one. Let's eat pumpkin cupcakes and sing Sufjan to JoLaz soon, all right?

Thank you to Erica Rutter for flying across the world, and to Susan Manly and Angus Stewart for always making an occasion for cake. Additional thanks to every friend who helped me celebrate the first book and get through a bad case of Second-Novel Syndrome, including Laura Gragtmans, Amanda Lanceter, Amanda Evans, Jennifer Brutosky, Jamie Cumby, and Maria Sequeira Mendes. I owe each and every one of you a coffee!

Last but never least, thank you so much to Rachel Holmes. You are a softer version of Rae and the better half of me. Thank you for taking me to all the places mentioned in this book and for sitting next to me on countless trains, late-night flights, and long journeys home. It makes so much sense that every love story I ever write will begin and end with you.